PENGUIN BOOKS
722
DARK DUET
PETER CHEYNEY

Dark Duet

BY

PETER CHEYNEY

*

PENGUIN BOOKS

HARMONDSWORTH · MIDDLESEX

First published 1942
Published in Penguin Books 1949
Reprinted 1950, 1951

To

MY STEP-SON

A-C2 WALTER, P.M.H.

R.A.F.V.R.

Made and printed in Great Britain
for Penguin Books Limited
by Hazell, Watson & Viney Ltd, Aylesbury and London

Contents

Faded the tinkling music of the minuet
And when its mincing cadences were sped
There echoed through that ballroom of the dead
Two ghostly voices in a dark duet.

CHAPTER I

IT DOESN'T HURT MUCH!

I

THE office was a small, square room on a third floor near Golden Square. It was sombre and unassuming. The furniture was nondescript. A suggestion of efficiency was provided by a steel filing-cabinet.

Outside, between this office and the corridor, was another even smaller room. In it MacMurray, a big, broad-shouldered, truculent-looking man, dozed over an evening paper. He wished Fenton would go home.

MacMurray – who had been 'lent' by C.I.D. Central Office, and who spent most of his time wishing he was back there – divided his attention between the Greyhound Racing news and wondering about Fenton. MacMurray was curious about Fenton. Damned curious. He wondered why it should be necessary for him to stay put in the outer office for twenty-four hours at a stretch whilst Fenton sat at the desk in the other room waiting for telephone calls that seldom came, or spent an odd hour going through the filing-cabinet making pencil notes on folders. Folders which MacMurray never saw.

He did not like being curious. But there was no way of satisfying his curiosity. His orders were to take his instructions from Fenton and to keep his mouth shut. Excellent orders, thought the plain-clothes man, and none the less excellent because he could not have done anything but keep his mouth shut. He had nothing to talk about.

Fenton, sitting at the desk in the other office, seemed at first glance to be as nondescript as the furniture. He was in the late fifties. His hair was thin, but what there was of it was plastered artistically. His moustache was small, well-brushed. When you looked at him carefully, noted his good, well-cut, if old, clothes, you thought he might have been a

7

senior Civil Servant or possibly a retired Army officer. It wouldn't matter what you thought anyhow. Fenton never answered any questions, maintained a background in which questions were not asked.

He moved the desk-lamp a little nearer so that the light fell on the papers he was examining. He looked at his watch. It was seven o'clock – a dark, cold, wintry night, with a sharp rain beginning to fall. He yawned. He leant back in his chair, produced a cigarette-case, lit a cigarette, wondered how much longer he was going to sit in the little office ... waiting.

Fenton thought that you were always waiting for something. From the moment you were born till the time when death was imminent, you were waiting for something – something good or bad. It might be the right woman, or a divorce to get rid of the wrong one – or some money, or revenge – or a chance to make good. But you were always waiting. And it was annoying. The telephone rang. Fenton sighed. He took off the receiver. He said:

'Yes. ... Yes, sir. ... I've got all the information we had on her ... there's nothing *new* on her at all, sir. ... No ... no real dossier and no official record. ... But we know quite a lot about her. ... Hold on, sir, I'll let you know in a minute ...'

He put down the receiver, went to the filing-cabinet, unlocked a drawer, pulled the steel file out and began to check through the carefully-filed folders inside. He took one out, went back to the desk, opened the folder, picked up the receiver.

He said: 'She's here as Mrs Marques. She came from Norway, a reputed refugee – a rich refugee. She's supposed to have money – both in Lisbon and New York. She's very clever, sir – awfully clever. The C.E. people definitely attri-bute the sinking of the *Maratta Star* to that quarter. ... You remember the *Maratta Star*, sir? It was one of the ships that were taking children to Canada. ... Yes, sir ... they got it ... a submarine was waiting for it. ... Not a very nice business, sir. ... They found a dozen of the children in an open boat twelve days afterwards, dead from exposure. ... That was Mrs Marques all right, sir. There are a lot of other things too – some of 'em not so bad – some, if possible, worse. ...

8

Oh ... she's done that too, has she, sir!' He began to smile a little. 'Well, if that's so, sir, then even *you* might begin to get annoyed with her. ...

'Well, what are you going to do, sir? You can't move through the Department of Home Security, can you? There is nothing official on the woman. ... You can't *prove* anything. ...' Fenton shrugged his shoulders. His smile became more incisive. 'Well ... if you think the case merits it you could always use Process 4 or 5. ...' He paused. 'In this case, Sir, I would suggest Process 5. ... You would probably save a lot of people's lives that way. ... Very well, sir. ... You needn't worry any more about it. I'll take the necessary steps. Just forget it ... write the lady off in your mind. ... Good-night!'

Fenton hung up the receiver. He was smiling. He sat for a little while looking straight in front of him at the expanse of black-out curtain that shrouded the window. After a while he pressed the bell-button on the desk. The man from outside came in. Fenton said:

'I'm going off now, MacMurray. If anything urgent turns up you can ring me at home. But I don't think it will. I think we've finished our urgent business for to-day.'

He smiled. MacMurray nodded and went back to the outer office.

Fenton went to the hatstand in the corner of the office. He put on his overcoat and hat. He went back to the telephone. He dialled a Mayfair number. After a minute he said:

'Hello .. Kane? How are you ...? There's a little business for you. ... You can get the details from your usual contact. ... I'll have a chance to talk to him on my way home. He'll make the necessary arrangements if he can. ... Yes, it's one of those things. ... Process 5. ... You understand? And remember this is England ... see? Play it carefully. ... Good-night, Kane. ...'

He hung up. He said good-night to MacMurray as he went through the outer office. He walked down the corridor towards the lift, whistling softly to himself.

When he'd gone MacMurray went into the inner office and looked round. He tried the locks on the filing-cabinet. He went into the outer office, closed and locked the door between the two offices. He set up a folding-bed in one corner and laid out some blankets on it and a pillow. He took an automatic pistol from his hip pocket and put it under the pillow. He locked the door leading to the corridor, lit a spirit stove and put on it a small kettle. Then he undressed. He lay on the camp-bed reading the last edition of *The Star*, waiting for the kettle to boil.

II

Kane was tying his tie in front of the cheval glass when the telephone rang. He answered it and afterwards resumed the process of tie-tying. He felt a little sick in the stomach. He was not quite certain whether this feeling was the result of the telephone call or too many double Martinis after whisky. He thought it did not matter anyhow.

He was tall and slim. But his shoulders were good and his hips very narrow. He appeared lithe. He moved as if he were putting very little energy into the process; as if he could produce much more vitality if necessary. His hands were peculiarly long, narrow and compact for so large a man, and his feet were small. He looked like a man who would be able to dance the tango very well ... to do most things well .. if he wanted to.

The sensitive mouth, the humorous and Celtic cut of the cheekbones, the set of the lips, indicated that he was not wanting in humour. Yet this attribute stayed with the lower part of his face. Above the cheekbones and nose – which was long and quivered at the end when he smiled so that you wanted to look at it all the time, especially if you were a woman – there appeared a peculiar indefinable grimness. Not a definite grimness associated with a heavy type of face, but something fleeting; certainly not permanent. Directly you had assured yourself that it was there it disappeared and the brow opened and the eyes smiled, and you believed you were wrong. You were ... but not the way *you* thought.

Kane opened a box of Player's cigarettes that stood on the dressing-table near the mirror, and lit one. One side of his face was almost framed in a wave of unruly dark brown hair. And the end of the eyebrow beneath it curled up in a mischievous Machiavellian manner. If you had been watching Kane you would have decided, if you were a man, that you liked him. And if you were a woman, that you liked him, but that you wouldn't take many chances about it. Not *too* many.

His clothes hung well on him. When he crossed the room to get an overcoat out of the wardrobe, his walk indicated that he was impatient about something. Yet the indication was belied by the almost casual way in which he put on the coat and a black soft hat.

With the hat on he looked more attractive than ever. He adjusted it at the right angle in front of the cheval glass. He liked it to be just so. He fumbled in his pockets for some gloves, and wondered if there would be a cab anywhere near Queen Anne Street.

Queen Anne Street. ... He looked into the glass and wondered why the devil he should have a bedroom in Queen Anne Street – that quiet and select backwater of Cavendish Square. He decided to take the question seriously, and sat down suddenly in a high-backed chair. He smoked the cigarette and wondered why the devil he should live in Queen Anne Street. After a little while he concluded that it was because it *was* quiet and a backwater. Maybe, thought Kane, he was getting a little old and beginning to think in terms of quietness and backwaters.

This thought made him laugh. Then he wondered if thirty-eight was old; decided that it didn't matter anyhow. He threw the cigarette stub away, lit another one and went downstairs.

It was cold outside in the street. He crossed Cavendish Square, went through Hanover Square, Conduit Street, Bond Street and down St James's Street.

There were few people about and Kane could hear his own footsteps distinctly. For some unknown reason the usual traffic noises of London seemed stilled. He began to think about Fenton.

Fenton was a one. He took you for granted. But then Fenton took everything for granted. Fenton was the type of Englishman who *appeared* to be a little grey and faded and undecided and odd, and who was, in reality, underneath, as hard as seven devils in hell. Definitely hard. You could depend on Fenton for damned little. He was afraid of nothing, but if it suited the book he'd walk out on you and leave you cold and dangling ... dangling was about the word for it too. ... A nice word ... dangling. ...

A sudden gust of wind almost blew him into the roadway. He thought November was a hell of a month. As if to justify this thought one or two large snowflakes began to fall. Kane moved nearer the shelter of the houses.

He came to the post office at the bottom of St James's Street. In the shadow between the post office and the Conservative Club a man in an old raincoat was leaning up against the wall. Kane stopped and said good-evening.

The man said: 'We'd better go round the corner. This isn't a good place to talk, is it?'

'Just as you like,' Kane said. 'It seems as good as anywhere else to me.'

The man in the old raincoat led the way down the narrow street by the side of the Conservative Club. He stopped fifteen yards past the side entrance to the Club. He leaned up against the wall. Kane stood facing him, his hands in the pockets of his overcoat, his shoulders drooped. 'I suppose Fenton's spoken to you?' said the man in the raincoat.

Kane nodded.

'Oh, yes,' he said. There was a peculiar sound of finality in the two words. They indicated somehow that whatever Fenton had said it produced a definite process of thought in Kane's mind – a process that was not subject to any alteration.

'Guelvada's in Surrey,' said the other man, 'playing around at some place called Tyrrell's Wood. I'm going to get a call through to him just as soon as I can. He's got a car down there. He can get back pretty quickly.'

Kane said: 'There seems to be an awful hurry, doesn't there?' He took out his cigarette case, lit a cigarette.

'Why not?' said the man in the old raincoat. 'Do you want to spin it out?' His tone was mildly sarcastic.

'I don't like spinning anything out,' said Kane. 'But I like to take my time.'

The other man shrugged his shoulders.

12

'I suppose Fenton didn't say anything to you about the *Maratta Star?*' he said.

'No,' said Kane. 'And anyway what's the *Maratta Star* got to do with it?'

'It was one of the boats that was supposed to take children to Canada,' said the man in the raincoat. 'A submarine got it. It was waiting for it. That was Mrs Marques – that was. That's her business. Well, maybe there'll be some more ships. Perhaps that's why Fenton's in a hurry.'

Kane moved his head slightly. He looked down the narrow street towards St James's Street. He said:

'That's all right, but I still don't approve of being too fast. I don't like all this quick movement. I don't like Ernie dashing back from Tyrrell's Wood in that car of his. One of these fine days somebody's going to ask how it is that a Belgian refugee –' Kane grinned suddenly – 'I beg his pardon – a free Belgian – is able to go dashing about the country in a high-powered motor car just at any odd minute. Then they're going to ask questions.'

The man in the raincoat shrugged his shoulders again. It was almost an imperceptible shrug. He looked rather bored.

'Well, supposing they do ...?' he said.

Kane echoed the words: 'Supposing they do. ... Well, hasn't it ever struck you that there might be people who are just as interested in Guelvada's movements and mine as we are in those of other people? Somebody's going to ask too many questions – somebody dangerous I mean – not bloody fools like you and Fenton who sit on your backsides in offices and think what smart fellows you are – but people like Guelvada and me. If anybody's going to take the rap then its going to be us, isn't it? You'll just go on sitting on your backsides.'

The other man yawned.

'Nonsense!' he said. 'I didn't lose my left hand sitting on my backside.'

Kane nodded.

'That's all right,' he said. 'You have it your way. I still think it's stupid. Well ... you're going to phone Guelvada?'

'That's right,' said the other. 'I think I can give him a tip or two about a very quick contact.' He grinned at Kane in

13

the darkness. 'Fenton suggested that it might be a good thing if you could finish this business off to-night.'

'My God!' said Kane. 'You fellows are getting impatient, aren't you?' He threw his cigarette stub away.

'I should think Guelvada would be back in town by nine o'clock,' said the other man. 'If everything is all right he ought to be at the 'Yellow Bottle' – that pub in Mayfair – somewhere around half-past nine. If I were you I should give him till a quarter to ten. Then you could telephone him there. If he's got on all right you ought to be able to go ahead from there – if he's seen the people I want him to see.'

'All right,' said Kane. 'Is that all?'

'That's all,' said the man in the old raincoat. 'Good-night, Michael.'

Kane said good-night. He walked down the narrow street into St James's Street.

III

Kane stood just inside the blacked-out stage door, an un-lit cigarette hanging from the corner of his mouth. He waited there two or three minutes; then the stage-door keeper appeared at the head of the stairway and beckoned him. Kane ran up the stairs quickly, followed the man along the corridor, went into the dressing-room. He closed the door behind him, stood leaning against it.

Valetta Fallon was sitting in front of her make-up glass doing her eyebrows. She was wearing a kimono which had fallen open and showed her legs. Kane looked at them appreciatively. He said:

'I don't know whether anybody's ever told you, but you've got the swellest pair of legs I've ever seen in my life, Valetta.'

She turned her head towards him and smiled.

'I've an idea that quite a few men have suggested something like that,' she said. She looked at him seriously, the eyebrow-brush poised in her hand, 'But *not* during the last nine months,' she concluded. 'Won't you sit down, Michael? There are cigarettes in the box,' She nodded towards it.

Kane hung his hat on the peg behind the door. He sat down. He threw away the unlit cigarette and took a fresh one. He said:

14

'And why *not* during the last nine months, Valetta?'

She looked at him sideways along her long eyelashes. Kane thought she was very beautiful. Her features were superbly chiselled; her mouth delicate, sensitive and almost tremulous. Kane, who liked looking at a woman's mouth, thought that he could look at hers for hours on end. It was that sort of mouth.

She said: 'You sound as if you're trying to be immoral.' She began to smile again. 'Possibly, Michael, you've forgotten I've been your mistress for the last nine months?'

He grinned. He looked rather like a mischievous schoolboy. He said: 'Why should I forget that?'

She raised her eyebrows.

'I don't know,' she said, 'except that I fail to understand why you should expect me to receive admiration from other people when I'm supposed to be in love with you.'

Kane nodded.

'Oh, *that* ...' he said.

He blew a smoke ring. She put down the eyebrow-brush and turned on the chair. She faced him. She said:

'I wish I knew about you. I wish I knew whether you really are a hard, cynical, extremely tough person, or whether the way you talk and behave is just a pose.'

Kane said: 'I don't think cynics ever pose. They don't have to. Who would want to pose as being a cynic? Nobody over the age of eighteen admires cynicism. Besides, you don't adopt it as a pose; it's one of those things that are forced on you.'

'I see,' said Valetta. 'And how much cynicism have *I* forced on you, Michael?'

'None at all,' he said with a smile. 'Just the opposite. If it weren't for you I would be absolutely and entirely submerged in the depths of cynicism.'

She said: 'You're an extraordinary person, aren't you? Don't you find anything good in life?'

'Nothing that lasts,' said Kane airily.

She picked up the eyebrow-brush again. She looked in the mirror. '*I've* lasted,' she said.

'You've lasted nine months,' said Kane. He stubbed out his cigarette end, put his hands in his overcoat pockets.

15

'I wonder what that means?' asked Valetta. 'Does it mean that you don't expect me to last much longer or that you hope I won't last much longer?'

Kane grinned. She found that grin maddening.

He said: 'I hope for very little and expect nothing. I'm damned glad of what I get.' He went on: 'Let's be constructive about you. When a woman falls in love with a man she has to get something out of it, doesn't she?'

She got up, slipped off the kimono, began to wriggle into her stage frock. She had a superb figure. She hoped he would realise that. It was some time before she said:

'Well, what does she have to get out of it? She doesn't *have* to get something out of it, does she, Michael?'

He nodded. He was smiling quite pleasantly.

'She must get something,' he said, 'otherwise it's no soap. When a woman definitely realises that a man is no soap she does something about it, expecially a woman like you, Valetta.'

She smiled at him. She powdered her nose, leaning forward so that the powder should not touch her frock.

'Has it never occurred to you that I may have got something out of you, Michael?' she said.

He raised one eyebrow. 'Such as ... ?' he queried.

'Such as a lot of fun for one thing,' said Valetta.

'I wouldn't describe myself as a particularly amusing type of man,' he said.

She sat down on the chair suddenly, her hands clasped in her lap, looking at him. She was concentrating.

'Neither would I,' said Valetta. 'You're not. But there is something damned fascinating about you. You're one of those men who don't require a background. Have another cigarette, Michael.'

He said: 'Thanks.'

She took a cigarette from the box, lit it, handed it to him. He noticed the mark of her lipstick on the end. He drew on the cigarette.

'This is interesting,' he said. 'So I'm the type of man who doesn't require a background. Elucidate that mysterious remark, Valetta.'

She thought for a moment.

16

'Well,' she said eventually, 'one meets some men and one's only really interested because one knows all about them. For instance, you meet a man. He's rather brusque; he seems hard. You wouldn't be attracted in the normal course of events; and then you find that he's a man who's done quite big things in his life. You realise that the things he's done have made him tough. They're responsible for his character. Knowing that, you're still prepared to be interested in him. If you didn't know you'd probably dismiss him from your mind. Do you understand? I'm not very good at explaining what I think,' she concluded.

'I understand,' said Kane. He blew a smoke ring, watched it sail across the dressing-room.

'But you'd be all right anyhow,' she said. 'Whatever you were, whatever your job was, whatever you did, you'd still be you. *You* are a fascinating person. *You* are an intriguing person. Quite independently of whatever it is you do ... which reminds me – –' she stopped speaking, looked at him. Her eyes were bright and a little wicked. Her mouth was smiling. Kane wanted to take her in his arms.

'Which reminds you of what?' he said.

'Do you remember the first time we met, Michael?' she said. 'The night they dropped that bomb and blew that place in, with all those people underneath? Do you remember how I flung myself into your arms for protection? *Was* I scared!'

'And was *I* scared?' said Kane.

'I don't know about that,' said Valetta. 'You weren't too scared to take full advantage of the situation.'

'I beg your pardon!' said Kane.

'There is no need to,' she said. 'I thought your technique was superb. But the point I was getting at was this: When we arranged to dine together and I was getting ready to meet you, I made up my mind to ask you exactly what it was you did, and somehow when the time came I didn't want to. I thought I'd like to keep you, in my mind, as a rather mysterious sort of person.'

Kane nodded.

'I see,' he said. 'So you'd already put me down as a sort of "steady," had you?' He grinned at her ironically. He showed a fine set of white teeth.

'What I thought is my business,' said Valetta. 'But the fact remains I didn't ask you what you were, and when I'd left you and we'd arranged to meet again, and I was lying in bed looking at the ceiling and thinking about you, I made up my mind that the next time I saw you I really would ask you.'

Kane said: 'What was it made you forget?'

'Oh, you wouldn't know, would you?' said Valetta.

'I've got an idea ... But go on ...' said Kane.

'Well,' she continued, 'I've sort of carried it on from time to time. One of these fine days I'll satisfy my curiosity.' She stopped speaking. Then quite suddenly said: 'Michael, what *do* you do?'

He blew another smoke ring. He said:

'I suppose one could say that you were fairly well experienced, Valetta. You're no fool, are you? You're a pretty good judge of character. Now, what would you think I was?'

She shook her head.

'I'm damned if I know,' she said. 'You might be anything. You're one of those people that you can't put in any sort of box. You're a type and yet you're not a type.'

Kane said: 'I suppose what you really mean is why aren't I in the Army, or the Navy or the Air Force?'

She said: 'All right. Why aren't you?'

Kane said: 'I'll tell you. I was run over by an express train when I was about seven. It cut my liver entirely in half, so they won't pass me fit.' He sat grinning at her.

She said: 'You're a pig, Michael, aren't you? But then you once told me you didn't like being asked questions.'

He said: 'Oh, I don't mind from you. So you really want to know what I am and what I do. Do you know' – he leaned forward suddenly – 'I think you're a marvellous woman, Valetta,' he said, 'to know a man, to get around with him, to sleep with him for nine months and only then to ask him what he does. I think it's too amazing.'

'Never mind about that,' she said. 'You tell me ...'

There was a knock on the door. 'You're on in two minutes, Miss Fallon,' said the callboy.

She got up.

Kane said: 'That interruption came just at the right moment. Now I've gots lots of time to think something up.'

She said: 'So long, Michael, I've got to go now. Am I going to see you to-night?'

He shook his head. 'I've got to meet a man I know,' he said. 'A little business. I'm sorry, Valetta. I'd have liked to have had supper with you to-night.'

'Me, too,' she said. 'I'll be seeing you, Michael. Take some cigarettes if you want some. *Au revoir*.'

He heard her high heels pattering down the stone passageway. He sat in the chair looking straight in front of him at the make-up table; his long, thin hands hung straight down between his knees. He presented a picture of ironic despondency.

After a little while he got up. He put on his hat, walked slowly along the passageway, down the stairs, out of the stage entrance.

IV

Presenting Mr Guelvada – 'Ernie' Guelvada – the Free Belgian. The gentleman with a mission.

Ernie was disquieting. Definitely disquieting. It was impossible to sit and talk to Ernie, or even to look at him or be in the same room with him, without experiencing a sense of vague discomfort. When you were not with him you wondered about this; concluded that you were suffering from nerves or imagination; that you were stupid. You became certain about the nerves or imagination until the next time you saw Mr Guelvada, when you noted that the effect of discomfort became greater as you got to know him better.

Of course you did not get to know him better. No one ever did. Except Kane. Kane knew him, and about the worm that lived in Mr Guelvada and spent its time wandering from the mind to the guts. When it was in the mind Ernie made people uncomfortable. When it descended to the stomach other – and possibly more interesting – things happened.

Guelvada sat at the corner table in the bar parlour at the Grain Tavern in Tyrrell's Wood. He was watching the proprietress. He was thinking that she had an excellent figure, a well-proportioned figure, that her breasts were absolutely in proportion to her hips and waist. Guelvada spent a great

19

deal of his time pondering on the figures of women. Not in any lustful or even mildly exciting manner but in a quiet and dispassionate way that was distinctly impersonal and almost remote.

While he was engaged in this process, he used, at the same time, to think about other things – things that were not disconnected from the object of his vision. Sometimes he would think in French or Walloon or Flemish or in Russian or Spanish or Portuguese or English. He spoke all these languages almost perfectly. Perfectly enough to get by. When he thought in English he would do all sorts of strange things to amuse himself. He would think in pedantic – or what he considered correct – English, or in English interlarded with slang and Americanisms that he had learned from the moving pictures. He was not the sort of man that you would 'put' with languages. He was not the sort of man that you would consider to be at all erudite. Yet he was extremely erudite.

He seldom talked about himself, and preferred to believe that he behaved in a mediocre and uninteresting manner. He was on the short side, and seemed a little plump. He was not in fact plump. He merely gave the impression. He was strong and nimble on his feet when he wanted to be. His face was round, pleasant and good-humoured. His mouth was mobile and good-natured. Seeing all these things accompanied by the half-smile that usually played about Guelvada's lips made you wonder more than ever *why* you felt uncomfortable when you were with him.

He had been born at a baconry near Ellezelles. It was a profitable baconry and had belonged to his father. His mother, who had noticed that Guelvada was not particularly happy with pigs, decided that he should go into the priesthood. She saw him as a curé. The picture of Ernie in a cassock delighted her. It was for this reason that he was educated so that he should be a successful priest. His mother, if asked, would not have known what a successful priest was, but to her education was a step in that direction. The World War of 1914 put an end to these dreams. It also put an end to his father, who was shot out of hand by the Germans for cutting the throat of a Corporal of Engineers, and to his mother, who was killed by the Corporal of Engineers because she put one of his eyes out with her thumb whilst he was endeavouring to rape her. Ernie, considering all these things in the light of the peace that followed, concluded that they were – in their way – quite logical, and became a courier.

Being a courier was an interesting business, he thought. You seldom stayed in any place long enough to become bored with it. You met a lot of people who passed on quickly. You had no time to become tired of anything. Your life became a kaleidoscope of middle-aged English ladies with dogs and money, surreptitious trips to the Casino with younger English ladies who wanted to see what night-life was like, and arguments about hotel bills with women of other nationalities who seemed to want to spend their lives arguing about a franc or two.

He picked up his glass and walked across the room towards the little bar that connected the bar-parlour with the saloon bar. Across the counter, in the other bar, he saw one or two men he knew casually. They grinned at him and he smiled back. When he smiled his face became almost transfigured. There was something cherubic about it. His smile was, in any event, prepossessing.

He put the glass down on the counter and asked in a soft voice for a gin and lime-juice. He watched the proprietress whilst she reached for the bottle. Reaching for bottles showed off a woman's figure, he thought, and it was for this reason that he always asked for drinks that came out of bottles on the highest shelves. One night, in Lisbon, at a place where they kept an egg-flip mixed with rum, that nobody ever wanted, on a high shelf, Guelvada had spent the whole evening ordering the foul stuff merely so that he could watch the girl who was serving, reach for the bottle. He was like that.

When the proprietress put the gin and lime on the counter in front of him she said: 'I haven't seen you for a day or two, Mr Guelvada. But then you've been busy, I expect?'

Guelvada smiled at her.

'Oh, no!' he said. 'Not at all, *Madame*. On the contrary. I have been walking about your so beautiful golf course, thinking.'

21

She laughed. He thought she was a very pleasant woman.

'What – in the rain?' she said. 'Whatever were you thinking about?'

Guelvada became suddenly serious. Then his round face lit up with a smile. He said quietly:

'Believe it or not, but one of the things I was thinking about was your figure. I think it is superb. I only hope the Germans don't invade England.'

'Why?' she asked. 'Whatever has that got to do with my figure?' She bridled a little. *She* thought she had a good figure too.

'It might have a lot to do with it,' said Guelvada. 'The Boches like figures like yours.'

She flushed.

'They could go on liking,' she said. 'I've got an axe in the tool-shed for Germans.'

Guelvada nodded.

'I know ...' he said thoughtfully. He smiled at her again. 'I knew another woman like that,' he said. 'She had an axe in the tool-shed too. They cut her breasts off ...'

He picked up the glass of gin and lime, carried it back to the table. As he was raising the glass to his lips, the barmaid from the public bar put her head round the door.

'Mr Guelvada,' she said, 'there's somebody wants you on the telephone. When I asked him who it was, he said to tell you it was Peter.'

Guelvada said: 'Thank you, honey ...'

He got up and went out of the bar parlour, down the little passageway. The wall-telephone was at the end of the passage. Guelvada picked up the receiver and said hello. The voice at the other end said: 'Is that you, Guelvada?'

'Correct,' said Guelvada. 'This is "E" for Ernie.'

'Right,' said the other voice. 'And this is "P" for Peter. There's a woman called Mrs Marques ...'

Guelvada interrupted. He said very quickly:

'Yes ...?' He was smiling a little – an odd sort of smile. His lips were drawn back over his teeth.

'*Yes!*' said 'P' for Peter. 'Process five. Does that please you?'

'Why not?' said Guelvada. 'It's logical, isn't it?'

22

'In this case definitely so,' said the other voice. 'I understand she'll be at a party at a place near Hampstead to-night. The party will start somewhere around ten-ish. It will be a late party. You and 'M' for Michael will have to get in on it somehow. Somebody wants this job done quickly.'

'I see,' said Guelvada. 'Do I have any contacts?'

'Unfortunately they're rather vague,' said the voice. 'But there's a pub in Mayfair called the Yellow Bottle. There's a woman goes there called Mrs Mallary. She's a friend of Mrs Jeanes who's throwing the party at Hampstead. This Mrs Mallary knows an awful lot of people. She might have met you some time. She was at Eden Roc three years ago and fell off the wooden jetty there. She broke her leg. Two nights afterwards, with one leg in plaster of paris, she went to a card party and won twenty-five thousand francs. Will that help?'

'It might,' said Guelvada, 'providing she goes to the Yellow Bottle to-night.'

'She'll be there,' said the voice. 'I can arrange that. I'll try and put a man in to make it easier. But after she gets there you'll have to play it on your own.'

'All right,' said Guelvada. 'But if you put a man in how shall I know him?'

'He'll know about your other identity card,' said Peter. 'He'll know the name on it is Pierre Hellard. You be Pierre Hellard and let him remember you. If he does, he's my man. But, remember, he'll get out before the business starts. He's an inexperienced one, that one. You can't rely on him for anything and he knows nothing – nothing that matters. Understand?'

Guelvada said: 'It's all right,' He smiled in that peculiar way again. 'I can do this on my own. If she goes to the Yellow Bottle it's easy.'

The voice said: 'You're not going to do it on your own. Sometimes you're a little too decided, Ernie. You'll do it with Kane. You'll take your orders from him. When you've seen Mrs Mallary at the Yellow Bottle you'd better hang about there. Michael will come through on the telephone. You can tell him what the position is. After that you two can carry the baby.'

Guelvada began to laugh.

'You're telling me!' he said. 'Carry the baby is good. Some baby! But we'll carry her. ... Tell me, what does she look like – this Marques I mean?'

'Pretty good, I believe,' said the voice. 'That sort always look good. They have to. You understand what you've got to do. You'd better get back to London right away.'

Guelvada said: 'All right. I'll be there in half an hour.'

'Take your time,' said the voice. 'There's no need to get picked up for speeding.'

Guelvada hung up the receiver. He went back into the bar-parlour, finished his drink, picked up his hat. He said good-evening to the proprietress and went out. When he had gone one of the men in the saloon bar said to her:

'He's a funny little fellow, isn't he, Mrs Soames?'

She nodded.

'I'm sorry for him,' she said. 'I'm sorry for all those Free Belgians. They've got no homes or anything. They've got nothing to do – just sort of sitting about waiting for us to win this war so that they can go back home and start cleaning-up.'

'He's a funny little devil,' said the man.

'He *is* strange,' said Mrs Soames. 'I think he's very pleased with himself about something. But you never know with these foreigners. ...'

It was raining when Guelvada drove through Berkeley Square. He parked the car at the end of Charles Street. When he got out the keen wintry wind cut his cheeks. He shivered a little. He did not like the cold. He began to walk towards Shepherd Market, his hands in his pockets, his head down against the wind; his round, good-humoured face concerned with some immediate problem.

The immediate problem was the weather. Guelvada was thinking that, in his part of Belgium, the wind was not so cutting nor the rain so cold. He wondered what life would have been like had he been a priest. He thought possibly it might have been more amusing; then again the lives of priests were not so amusing after all.

He traversed Shepherd Market and, on the other side, turned into the street that led to the cul-de-sac – the end of

24

which was formed by the Yellow Bottle. He went into the saloon bar. The place was full of people, and inside, standing to the right of the black-out curtain, he was able to look quickly at the bar and to see that there were two people serving behind it – one a potman of indeterminate age and, at the other end, an attractive barmaid.

Guelvada went quickly to the nearest end of the counter, bought a double brandy, carried it to a table in the corner of the room. He lit a cigarette; sat quietly looking about him.

You would not have noticed Guelvada. You would not have noticed him because at that moment he was busy making himself inconspicuous. He could do that. He belonged to that lucky class of people who, by merely thinking along certain lines, by presenting a mental attitude, could either become obviously present or inconspicuous, as they willed.

The Yellow Bottle was one of those places where the Saloon Bar has an atmosphere of its own. When you went in you wondered where the people came from, who they were and what they did. You were surprised that so many people could have nothing to do except drink at the same time.

Most of the young men appeared effeminate and slightly odd. The women, with some exceptions, of course, were those sort of women that you see in the company of young men who are effeminate and slightly odd.

Soldiers, sailors and airmen were remarkable for their absence. Real soldiers, sailors and airmen. There were a sprinkling of those young, and apparently fit, individuals who, garbed as army officers, perform mysterious and doubtless – to them – important tasks which ordinarily might be achieved by an efficient typist; a type produced by any war which, whether brainless or not, shows a remarkable aptitude for wearing a uniform and for keeping as far away as possible from any sort of lethal weapon.

In the far corner, two or three young men 'of either sex' were engrossed in a conversation on the trend of fashions. One of them said he was a dress-designer. He was there every night talking about himself, wearing different coloured sweaters.

He was talking to another young man who, judging by his

conversation, was an interior-decorator. Guelvada thought that the descriptions 'interior-decorator' and 'dress-designer' were like charity, inasmuch as they often covered a multitude of sins. He wondered how British stock, famous for its virility, could produce specimens of manhood like these. He wondered just what these young men would have been doing in Victorian days when, no matter what other failings obtained, there was a definite prejudice against young men who behaved like women, who did jobs that could be described as effeminate, concerned themselves only with each other, and left the real dirty work of life to other people. Possibly they would have been 'remittance men,' and toughened a little in the process.

Guelvada sighed and turned his eyes away. In another corner of the bar he noticed a man of mature years with curled hair and carefully made-up lips. He was drinking Benedictine and smiling vaguely at any one who cared to look in his direction. Guelvada, with a little smile, thought that he would very much like to cut the Benedictine drinker's throat; that it might be amusing; that it would be a good deed.

His eyes wandered slowly round the bar. There were little parties of women, well dressed and certain of themselves, belonging to that select circle, to be found in every town and city, that does little to justify an easy and aimless existence in days of war. Women who always have money either from divorce alimony or from some sort of allowance, and who are always going to begin doing some sort of war work next week. Sometimes they get as far as going to a Civil Defence or other national centre to make some enquiries about it; sometimes they get as far as taking away a form to fill in. They seldom get any further. Their lives usually begin in the evenings and they always know which 'club' serves the best dinner, and where you can go on afterwards. For reasons best known to themselves they consider they are remote from war and its alarms, and even a thousand-kilogram bomb in the next street fails to shake this conviction. Unable to interest themselves in either fearing, hating, or desiring to checkmate the enemy, they are careful to eschew conversation, films, books, or newspapers that tend to bring the war into the radius of their small vision. And if the enemy were busy in the next house they would be certain that for some good, if mysterious, reason he would miss their domicile and go on next door. They suffer inordinately from headaches, and invariably carry in their handbags little boxes containing some sort of sedative which, followed by a whisky and soda, invariably puts the trouble right for another couple of hours.

In spite of coupons and restrictions, they are always well and stylishly dressed and manage to buy new clothes when they want them. They possess an extraordinary ability to fulfil their own desires; an amazing disability to understand anything or anyone not connected with the small orbit in which they revolve.

Guelvada began to wonder about Mrs Mallary. He wondered what type of woman she was; whether she would react easily or whether she was one of those cynical women who were not prepared to take a man on his face value. He thought about this for a little while; then finished his drink, picked up his glass, and went to the far end of the bar. He ordered a double brandy from the barmaid. His smile was so charming, so childlike, that almost in spite of herself she smiled back. Guelvada said: 'Hello, honey. I haven't seen you for a long time. How have things been cooking around here?'

'All right,' she said. She didn't remember having seen Guelvada before, but he was so sure of himself that she thought he *must* have seen him. Possibly he was an old customer who hadn't been in much lately.

Guelvada went on: 'There are a lot of new faces in here. Does Mrs Mallary still come here as much as she used to?'

The barmaid nodded. 'Quite a bit,' she said, and such was Guelvada's power of suggestion that she now remembered that she *had* seen Guelvada with Mrs Mallary in the bar at some time.

Guelvada said: 'If a telephone call comes through for Mr Guelvada, let me know, will you? I'm expecting a friend to call me.' He picked up his glass; went back to his seat. He sat there patiently smoking a cigarette.

Ten minutes later the black-out curtain was pushed aside. A thin weedy-looking young man, with the red flush of tuberculosis about his cheek-bones, came in; stood aside for a woman to pass. He said in a quiet but very distinct voice:

'It's marvellous seeing you again, Mrs Mallary – such a *lovely* surprise.'

Guelvada looked up quickly. So this would be the contact. His casual eyes swept over the weedy young man. Guelvada wondered where the devil Fenton or whoever it was had picked *him* up. But then you never knew – some of these weedy young men were tough.

Mrs Mallary was what is usually described as a good sport. Her first name was Eloise, which she liked very much. She was broad-minded about what she called 'fun and games.' She could drink quite a lot without becoming tight. She liked drinking because it made her feel care-free, and gave her a peculiarly attractive mental abandon which she found amusing.

She was in the late thirties and was good-looking. She had fine eyes which she could use in a most devastating manner, and a shape that was, at one time, popular in France. Her bosom was extremely well-developed, which fact, coupled with her trim waist and small hips, gave her an appearance of being most attractively top-heavy. Sailors – possibly for some mysterious nautical reason – always looked at her with the frankest admiration, a process which pleased Mrs Mallary because she had always admired the Navy, although – as she put it – she liked a service that wasn't *too* silent.

Many heads turned to look at Mrs Mallary. She liked that too. She was, in fact, a delightful sight. She wore a plain but very well-cut coat and skirt in black velvet, a fox-fur cape reaching to her hips, a small tailor-made hat in black velvet with a pin-spot veil which, turned back from her face, gave the required touch of mystery. Her stockings were of gossamer black silk; her shoes glacé kid with four-inch heels.

Guelvada watched them as they went to a table at the other end of the room.

He waited five minutes; then he picked up his glass, walked to the far end of the counter, ordered another drink. He turned and, on his way back to his table, stopped suddenly as he passed the pair. A smile of recognition lit up his face. He said:

'Well, of all the wonderful things ... Mrs Mallary ... and after all these years!'

She looked up at him. She said:

'Well, I'm going to be very rude and say that I don't remember you. I expect I ought to.'

Guelvada looked disappointed. He said:

'I think you ought to.'

The weedy young man said: '*I* feel I ought to too. I've seen you somewhere. In fact, I'm *certain* I've met you – I just can't remember where.'

Guelvada gave him a quick smile. He realised the young man was trying to help; was afraid of saying too much.

He drew up an empty chair; sat down. He did this almost unobtrusively. He was smiling at Mrs Mallary. She smiled back. Already in her mind she had decided that Guelvada was 'interesting.'

Guelvada, smiling diffidently, looked straight into her eyes. His own were very dark brown, limpid, almost appealing. He was unconscious of the fact that, where women were concerned, he possessed a power of suggestion that was akin to a natural hypnotism. Mrs Mallary felt this. She was very conscious of Guelvada's eyes, of his round, good-natured face. She thought that his mouth was well-shaped. She liked the fastidious neatness of his collar and shirt, his beautifully tied tie, his well-fitting clothes. Definitely 'interesting,' thought Mrs Mallary.

Guelvada said: 'I'm fearfully disappointed. Don't you remember falling off the little wooden pier at Eden Roc and breaking your leg – and then a couple of nights afterwards so bravely going out with the same leg encased in plaster of paris and winning a whole lot of money? Don't you remember that?'

'My God!' said Mrs Mallary. 'Were you there? don't say ...' She searched her memory. 'Good heavens! You're not the man who waded in waist-deep to pull me out, are you?'

Guelvada looked modest. The weedy young man said:

'My God ... of course he is! Now I remember.'

'Life is a scream, isn't it?' said Mrs Mallary. 'Just fancy! They were the days, weren't they? I wish we could go back to them.'

Guelvada nodded.

'I wish we could,' he said. 'In the meantime I think we ought to celebrate. What about a little drink?'

The weedy young man came in again quickly. He said:

'This is definitely an occasion for celebrating – a link with the past. Believe it or not, I'm going to buy a bottle of champagne.'

'My God ...' said Mrs Mallary. 'You've got something there, Johnnie. That's *definitely* an idea.'

Guelvada thought that whoever he was Johnnie had been well trained. He never missed an opportunity. Guelvada wondered who he was; what *his* particular job was. He said smilingly:

'Oh, no, *I'm* going to buy the champagne. This is my treat.' He went over to the bar.

Twenty minutes afterwards Mrs Mallary, her eyes a little brighter, said: 'You know, it's damned funny, but I can't even remember what your name is.'

She toyed with the stem of her champagne glass, twiddling it round and round.

Guelvada said smoothly: 'My name's Hellard. I'm a Belgian.' He smiled. 'A Free Belgian. I have a post here under our Government. I was lucky to get out of Belgium.'

She nodded.

'You had a pretty thin time, I should think,' she said. 'I'm fearfully sorry for the Belgians.' Her tone indicated that she was sorry for the Belgians in the same way as she might have been sorry because the laundry came home late.

Guelvada nodded appreciatively.

'I'm sorry too,' he said. 'But one day we shall get our chance. We shall rise again, *Madame*.'

'Of *course* you will,' said Mrs Mallary. She finished her champagne. 'I suppose you're not having very much of a time over here,' she went on. 'Life's very dull in London, isn't it? But I think you talk English awfully well ... but then all Continentals are good at languages, aren't they?'

Guelvada said: 'I'm not very good, but, of course, I've had to learn to speak English fairly well. I'm still taking lessons.'

She said: 'I shouldn't think it was necessary.'

'It is,' said Guelvada. 'One can speak a language but one has to go on learning it. You know, when I tell a story or listen to one I like to be able to understand the point.'

The weedy young man said, with a knowing look: 'And I bet you could tell some stories too.' His face suddenly lightened. 'By jove,' he said, 'isn't your first name Pierre – Pierre Hellard? I've remembered it at last.'

'That's right,' said Guelvada, 'Pierre Hellard.' He smiled at Johnnie. Here was the identification. Johnnie was letting him know who he was. Only a few people knew that Guelvada carried three identity cards in his pocket – one of which indicated that he was a Free Belgian – Pierre Hellard. He said:

'Well, in my travels I've picked up one or two good stories. This might amuse you.' He looked at Mrs Mallary wickedly. He told a story – a very clever story – not too risqué – just right.

She laughed heartily. She wanted more stories like that. Guelvada produced them. Mrs Mallary and Johnnie were delighted. Guelvada began to put his personality over. He became charming and pleasant and a rather brilliant conversationalist. Johnnie helped him, subtly interposing a word here – a little encouragement there. Mrs Mallary began to think that Guelvada was more than 'interesting.' He was definitely *amusing*. She thought she might even begin to like him in a little while.

He ordered another bottle of champagne. Whilst it was being uncorked she said:

'I'm going on to a party to-night. Johnnie's coming. Why don't you come too – it'll be amusing – that is if you're not doing anything more exciting?'

Guelvada said: 'I'd like to very much.'

Johnnie grinned.

'That's fine,' he said. He turned to Mrs Mallary. 'Pierre can take you there, Eloise,' he went on. 'I've been wanting an excuse to duck. Now I've got it. I've got a date to-night.'

'Have you?' said Mrs Mallary. She looked slightly aggrieved. 'Is she very nice?' she asked.

'It's not a she,' said Johnnie. 'It's a he. It's business.'

'I bet it is!' said Mrs Mallary. 'I expect it's that blonde I

31

saw you with last week. ... What was her name – Virginia something or other ...?'

'Oh, her ...' said Johnnie. 'Oh, no, that's all over. She was a funny girl. She had a job in one of the Ministries some time as a secretary. They called her Virgin for short – but not for long ...!'

'You're telling me,' said Mrs Mallary. 'But, still, if you can't come, Johnnie, you can't. I don't mind now that I have got Pierre. ...' She shot an arch look at Guelvada.

He felt satisfied. He was pleased that Johnnie was ducking. He had no doubt that Johnnie had had his orders to make the contact between Mrs Mallary and himself and then get out of the business. Quite right, thought Guelvada, the less any one knew the better.

He said: 'There is only one thing ... I'm expecting a friend of mine to call me. We were going to spend the evening together, but I'll get out of that. I'd much rather go to the party with you.' He looked at Mrs Mallary. His eyes were smiling.

She said casually: 'What's your friend like? Is he nice?'

Guelvada said: 'He's wonderful. I wish I were like him.' She laughed.

'You're not so bad, Pierre,' she said. 'But, anyway, if your friend rings up ask him to come too.'

'Thank you,' said Guelvada. 'I think he'll be delighted. By the way, where is this party?'

'At Charlotte Court, Hampstead ... Mrs Jeanes' flat. But don't worry, I'll take you there.' She smiled at him. 'You ought to be fearfully popular with those stories of yours,' she went on. 'Mrs Jeanes likes stories like that.'

Guelvada raised his eyebrows. He looked *very* whimsical. He said:

'Then we ought to be friends. I've got a lot more stories. ...'

'My God!' said Mrs Mallary. 'You don't mean it? Tell me some more.'

'Not now,' said Guelvada. 'We'll save those for the party.'

He began to pour out the champagne. As he put the bottle down, the barmaid beckoned to him. He excused himself; went over to the bar. 'Your friend's on the line,' she said, 'a Mr Michael. You'll find the telephone on the other side of that door.' She indicated a door in the corner.

'Thank you,' said Guelvada. He walked across the room through the doorway. In the passage was a telephone box. He picked up the receiver.

'Hello,' he said. 'This is Ernie. ...'

Kane's voice came quietly through the receiver.

'Have you made that contact?' he said.

'Yes,' said Guelvada. 'I've met Mrs Mallary. She's here now. She's all right. I'm going along with her to a party at a Mrs Jeanes' flat at Charlotte Court, Hampstead.'

Kane said: 'What's the set-up like? What's this woman like?'

'Easy, I should think,' said Guelvada. 'She's *that* sort – casual, well-dressed, not bothering very much, rather bored ... and she likes a drink. She drinks a lot. Perhaps they'll all be like that.'

Kane said: 'That looks all right. How long do you think you'll want?'

Guelvada thought for a moment. Then:

'It's a quarter to ten now,' he said. 'Give me another hour. I want to put in a little more work on Mrs Mallary. If you come to Charlotte Court at half past eleven or just after, that ought to be all right.' He paused for a moment; then said: 'You know they want this to be quick?'

Kane said: 'I know.'

There was another pause. Guelvada asked: 'How are we going to play this?'

'I don't know,' Kane answered. 'It depends on Mrs Marques. When you've met her, and had a chance to see what sort of woman she is, you'll get an idea. You know,' he went on, 'people like Mrs Marques always have to have lots of allure, and women with allure always leave themselves open, don't they? They're always expecting admiration. It doesn't matter how experienced she is, she might still fall for that old line.'

Guelvada said: 'You mean play it like we played that thing seven months ago?'

'That's what I mean,' said Kane. 'It's the best way to do it in this country.'

'All right,' said Guelvada, 'that suits me very well. I like that way,' he said. 'It's artistic.'

Kane said bitterly: 'Like hell it is!' He had a mental picture of Guelvada standing at a telephone smiling, with his lips drawn back over his teeth.

Guelvada said: 'I *like* being artistic. By the way, I'm Hellard to-night – Pierre Hellard.'

'I see,' said Kane. 'And that means we'll use the Hellard flat?'

'Excellent,' said Guelvada. 'That's in St John's Wood – not too far from Hampstead. It all fits in. It looks quite good to me.'

Kane said: 'I'm glad you like it.'

There was a silence; then Guelvada asked: 'Who are you to-night?'

'I'll be Singleton,' said Kane. 'George Singleton. I was in the car business – on tank production now. ... And, for God's sake, Ernie, see you only have one identity card on you – the Hellard one.'

'Don't worry,' said Guelvada. 'Have you ever known me to make a mistake?'

Kane answered rather bitterly: 'No, damn you, Ernie. You never have!'

Guelvada grinned.

'Then you should worry,' he said. 'I'll be seeing you.'

He heard the receiver click.

VI

It was ten minutes past eleven when Kane rapped on the glass partition of the taxi-cab and signalled the driver to stop. He got out, paid the man, began to walk towards Ormesby House – the apartment block in St John's Wood where 'Pierre Hellard' was supposed to live. It was raining a little and very cold. Walking along, his hands thrust deep into his overcoat pockets, Kane thought of all the flats in the many parts of the world that had been used by himself and Guelvada for different purposes. Each job they had done together, each bit of 'business' – humorous, distasteful, macabre, or merely tragic – was impressed on Kane's mind by the atmosphere of the place in which the work had been done. A series of mental pictures, of flats and apartments, flashed through his mind – in unoccupied France, Belgium, Switzerland.

One of these days, thought Kane, something would go wrong. It had to. You could toss up a penny a dozen times, and eleven times it would come down heads, but the twelfth time tails would turn up. One of these fine days, if they went on long enough, tails would turn up.

If they went on long enough! He smiled grimly and dismissed the thought. He turned into Ormesby House by the side entrance. In the passageway, dimly lit with blued-out lights, he stood, motionless, watching for the hall porter. Satisfied that no one was about, he walked quickly to the foot of the staircase. He passed the indicator which showed that Mr Pierre Hellard lived on the first floor, and was 'Out.'

Kane moved up the stairs quickly, meeting no one. On the first floor he walked along the passageway, opened the door of the flat quickly with one of the keys on his chain-ring; stepped inside, closing the door quietly behind him. He put on a pair of kid gloves before he switched on the hall light.

The flat was the normal suite of apartments in a good middle-class block of flats. There was a hallway with a short passageway each side of it – that on the left leading to the kitchen, bathroom, spare bedroom; that on the right leading to the best bedroom. Immediately opposite him was the door leading to the drawing-room, and on the right of that, that leading to the dining-room.

Kane went into the drawing-room, switched on the light, took off his hat, lit a cigarette. He looked round the place. It was a little cold and there was a slight atmosphere of damp – the atmosphere of a place which has not been lived in for a while. Kane switched on the electric fire in the drawing-room; went into the dining-room, switched on the fire there; went into all the rooms switching on the electric fires. Then he came back to the drawing-room. He stood for quite a while in the middle of the medium-sized, comfortably-furnished room, drawing on his cigarette, occasionally blowing an artistic smoke-ring. When he wanted to knock ash from his cigarette end, he did not place it in one of the ash-trays that were sprinkled about the place, but dropped the ash carefully into the right-hand pocket of his overcoat.

He stood in the centre of the room looking about him. He was standing with his back to the door that led to the hallway. Immediately facing him was a large settee. The electric fire was on his left. Kane moved over behind the settee, pushed it a little nearer the centre of the room. It was now directly in line with the door leading to the hallway, and nearer to the fire.

He went over to the sideboard, opened the doors, looked inside, examined the bottles. Most of them were empty. He took these bottles to the kitchen, stacked them underneath the sink. He opened a store cupboard and took fresh, full bottles back. He took brandy, whisky, gin, Martini, soda-water. He put these in the drawing-room sideboard, and on the top a silver tray with a dozen glasses and a water jug.

He put out the stub of his cigarette against the sole of his left shoe. He put the stub end into the right-hand pocket of his overcoat; then he sat down in the centre of the settee, noted his position carefully. From where he was sitting he was practically directly in line with the doorway leading to the hall. Immediately on the right of the settee, near enough for him to feel the rays of heat, was the large electric fire. On this side of the fire, nearest the end of the settee, was the sideboard.

Kane got up and paced towards it. Two long steps brought him to the sideboard. With his gloved hand he opened the centre drawer and examined the contents. There were some table mats, some freshly-laundered napkins, a few odd silver fruit knives and one or two old copies of magazines. Kane left the drawer open and went back to the kitchen.

He opened the store cupboard, knelt down before the bottom shelf and began to move away the pile of house-linen and napery that was stacked there, filling the shelf. When he had cleared the space, he put his hand towards the back of the cupboard and opened a little door that fitted flush with the wall. He put his hand in his top left-hand waistcoat pocket and produced a small electric torch. He flashed it into the cupboard. In the little trap at the back of the cupboard was a curious collection of weapons. There were a couple of German 3 mm. pistols, four or five assorted automatics of American make, two .45 service revolvers and a collection of knives, ranging from one that looked like a Malay *kris* to the straight-bladed razor-edge type used by British paratroops. Neatly stacked against the side of the trap was an assortment of boxes of ammunition.

Kane took out a Spanish .32 automatic with a Guernita registration mark on it and a box of .32 ammunition. He put both the gun and the box of ammunition on the kitchen table under the light. He picked up the gun, holding it gingerly by the end of the barrel in his gloved fingers, and he removed the ammunition clip with care. He was using care so as not to disturb the natural layer of dust that was on the gun.

The clip was empty. Kane opened the box of ammunition, which was three-quarters full of live shells and a quarter with the empty cases of fired rounds, and took out nine empty cartridge cases and one live round. He inserted eight empty shells into the ammunition clip; then the live round; then on top of it another empty shell. He loaded the clip back into the butt of the automatic; then holding the pistol firmly in his right hand he pushed back the recoil action, thereby forcing the empty case at the top of the automatic into the breach. He pulled the recoil action back again and extracted the empty cartridge case. He worked the recoil action a third time, thereby bringing the live round into the chamber of the pistol.

He carried the automatic to the drawing-room. He laid it on top of one of the old magazines in the sideboard drawer. He closed the drawer carefully. He went back to the kitchen, closed the trap at the back of the linen cupboard, replaced carefully the linen and napery, looked about him to ensure everything was as it should be, turned off the electric fire and went out closing the door behind him.

He went round the rooms of the flat, turning off the electric fires, except in the drawing-room, where he left it burning. He turned off the electric light, went into the hallway. Very quietly, very gently, he opened the front door of the apartment and stood listening. He could hear nothing. He closed the door as quietly behind him, walked silently along the passage, quickly down the stairs and out of the side door.

Outside, in the darkness, he smiled to himself. No one had seen him go in. No one had seen him come out.

VII

Kane stood before the door of Mrs Jeanes' apartment in Charlotte Court, Hampstead. He looked at his watch and saw that it was a quarter to twelve.

The door opened. On the other side of the threshold a man stood looking at him inquiringly. Kane, at ease, his hands in his pockets, looked the man over almost casually.

The dress suit was old, and it did not fit. The lapels were not faced with silk. The stiff shirt front was faded and looked like a dickey. The tie was black. Kane thought that the man might have looked like a butler if he had not, all over him, on clothes and face, all the hall marks of a hired waiter. Kane wondered vaguely just where you went, in war time, to hire a waiter.

He said: 'I'm Mr Singleton. I think my friend, Mr Pierre Hellard, is expecting me.'

The man smiled. Kane thought the smile was intended to be charming. It lit up the thin face, removed the deep lines between the eyebrows. It showed a mouthful of odd teeth; some broken, some marred with decay. When the man spoke his voice was soft and reassuring, the accent just distinguishable. A Swiss, thought Kane.

The man said: 'Please come in. M'sieu Hellard told me you would arrive. Please to come this way.'

Kane stepped into the hallway, followed the man into a room on the right. It was a large, well-furnished room completely covered with coats and hats of every shape and description. A woman's fur coat, of the latest *chic*, rubbed shoulders, on the table, with an old, wide-brimmed soft, black hat. Kane looked about him quickly. So it was *that* sort of party. In one corner of the room, stacked in lines, like soldiers, stood bottles of champagne, whisky, brandy, and gin.

He took off his overcoat, dropped it, with his hat, on a vacant spot on the floor. When he turned towards the door, the waiter was standing directly in front of him, a tray filled with glasses held invitingly.

Kane grinned and took one. He drank champagne cocktail almost in a gulp. Its sharp, almost acid, taste pleased him. He took another, swallowed it as quickly.

The waiter said: 'I'm so glad you like the cocktails, M'sieu. They are of my own making. My own particular mixture.'

Kane said: 'They're very good. I congratulate you.'

From across the hallway, from the open doors of the other rooms, came a confused jumble of voices.

The waiter moved to one side. He began to walk towards the door. He said over his shoulder:

'Mrs Jeanes is in the room on the right, M'sieu ... your hostess. If you want anything during the evening – anything *special* – I shall be very much at your service.'

He went off with his tray.

Kane moved out into the hallway. Immediately opposite him was an open door, and in the room beyond a crowd of men and women, packed like sardines, talked, all at once, producing a noise that sounded like a high-pitched gramophone record of a football crowd. On the right-hand side of the hall, facing the entrance door, two folded doors were opened, showing a wide area of another room – a large one, not nearly as full of people as the first, but full enough to be uncomfortable.

Just inside the doorway Kane saw an extraordinary woman. As his eyes fell on her, he saw the waiter sidling sideways to reach her, like an eel; whisper something to her. Immediately she looked towards Kane. This, he thought, is my hostess. He moved towards her, and she advanced to the threshold of the room to meet him, walking with a mincing gait, induced by shoes that were too small and with heels too high.

She was a strawberry blonde. Kane, who had often wondered exactly what a strawberry blonde was, now saw and wondered even more. Her hair, piled high in a fashion almost rococo, gave her the appearance of a clown with horns. The idea was confirmed by the extreme whiteness of her complexion, produced by a dead white face-powder, and lips that were made up with a colour like a Guardsman's dress tunic. She had painted them in the shape of a Cupid's bow, but, in order to make her mouth appear smaller, had tailed off the make-up before it actually reached the ends of her lips.

The effect was to give her the appearance of an astonished codfish, and it was heightened by the oddity of her eyes, which, edged with mascara and shaded blue on the lids, were thrown out of proportion and shape by the dead white beneath them. They were staring, brassy eyes, slightly bloodshot. They protruded as if they might drop out at any moment.

Kane said: 'Mrs Jeanes? My name's Singleton. It's very nice of you to let me come to your party.'

She smiled at him. The smile was intended to be devastating. She said in a very raucous voice:

'That's all right. I'm glad to have you. I'm sick of this bloody party. None of the people I don't want will go away, and I can't talk to the people I _do_ want. Life's hell, don't you think?'

Kane murmured something.

'My parties used to be fearfully nice,' she went on. 'Until I met a lot of people I didn't want to meet. People who don't really do anything artistic. Stuffed shirts. And now they all come and drink and talk a lot of rubbish about things nobody gives a damn about. This War's going to be the end of Art, you mark my words. Ask Veteria to give you a drink. He's the waiter. He's got the real stuff locked up. I'm damned if I'm going to give my best drink to a lot of bloody _bourgeoisie_.'

She gave him a quick smile that showed a mouthful of false teeth, turned away, lost herself in the crowd. Kane smiled and moved away in the opposite direction. He was looking for Guelvada.

He was a little perturbed about Ernie. It was quite obvious that it would be impossible for the Belgian to start work seriously on Mrs Marques in a crowd. The only chance would be for him to wait until most of the people had gone. But it was late now, and Mrs Marques might be one of the first to go because, if she was the sort of woman Kane thought she was, she would not stay on at a party like this unless she had good reason. She would have too many things to think about – serious things – to dissipate her energy, mental and physical, on a party such as this one.

Guelvada might be thinking along the same lines. If he were he might try to rush things, and Guelvada was not at his best when he was in a hurry. This was why the Belgian was never allowed to work alone. He became impatient and tried to take short-cuts to a desired end, a process which, in their peculiar business, was not a good one.

Kane moved in the direction of the hallway. He was relieved to see that a number of people were getting their hats and coats, and to hear the hoarse voice of Mrs Jeanes bidding hearty and artificial farewells. He went across the hallway into the other room. Quite a third of the crowd had gone, and it was possible to move.

He went over to a big sideboard on which lines of freshly filled champagne cocktail glasses were set out. He helped himself to a brandy and soda; stood leaning against the sideboard, looking about him.

At the far end of the room was an alcove. An alcove that appeared incongruously Turkish. Inside, set against the wall, was an immense settee covered in yellow brocade, and on it Guelvada and a woman were seated. Guelvada, a charming and childlike smile playing about his lips, was leaning forward and talking to the woman.

So that was Mrs Marques! He found himself vaguely surprised. He had not thought that Mrs Marques would look like that. For some unknown reason he had imagined her to be a slim, beautiful and alluring woman of a more or less conventional type. Alluring and beautiful and intelligent – a combination which certainly does exist, whatever American film-writers may say, and which, in times of war, finds itself properly appreciated. Kane thought for a moment about the people who properly appreciated Mrs Marques.

She was a big woman of the type usually called Junoesque. And she was good-looking. But her attraction and allure were not immediately apparent. Her figure was good but was of the type that required a good corsetière, and her legs tapered down from well-rounded hips to very slim ankles and feet which seemed almost too small for her size.

She was a brunette. Kane wondered if she was a blonde who had decided to become a brunette. Her type was blonde. Her face was handsome enough when you looked at it carefully, but at first glance her head and features appeared too large for her size, although this appearance was probably due to the manner in which her hair was dressed.

The more you looked at her the more attractive she appeared. Kane suddenly realised that she was one of those extraordinary women who, at first glance, appear for some reason to be vaguely unattractive and rather lumbering; but in whom, when you examined them, you found yourself interested, and who were, in fact, large-size replicas of beautiful women. When you got used to the large size you were perfectly prepared to accept the fact that they were beautiful and alluring.

She was laughing at Guelvada, and her mouth and teeth were quite perfect, Kane thought, and when she moved she moved gracefully, in spite of her size.

Kane became suddenly aware of what it was that Mrs Marques had. She was the pseudo-mother type. Your first interest in her was because she was interested in *you*. You were attracted to her because she had, you would think, some quality of mothering which appeals to the great majority of men, and then, when you had got to know her, when it was too late, you would become aware of the fact that she had *sex* with a big S, and that it would take a great deal of talk to explain that you had been unaware of that fact in the first place. After which Mrs Marques would probably handle the situation in the way *she* wanted.

Her clothes were good and superbly cut. She wore a dark red dress under a three-quarter coat of the same colour. The coat was trimmed at the collar and cuffs with black Persian lamb. The effect against the yellow settee was striking. Her stockings were of a light tan, and she wore very beautiful black glacé kid court shoes with high heels which threw her instep forward and made the foot appear even smaller than it was. Apparently she was proud of her feet.

There was a suggestion of a small lace ruffle at her throat, and over it, showing against the dark red of her breast, hung a string of pearls. She wore several valuable rings on her fingers, and Kane could see the glint and sparkle of the precious stones when she moved her hands.

She used her hands gracefully. She was leaning back against the end of the settee, looking at Guelvada and smiling and gesticulating with her hands. Kane could see that the fingers were slender and expressive.

Ernie had not wasted much time, Kane thought. He had got to work quickly. But this time, for once, he was, possibly right. He had seen that Mrs Marques would, in all probability, be bored with the party. He had headed her off, parked her effectively against the carefully selected background of the yellow settee, from which she would be disinclined to move, and had begun to do his stuff, hoping he could hold her there until Kane arrived and they could handle the next step.

Kane thought she looked fascinating. Yes ... definitely ... fascinating would be the word for Mrs Marques, he thought. And fascinating women were a damned sight more dangerous than beautiful or alluring or merely intelligent women.

In order to be fascinating a woman must have intelligence. Kane wondered about this for a moment, concluded that fascination was a kind of physical intelligence plus charm.

He looked at the Belgian. Guelvada was busy. He was leaning forward talking rapidly whenever Mrs Marques stopped talking. He was putting a great deal of energy into his words, and his face radiated good humour. He would be telling Mrs Marques a story, thought Kane – one of the stories of which he had so many, most of them with two or three alternative endings so that they could be adapted to the state of mind or sobriety of the hearer.

Kane helped himself to another brandy and soda and looked again at Mrs Marques. She seemed to be reacting to Guelvada. Kane realised how necessary it was that Mrs Marques *should* react. Everything depended on that.

But women usually reacted to Guelvada. Kane wondered what it was, what hidden quality or virtue or quirk or attraction, caused women – even clever women – to fall for Guelvada's line. Shadowy figures of past women paraded through Kane's mind ... the short, plump woman in the Valdez *affaire*, the one who had been stabbed; the woman at Arquesnes who had got Ernie out of a nasty hole; the *grande dame* in the Loughborough business ...

It was damned funny, but Ernie usually managed to pull it off, although it was not a good thing to rely on luck – if it was luck. Sometime, Kane thought, the penny that invariably came down heads for them might decide to come down tails – just for once. And once would be quite enough!

He wandered back into the hallway. More people were going, saying good-bye or good-night to Mrs Jeanes, mouthing artificial insincerities, talking about 'after the War.' Kane looked at them sourly and wondered just what the War meant to them. A certain amount of inconvenience, and that was all. Suddenly the contrast of himself and Guelvada came into his mind. He grinned wickedly. The War certainly meant a hell of a lot to him and Ernie. It meant *too* much. It meant so much that sometimes when you were not in a particularly good humour you did not want to think about it.

It was not good to think about things. Fenton had once said in Kane's hearing: 'I don't like men who think too much ... not in our business anyway ... *I'll* do the thinking ... providing they do what they're told to do and don't ask questions and don't think. Directly one of my people begins to think he's finished. ...'

Kane shrugged his shoulders and went back into the room he had just left. Now there were about twelve people – including Guelvada and Mrs Marques – in it drinking and eating and talking. Most of them were a little tight. Kane ran a practised eye round the room. He was looking for someone – for a type. There were two people standing by the sideboard, helping themselves to champagne cocktails. Kane had noticed them earlier. They seemed to talk and drink an awful lot. They looked artistic. They looked as if they might do.

He went over to the sideboard and took a cocktail. He said to the man: 'Veteria makes damn good champagne cocktails. They're a mixture of his own. I think they're rather unique, don't you?'

The man looked at him. He was a short, broad-shouldered

man with unruly dark hair that was a little dank about the forehead. He wore a tie made of rough tartan plaid, and his collar was not particularly clean. He was tight. He said:

'I agree. I've drank champagne cocktails all over the place and I find them very good here.' He glanced quickly at Kane in a manner that was intended to be knowing. 'That's why I come here,' he concluded.

Kane grinned at him amiably. 'Just for that?' he asked.

The man became confidential. 'I don't know if you've been to a lot of Sonia Jeanes' parties,' he said. 'But they used to be damned good. One met intellect – or at least intelligence – here. My wife and I' – he indicated the woman with him, who was leaning against the wall by the sideboard leering at a man on the other side of the room – 'used to look forward to coming. But now—' he shrugged his shoulders. 'Look at the people who were here to-night. My God! I ask you. Look at 'em. ...'

Kane nodded ponderously. He was thinking that the man in the plaid tie was a squirt. He was also thinking that he might do. He and his wife. He said:

'I understand how you feel. I know just how you feel. I imagine you're an artist of some sort?'

The other nodded.

'My name's Kelzin,' he said, rather archly. 'I'm a critic. I write. I dissect. I analyse. I am a student of life and art, and so, in a lesser degree, if I may say so, is my wife. ...'

The woman looked at Kane and smiled. She took a step towards them.

Kane said: 'My name's Singleton. I make motor cars in normal time ... now I'm interested in tanks. But I've an intense admiration for artists. I think people like you and your wife are the salt of the earth. Art is really the only thing that matters ...'

Mrs Kelzin looked at her husband and smiled. She had thick lips and a spatulate nose. Her skin was olive and not very clear. Quite obviously she was pleased with Kane's flattery.

So was Kelzin, who said: 'Naturally any artist likes to be appreciated – especially by someone like yourself who isn't connected with art. There's too much jealousy in art –

especially where critics are concerned. Early this evening I had a hell of a row with a fellow who had the impertinence to suggest that a critic was a sort of parasitic growth, someone who lived on other people's work, who criticised work that he couldn't produce himself. He said that if there weren't artists, critics would either starve or have to find themselves an honest job ...'

Mrs Kelzin interrupted. She said:

'It was just jealousy, Fern dear. He was envious of you. Besides, you can always take it out of him at any time you like.'

Kelzin grinned. 'Quite,' he said. 'A critic does have the last word anyway – in print, I mean.'

Kane pushed another champagne cocktail towards the critic. 'Do you criticise pictures as well as books?' he asked pleasantly.

Kelzin nodded.

'Yes,' he replied with a badly-concealed hiccough. 'I review all art forms. I believe that the mind of a critic should embrace everything.' He spread his fingers on the top of the sideboard and looked at them diffidently. Kane noticed that the fingernails were dirty. 'But why do you ask?'

Kane grinned to himself. It was impossible to lay it on too thick for the Kelzin type. He said:

'Some time ago somebody, I forget who it was, mentioned your name in connection with pictures. I forget what the conversation was about, but I do remember that my informant suggested you were pretty good at your job. ...'

Mrs Kelzin said quickly: 'He is ... he's damn good. *I'd* back his opinion any day.'

Kane smiled at her.

'I'm sure you would,' he said, 'and rightly. But the thing I wanted to talk about was this. A man I know wants to sell me some pictures and before I buy them I'd like an opinion. They're a mixed lot and not awfully valuable, but still I'd like to know what I'm doing. I wonder if you'd have a look at them. Naturally you'd want a fee?'

Kelzin grinned.

'The labourer is worthy of his hire,' he said portentously. 'I'm your man. Where are the pictures, and when d'you want me to look at them?'

46

'I'd be glad if you could do it to-night,' said Kane. 'You see I'm due to go off in the morning, and they're at a place I'm using not far from here – in St John's Wood in fact. If you and Mrs Kelzin would come along and have a drink ...?'

She said: 'Why, that's on our way home. Perhaps we could leave here together and share a cab?'

'Marvellous,' said Kane. 'That's wonderful. Let's leave here together.'

Kelzin took another champagne cocktail.

'That suits me,' he said. He was beginning to talk thickly.

'I've got to talk to one or two people before I go,' said Kane, 'and then I'll collect you and we'll go along to St John's Wood.'

Kelzin nodded.

'Excellent,' he said. 'If we're sober enough by then we'd love it. Look out for us before you go.'

The woman smiled at Kane and the pair went off. In a minute they were deep in conversation with a woman on the other side of the room.

Kane drank another brandy and soda. He thought that by now he'd had enough. He'd been drinking quite a bit ... quite enough to *appear* to have drunk too much. He looked over towards Ernie.

Guelvada looked up, and his eyes met Kane's across the room. Guelvada smiled suddenly and waved his hand to Kane. He waved his left hand, waggling the hand up and down on the wrist. The greeting of a man who has drunk just a little too much.

It was an old signal. It meant *all right, go ahead.* Kane grinned back, put down his glass on the sideboard, and walked across the room towards the yellow settee.

On his way he could see that Ernie and Mrs Marques were sitting a little closer together, that their hands, lying on the settee between them, were almost, if not quite, touching. She was lying back against the settee, relaxed, looking at Kane as he approached. He could see that her lips were slightly opened and moist. She was smiling.

Kane stopped and stood facing the pair on the settee.

Guelvada said: 'Hello, Jack ... It's nice to see you, Jack ... you probably know why.' He smiled wickedly at Kane;

then looked quickly at Mrs Marques. He said: 'Mrs Marques, this is my friend Jack Singleton – a great friend of mine. Jack, this is Mrs Marques – Mrs Helda Marques – a Norwegian ... a delightful and charming person.'

Kane said: 'How do you do?' He went on: 'Mrs Marques, I think you are a very lucky and also a very unlucky lady.'

She began to speak. Immediately words fell from her mouth, Kane realised that possibly her greatest attraction was her voice. It was a low, rather hoarse voice, with a peculiar quality of richness – a voice you wanted to listen to. She spoke good English, with an obvious accent that made her speech even more charming.

'Please to tell me, Mr Singleton, why I am both lucky and unlucky.'

Kane placed one hand against the side of the alcove and leaned on it. He looked down at her. He said:

'Lucky for obvious reasons. Any woman who looks like you look, dresses like you dress, speaks like you speak, is lucky. As for the "unluck," that is merely temporary. Any woman who has to talk to Pierre here is unlucky.'

She laughed in her throat. She said: 'Tell me why.'

Kane grinned.

'Pierre is obvious,' he said. 'He is one of those cheap Belgians ... you know! He thinks he's marvellous with women. It takes a woman like you, Mrs Marques, to see through him.'

Guelvada leaned back against the yellow settee and exploded with laughter. Kane could see that he was squeezing Mrs Marques' hand. He noted quickly that she did not seem to mind the process. Guelvada said:

'You remember, Helda, I told Jack that I was particularly glad to see him to-night. I'll tell you why. I'll make him even more angry. Always when we arrange to go to a party together he's late. That's because he's stupid. But I am the wise bird. I am the early bird. The stupid Free Belgian Pierre arrives first, and when he arrives, what does he do?'

Guelvada sank his voice almost to a whisper. 'Being an artist he selects the one woman in the place who is worth talking to – except, of course, his hostess – and he talks to her. Afterwards fool Englishmen, like my friend Jack here, arrive and find there is nobody to talk to – no woman with intelligence or worth looking at, I mean.'

Mrs Marques said: 'You two are, how do you call it – in-corrigible. ... You like to pretend to fight with each other.'

'Don't you believe it, Mrs Marques,' said Kane. 'We do not *pretend* to fight with each other. We're the sort of friends who spend most of our time quarrelling. We have occasional splashes of ordinary conversation – very occasional.'

She said: 'And do you usually quarrel over women?'

She looked at Kane; her eyes were amethyst and very clear. Guelvada exploded with laughter again.

'I do not have to quarrel, Helda,' he said. 'He quarrels. You see, the ladies are always very kind – they want to talk to me. They never want to talk to him.'

She said: 'That's unfair, Pierre.'

Kane thought: 'So they're Pierre and Helda already. Ernie *has* been working fast.' He wondered if Guelvada had caught Mrs Marques off her guard; wondered whether she was not working at this moment – whether she was taking a 'holiday' and therefore prepared to be amused.

'I am most certain that I should like to speak to Mr Singleton about all sorts of things,' she went on.

Guelvada said: 'Like hell you would. He hasn't anything to talk about – only those ridiculous tanks he makes.'

Her eyes widened.

'So he makes tanks?' she said. 'Wonderful! Mr Singleton, it doesn't matter if you do-on't talk so long as you make lots and lots of tanks so that my beautiful country may be freed from those accursed Germans.'

Kane said: 'There you are, Pierre. I have scored a point. My lack of conversation and charm is made up for by the fact that I make tanks. I go up one.'

She said: 'Don't let Pierre annoy you, Mr Singleton. He is one of those frothy and quite delightful people that women like to talk to ... but merely to *talk* to, you under-stand?' She threw a sidelong glance at Guelvada.

He said: 'Me – I am a modest person. I never even hope that any woman would want to do anything except talk to me.' She was still looking at him sideways.

Kane altered the tone of his voice. He made it a little

bad-tempered. He said: 'You think a hell of a lot of your-self, don't you, Pierre? A lady-killer, aren't you?'

Guelvada looked a trifle hurt.

'Now,' he said in a deprecating voice, 'please, Jack, don't be like that.'

'All right,' said Kane. 'I won't. I think I'll have another brandy and soda.'

'Yes,' said Guelvada, 'that's a good idea. Come back and see us again – sometime next year.' He winked at Mrs Marques.

Kane turned away. He walked across the room out into the hallway. On his way he saw Kelzin and his wife deep in an argument with another woman. The hallway was empty. Mrs Jeanes had disappeared. Kane walked into the large room that was used as a cloakroom. In a corner the waiter, Veteria, was stacking empty bottles. Kane went over to him. He said:

'I think the time has arrived, Veteria, when I'd like one of your special drinks.'

Veteria looked up. He smiled. Kane thought he was a nice-looking old man. Veteria said:

'I have some very good brandy, M'sieu. Not the brandy that you mix with soda – the stuff I've seen you drinking this evening – but something very good. Wait just a moment, please.'

He went out of the room; returned after a minute with a balloon glass in which there was a good three inches of brandy. He handed the glass to Kane.

'I did not bring the bottle,' he said. 'Otherwise somebody, like Mr Kelzin for instance, might have wanted it for him-self. I think you will find that very good, M'sieu.'

Kane held the glass in his hands, warming it between the palms. The brandy smelt very good. He drank a little.

'It's marvellous,' he said. 'Very, very good. One doesn't often get brandy like that these days.'

The waiter said: 'One doesn't often get anything that's *good* these days, M'sieu.' He stood looking at Kane, his hands hanging straight down by his sides.

There was something pathetic about him – something pathetic about the meagre but carefully tied black tie, the faded shirt front, the well-brushed but shiny dress suit.

Kane asked: 'Do you like being a waiter?'

Veteria looked over his shoulder. He looked towards the hallway as if to make certain that no one could hear what he was going to say. Then he said:

'M'sieu, did you ever meet in the whole of your life a man who *liked* being a waiter? Is there such a fool as a man who would *like* to belong to a lost tribe?'

Kane grinned.

'Are waiters a lost tribe?' he asked.

Veteria said: 'If a man could do anything else he would do it. No waiter is quite certain as to how he ever became one – a *real* waiter. I mean – not one of those young gentlemen who wear an apron for a few months because they are learning to run an hotel or manage a restaurant – but a real waiter, M'sieu.

'People become waiters because of some incident in their lives; always it is going to be a temporary job; always tomorrow they are going to find some other job, be something that matters. But they never do. They go on being waiters. They eat at times when no one else eats. They are hungry when other people are eating. Always they are trying to please, always they feel they have not succeeded. Nobody ever tells a waiter that he is a good waiter; they only tell him that he is bad or has forgotten something, *n'est-ce pas, M'sieu?*'

Kane smiled. He said: 'I believe you're right. Do you know, I've never thought of that before!'

Veteria said: 'Why should you, M'sieu? Who does? Who wants to think about a waiter?' He paused for a moment.

Kane drank a little more brandy. Veteria went on:

'As for me, I am placed more badly than any other waiter to-day.' He shrugged his shoulders.

Kane said: 'How do you mean?'

'I am a Swiss,' said the waiter. 'Not only am I a waiter, M'sieu, but I am a Swiss waiter.'

He paused for a moment to let his words sink in. 'Figure to yourself, M'sieu,' he said, 'when practically every other country in the world is fighting or concerned with this war, mine is not. There are other waiters in the world – French waiters desiring to be free, or German waiters exulting in what they think is their Führer's victory, or Italian waiters – members of that race of waiters – acclaiming that head of a race of waiters – Mussolini. But I have no place even in an argument amongst waiters about this war.'

He looked again over his shoulder; then went on: 'Consider, M'sieu. I work sometimes in a place where there are two Italian waiters – they are naturalised British and they dislike the Fascist regime. There are also some French waiters, one Hungarian waiter, and two or three Czechs. Occasionally, there is a talk about the war. They listen to each other, but when I want to say something, somebody says: "What do you know? You are a Swiss. Your country never fights anybody." '

Veteria stopped speaking. He looked pathetically at Kane; then he turned and walked slowly away.

Kane finished his brandy. He put the glass down; walked across the hallway into the large room. It was empty now except for Mrs Marques and Guelvada, whose heads were close together in deep conversation. Kane could see Guelvada was talking quickly and smiling. He stood for a moment in the doorway watching them; then unsteadily he advanced towards them. Mrs Marques looked up as he approached. She smiled at him. Kane said thickly:

'Haven't you got tired of this fool yet?' He indicated Guelvada with a jerk of his thumb. 'You don't mean to say you're falling for that line of his, are you?'

She laughed.

'I do-on't know what you mean, Mr Singleton,' she said. 'And I do-on't know what you mean by Pierre's "line." I think he is mo-ost amusing.'

'Yes?' said Kane. His voice was insolent. 'And so have a hell of a lot of other women. But I haven't worried so much about *them*.'

'No?' queried Mrs Marques softly. 'Then tell me why you are worrying about me.'

Kane flopped down on the settee beside her. He said, with a hiccough:

'I'll tell you. ... You remind me of a woman I used to know a long time ago. She was a hell of a woman. I nearly married that woman ... I said *nearly* ... I wish I had. ...' He hiccoughed again. 'That's why I take a sentimental interest in you,' he went on, 'and that's why I want to tip you off about him.' He pointed to Guelvada, who was leaning back against the far end of the settee, his hands folded behind his head, smiling at Kane patronisingly.

'That fellow is a friend of mine,' said Kane, 'but not where women are concerned. Where women are concerned there's only one word that adequately describes him ...' He had a certain amount of difficulty in pronouncing the word 'adequately.' He looked solemnly at Mrs Marques for a moment. Then he went on:

'That word is bastard. He's just an ordinary common or garden bastard where women are concerned. His nickname ought to be "Love 'em and Leave 'em Joe." '

Mrs Marques said softly and comfortingly: 'But there are a lot of men like that, Mr Singleton, aren't there? Do-on't you think?'

'Perhaps,' said Kane. 'But there's none of 'em as bad as he is. When I said, "Love 'em and Leave 'em Joe" I didn't mean just that. When he leaves 'em he leaves 'em with *nothing*. He's an expert at separating *every* fool woman that falls for him from everything she's got. He's just a low, lousy, low-life Belgian – a Free Belgian.' Kane gave a sarcastic laugh. 'A Free-for-all Belgian!' He pointed solemnly at Guelvada.

Guelvada said: 'Listen, Jack, why don't you go home? You're beginning to bore us.' He looked at Mrs Marques knowingly.

'I'll go home when *I* want.' said Kane. 'Don't you think I'm trying to force my company on you, Mrs Marques. I'm just warning you ... that's all. And I'm only doing that because you remind me of a woman I very nearly married.'

Somebody said: 'Mr Singleton. ...'

Kane looked up. It was Mrs Jeanes. She stood over him like an apparition. On her face was a look of extreme distaste. She said:

'There are some people in the other room called Kelzin. The man professes to be an art critic. I want them to go. I don't think I like them.'

Kane said: 'I'm sorry about that, Mrs Jeanes.' He leaned towards her confidentially. 'I'll tell you something. ... I don't think I like them either. But you wouldn't tell 'em, would you ... just keep it a very great secret between you and me ...' He sounded very drunk. 'Anyhow, Mrs Jeanes,' he said, 'will you tell me what all this has got to do with me ...?'

'Nothing very much,' she replied acidly, 'except that Kelzin says that he's an appointment with you to go and see some pictures. I must say it seems an extraordinary time to look at pictures. But I don't suppose it would make any difference to Mr Kelzin's opinion what time it was. I was only hoping that you might take him away to see them.'

Kane said: 'Thank you, Mrs Jeanes ... I think you're swell. ... I'll go and talk to Kelzin. I'll take him away. Sorry he's annoyed you.'

He moved two unsteady steps; then turned. He said to Mrs Marques:

'Remember what I told you about him. You be careful. He's bad medicine.'

He waved his hand; negotiated the way to the folding doors with difficulty; moved out of sight. Mrs Jeanes went away.

Mrs Marques looked at Guelvada. She said softly:

'Pierre ... shall we go?'

Guelvada nodded.

'Let's go away, my dear,' he said. 'I'm sick of all the Singletons, the Jeanes, the Kelzins ... all of them ... *pouf!* I am only interested in the Heldas ... *allons donc!*' He got up.

In the other room Kane was deep in conversation with Mr and Mrs Kelzin. The Kelzins were leaning against the sideboard. They found that the most convenient method of standing. Kane stood in front of them rather unsteady on his feet, waving his hands benignly. They were deep in some argument on art. After a few minutes it seemed that they had forgotten what they were talking about. Kelzin suggested they have another drink. Veteria, the waiter, hovering about, brought them brandies and sodas. He said to Kane:

'Excuse me, M'sieu ... I know you will not think this an impertinence, but *Madame* ... Mrs Jeanes ... has indicated that she would like to go to bed. It is very late and every one else has gone. ...' His voice trailed away.

Kane said: 'Fancy that now. So everybody's gone.' He turned to Kelzin. 'We'll go too,' he said. 'Let's go and look at those lousy pictures.'

The three of them moved off towards the cloakroom.

When they had gone, Veteria, the waiter, began to walk about the large room, picking up glasses, emptying ashtrays. He looked very tired.

When he came to the occasional table that stood by the yellow settee he noticed a tiny handkerchief in the crevice between the cushions. He picked it up. The small piece of cambric and lace emanated a subtle perfume. He held the handkerchief to his nose. He thought the perfume was very good. The handkerchief, he thought, must be Mrs Marques's.

He stood in the deserted room, turning the tiny handkerchief over and over between his fingers, thinking of Mrs Marques, thinking about women and scent, and other delightful things.

He looked a pathetic and forlorn figure. He stood there for a few minutes, thinking; then with a sigh he put the handkerchief into his pocket, went on with the emptying of ashtrays and collection of used glasses.

VIII

Kane stopped the cab about fifty yards from the side entrance of Ormesby Court. He got out and searched his pockets for money. Eventually he found some silver. He stood, swaying a little, in front of the cab, the hand with the coins held under the head-light whilst he fumbled for the fare. He was giving the driver ample time to see that he was tight.

Kelzin and his wife got out. Kelzin was very drunk – the air had upset him – and his wife was nearly as bad. The cab drove away.

Mrs Kelzin said: 'Fern, if you can even *see* those goddam pictures you'll be lucky. I don't even know where I am. ... Who cares!'

Kane said: 'I stopped the cab too soon. But it's not far,

55

just along here.' He led the way along the dark pavement, waited for them at the side door.

They turned into the entrance. Kane, walking quickly, with an occasional lurch, began to mount the staircase. Kelzin and his wife came after him, negotiating the stairs with difficulty.

They walked along the passage. Kane pulled out his key chain and selected the key. He had it ready in his hand as they reached the door of the flat.

He opened the door. In front of them the hallway was dark. Kane said softly: 'Let's go right in and have a drink. We'll take our things off afterwards.'

He put out his hand and snapped on the light, shut the front door quickly immediately the Kelzins were inside. Then he crossed the hallway, threw open the door of the drawing-room. He said in an odd voice: 'My God!'

He stood, looking into the room, the art critic and his wife close behind him.

Guelvada and Mrs Marques were on the settee in the middle of the room. She was lying back against the sloping end of the couch. Guelvada was leaning over her, his lips pressed to hers. Her arms were round his shoulders. The scene was definitely voluptuous.

Kelzin laughed nastily. He said:

'Nice work if you can get it. ...'

'If you can *get* it. ...' said Mrs Kelzin.

Kane moved a step into the room. Guelvada disengaged himself. Mrs Marques swung her legs off the settee on to the floor. She looked from Kane to Guelvada and back again. She was quite poised. Her eyes did not indicate surprise, merely an amused curiousity.

Kane looked round the room. Then he glanced from the small table with the whisky decanter and two glasses, placed near the pair on the settee, towards the sideboard. For a split second his eyes looked straight at the centre drawer of the sideboard.

He said thickly to Guelvada: 'Hellard ... get out of here and take that harlot with you!'

Guelvada stood up. He moved slowly. He stood in front of the settee looking at Kane. There were some beads of sweat on his forehead and his lips were twitching. His face was dead white.

Mrs Kelzin mumbled: 'Fern ... let's get out of here.'

Mrs Marques smiled a little. She said, addressing Guelvada's back: 'Pierre, your friend is a leetle stra-ange ... do-on't you think so?'

Guelvada looked straight at Kane. He said, very slowly: 'Who the hell do you think you are talking to like that? And this is *my* flat. *You* get out!'

Kane said rudely: 'Nuts! I pay the rent and you know damned well I've been using the place for the last three days. You get out and take that fat harlot with you. ...'

Guelvada took a step forward. He put up his hands. Kane slapped him across the face. The blow caught the Belgian off balance and he fell, sideways, on top of Mrs Marques. Kane began to laugh.

Guelvada scrambled up again. His face was livid. He was mouthing in Belgian. Obscenities tumbled out of his mouth.

'You son of a bitch, I'm going to kill you for this,' he said thickly. He lurched towards the sideboard.

Kane said: 'You couldn't kill pussy. You half-witted pimp. Get out of here and take her with you ... there's a nice piece of waste ground at the back of here. Why don't you use that? And be quick ... or I'm going to smash your face in. ...'

Guelvada yanked the drawer open. He put his hand in. It came out with the gun in it.

Kelzin said: 'Christ ...!'

Kane murmured over his shoulder: 'Don't worry. He hasn't enough guts to kill a fly. He's just a big false alarm. ..'

Guelvada was almost frothing at the mouth. He yelled: 'So I'm a big false alarm, am I? By God, I'll show you!'

He pointed the automatic at Kane.

Mrs Kelzin shrieked.

Kane said: 'Don't worry. It isn't loaded. He's playing cowboys.'

He stepped forward quickly, moving out of the line of the gun. He hit Guelvada on the side of the neck with a short-arm jab.

Guelvada fell. He fell towards the settee. He caught the end of it with his left hand, tried to save himself, lurched

57

sideways. His right arm came up. As he fell the gun went off. ...

A look of intense surprise came over Mrs Marques's face. Just for a second. Then her mouth opened. But no sound came out of it. She tried to raise her hand to her body. She could not. Her face twisted in supreme agony for a split second; then she slumped sideways on the settee. A little blood ran out of her mouth. Kane saw the darker red stain begin to cover the front of her red frock.

Kelzin said: 'Oh, my God. ... My God ...!'

Mrs Kelzin turned and tried to run out of the room. She stumbled over a chair by the door and fell down. She stayed on the floor, moaning softly.

Guelvada looked round. He saw Mrs Marques. His fingers opened and the automatic dropped on the floor. The Belgian's eyes were wide. His mouth sagged open. His gaze was riveted on Mrs Marques, whose eyes, already glazing, looked absurdly towards the fire.

Guelvada dropped on his knees. He began to cry. He remained on his knees, waving backwards and forwards, making odd noises ... whimpering.

Kane turned round. He looked at Kelzin. He said:

'This is damned awful. ... Go downstairs and get the porter ... be quick. ...'

Kelzin went away. His wife, still on the floor, began to shriek hysterically. Kane picked up the water jug off the sideboard and poured some water over her. She stopped shrieking and began to moan softly to herself.

Kane walked to the telephone by the window. He picked up the receiver and dialled 999. After a minute he began to talk. ...

IX

Kane stood in front of the electric fire looking at the inspector from the C.I.D. Somewhere in the neighbourhood a church clock struck four. From outside came the noise of changing gears as the police van removed what remained of Mrs Marques. Kane was thinking that it must be damned boring to be a C.I.D. officer, and get called out on messy business at this time in the morning.

The detective-inspector sat at the card table that he had pulled into the centre of the room. He wrote carefully and slowly. Just behind him a young detective-constable was putting the sheets of foolscap into a document case.

The detective-inspector had a thin and rather good-looking face. He was grey about the temples and his knuckles were a little swollen. Kane thought he probably suffered from rheumatism.

Guelvada was sitting on the settee, at the end nearest the fire. His eyes were red. His face was quite drawn and lined. He looked an old man. His hands were clasped between his knees. All the time he ran his tongue over his lips. Kane thought he was marvellous.

The detective-inspector got up. He put his note-book into his overcoat pocket.

He said: 'Well ... that's all we can do to-night.' He looked at Kane. 'Needless to say, both of you gentlemen will be available when we want you. There'll be the inquest ... next week I should think.' The detective-constable handed him his soft hat.

Guelvada said, without moving his head: 'Jack ... why did you say that ...? Why did you say it ...? Oh my God ...!' His voice rose. 'If you hadn't said that ...' He began to cry. He made a hoarse, croaking noise. It was not nice to listen to the noise he made.

The detective-inspector said, not unkindly: 'I should take it easy if I were you. You don't want to get angry with any one any more to-night ... do you?'

He went towards the door.

Downstairs, Kane said: 'Good-night, Inspector, and thank you for everything. It's a pretty damned awful business. It's difficult to realise it's happened.'

'It's always difficult to realise these things – afterwards,' said the inspector. 'It's a pity that live round got into the gun.' He shrugged his shoulders. 'I should give Hellard a bromide,' he said. 'He looks to me to be in a state where he might do anything. ...'

'I'll look after him,' said Kane. 'Poor devil. ... It's pretty bad to kill a woman like that.'

The detective-inspector nodded.

'She was a good-looking woman too,' he said, inconsequently. He smiled at Kane. The smile was not unsympathetic. 'Well. ... Good-night ...' he said.

He and his man went off into the darkness.

Guelvada came out of the bathroom. He was drying his hands on a towel. He went over to the sideboard and poured a stiff one. He drank it at a gulp. He took out his cigarette case and lit a cigarette. He inhaled with obvious pleasure.

He said: 'I've never done that before ... taking a shot whilst I was actually falling over, I mean. ... It must have looked pretty good ... eh?'

Kane said: 'You took a chance to do it like that. You might have missed her. Why the hell d'you have to take chances?'

Guelvada shrugged.

'It's artistic,' he said. 'I like to be artistic ...'

Kane picked up his hat.

'Don't be too artistic at the inquest,' he said. 'Just stick to what we arranged, and don't try to be clever. Good-night, Ernie. ...'

He went out. He closed the front door softly behind him.

Outside it was very dark and very cold. He lit a cigarette, and began to walk towards Queen Anne Street.

He was whistling softly to himself.

CHAPTER II

SWEET CONGA

I

THE MUSIC sounded far away. When somebody – a waiter or a chambermaid – opened the service door at the end of the hotel corridor it came closer. Then the beat and rhythm of the Spanish music floated in at the half-opened door.

Guelvada said: 'I like that music. Spanish stuff – hey! Warm and full of colour. A *Conga*. What, I wonder, is the name of the piece? It makes me feel very soulful, a little artistic. I think I could make love to somebody to-night ... or ...'

'Cut somebody's throat ... ?' Kane finished the sentence.

Guelvada shrugged his shoulders. He went to the sideboard and began to mix two stiff drinks. He put a lump of ice in each glass, and a sprig of mint leaf. He brought the two glasses across the room, handed one to Kane, who was lounging in an over-stuffed divan chair reading a four days' old copy of the *Evening Standard*.

Kane said: 'One of these fine days I want to take a real look at this city. I'd like to look at it when there isn't a war. It looks a good spot to me. It has atmosphere. So has this hotel. So have the women. One of these fine days I'm going to come back here.'

Guelvada nodded.

'One of these fine days ...' he repeated softly. He grinned at Kane. 'In the meantime, *mon vieux*, you remain cooped up in this hotel suite, waiting for something that does not happen, for somebody who does not come; somebody who, perhaps, will not come.'

He sat down on the arm of a chair. He leaned towards Kane. He had an idea. Excited, he developed a suggestion of Belgian accent.

'Listen,' he said. 'How damn funny it would be – how *goddam* funny – if they were to forget about us. Forget that we were here; left us here. We could have a marvellous time, Michael, especially if they also forgot to stop sending the money.' He lit a cigarette. 'Lisbon is a good place. I know it. You forget sometimes that I was once a *courier*. I tell you this is one hell of a place and if one knows one's way about ...'

Kane said: 'Tell me about it. I've never even taken a real look at the place. ...' He went to the sideboard and poured another drink. He drank it quickly, poured another, went back to his seat.

Guelvada said, reminiscently: 'I'd like to take you all around the place. To the Alfama – the old town; to the Cidade Baixa – that's the lower part of the place, and then to the high part – the Bairro Alto. But you can always look out of the window here and see the Avenida. There are always a lot of good things to be seen on the Avenida.'

Kane said suddenly: 'The place stinks. It stinks of Germans. Everybody knows that. They're getting away with everything here. Everybody knows *that*. ...'

Guelvada raised one eyebrow.

'Everybody?' he said. He smiled cynically.

Kane picked up the newspaper.

'This is the *Evening Standard*,' he said, 'the edition of four days ago. Listen ...' He read:

'*Nazi propaganda is now unchecked and it is daily becoming bolder. A social layer has also been imported, including many-lingual Aryan titled women, whose morals are also at the service of the Führer. The line is to attract the snob element among the Portuguese.*

The Nazis always ask themselves in a case such as this: Where does the real power of the State reside? In Portugal they have come to the correct conclusion that it is not the Dictator's Government or the country's economy which rules the country – but the police. So the Nazis have set themselves to win the police. The highest officials have as yet received little attention. The main effort has been directed at those doing the administrative work and handing out daily orders.

These second-grade officials are being invited to the German Embassy, treated as equals with the highest in the land, flattered, invited to visit Germany at the Nazis' expense, presented with motor cars, expensive cameras, and with casual hints how much more men of such ability earn in German-controlled countries than, for example, in Portugal or Spain. ...'

Guelvada shrugged.

'What do you expect?' he asked. He grinned at Kane. 'The Boches may be getting away with some things,' he went on. 'But there is one thing, *some* thing, that they will not get away with.'

Kane took a drink. 'What?' he queried.

Guelvada said: 'How should I know? But we're here, *n'est-ce pas*? And doesn't it usually mean when we come to a place that somebody does *not* get away with something?'

Kane nodded. He finished his drink. He said:

'I was reading a book to-day. Some goddam silly book

62

that somebody left in the bedroom here. There was a bit in it about us. A nice bit.'

Guelvada was getting out a fresh bottle of whisky. He turned his head over his shoulder and looked at Kane. Something in Kane's voice intrigued him. He said softly:

'What was the nice bit?'

'It was a bit of poetry,' said Kane. 'Listen ...

> *'Faded the tinkling music of the minuet,*
> *And when its mincing cadences were sped,*
> *There echoed through that ballroom of the dead*
> *Two ghostly voices in a dark duet.'*

That's what we are, Ernie,' said Kane. He was smiling, almost cheerfully. 'Two ghostly voices in a dark duet ... a hell of a duet. ...'

'Why not?' said Guelvada. 'Personally, I desire nothing better than to be a ghostly voice. I think it's artistic. ...'

Somebody opened the door at the end of the corridor. The music swept along the passage, came in at the door. They both listened.

'That's a damned good band,' said Kane. 'It must cost a whole heap of money.'

'But yes,' said Guelvada. 'Why not? This is the best hotel in Lisbon. It has everything. It even has fat blonde German spies all dressed in black velvet gowns hiding behind the palms in the lounges. It only needs William Le Queux here to write a book about it. It's a scream, *n'est-ce pas?*'

He took a very thin platinum cigarette case out of his pocket and opened it. Inside there were a few cigarettes, a tiny flat phial of some colourless liquid and an inscription. The inscription said: *'To my most beloved Ernest. From A.'* Guelvada took out a cigarette and lit it. He smoked for a while, then he asked:

'Exactly what are we supposed to do here, *mon cher* Michael?' He asked the question diffidently, as if he expected no reply. When none came he continued smoking placidly.

There was a long silence. Then, surprisingly, Kane said:

'We've got to wait for somebody. An American. He knows. He's a bird called Gallat.'

Guelvada said: 'Ah ...! A delightful name, Gallat ...'

The telephone rang. Kane got up and answered it. He listened. After a while he said:

'Yes, Mrs Lahn ... certainly ... I'd like that a lot. Mr Guelvada? Oh, yes ... he's here. I'll bring him along to. ... Yes ... in a few minutes.' He hung up.

'That was Mrs Lahn,' he said. 'The nice American woman – the one with the daughter. She wants to know if we'd like to join her for supper. I said yes. Don't start anything with the daughter, Ernie.'

Guelvada raised his shoulders deprecatingly.

'But why should I start something?' he asked plaintively. 'Me ... of all people. Nothing would be further from my mind.'

'Like hell it wouldn't,' said Kane. 'But in any event don't start anything. I don't want to attract too much attention here. There are too many curious people in this place as it is. If we go down and have supper with the Lahns and a dance or two it looks more normal than sticking in this suite and not showing our noses.'

'Excellent,' said Guelvada. He smiled suddenly at Kane. 'But supposing, for the sake of argument, the daughter should make advances to me. What do I do then?'

'Nothing,' said Kane. 'Tell her you're married.'

'That often makes them worse,' said Guelvada. 'Much worse. All women believe that stolen fruit is the sweetest.'

'I don't care what they believe,' said Kane. 'Any woman who takes a look at you and thinks you're "stolen fruit" ought to get her brain examined. In any event you'll do what you're told. No nonsense with the daughter. If you start something I'll finish it – possibly in a way you won't like. Understand?'

'Perfectly,' said Guelvada. 'I think it is such a pity that I am so often misunderstood.' He went off, in the direction of his bedroom, whistling.

Kane went into his own room on the other side of the sitting-room. He laid out his dinner clothes and began to change. When he took off his sock, he fumbled in the bottom of it and produced a telegram. The telegram read:

'*Kenneth Michael, Hotel Estrada, Lisbon.*
Operations on Sally successful according to American

64

specialist's report. Doctor Gallat will remain in charge till she is convalescent. Your uncle arrives 27th. Love from us all. Mary.'

Kane took a pencil from his pocket, crossed out some of the words on the wire, leaving:

'Operations according to American Gallat arrives 27th.'

Kane took a cigarette from the box on the dressing-table. He lit it and burned the telegram with the same match.

Gallat should have arrived on the 27th November. It was the 28th. Kane did not like that. Sometimes a day's delay could be dangerous.

He put on his evening shoes and trousers, walked into the sitting-room and took another drink. Guelvada was singing in the bathroom. He was singing, very fluently, a Portuguese love song.

Kane grinned. He went into his bedroom, shut the door.

II

Meet, if you please, Marcel Du Puisse – at seven-fifteen on a cold and rainy evening – short and slim, very neat, very well-dressed. Almost the conventional film Frenchman ... almost, not quite. ...

Marcel's face was long, peculiarly heart-shaped. His eyes brown, attractive – sometimes pleading – often a little hard. His skin had that peculiar soft appearance possessed by a few men who seldom need to shave very seriously. His feet and hands were small.

He was essentially a Frenchman. Everything about him proclaimed the fact. Any conversation about the Germans had a peculiar effect on him. His eyes would become hard; his mouth would set in a thin line. It was apparent to everybody that he hated the enemy.

And he made it very apparent to the charming W.A.A.F. with whom he was drinking cocktails in the lounge at the Marigold Club. She was a nice girl. She was thinking it was a pretty tough thing to be a decent sort of Frenchman like Marcel these days.

The waiter hovered discreetly. He said:

'Your table is waiting, M'sieu.' He put a plate with a

folded bill for the drinks on it before Marcel. He went away.
Marcel said:

'Shall we go in? I am hungry, aren't you?'

The W.A.A.F. said yes she was. She got up. Marcel
flipped open the bill. It told him that he owed eight and
ninepence for cocktails. At the bottom of the bill on the
blank space under the total, pencilled very lightly, were the
words '*Sweet Conga.*'

Marcel put a ten-shilling note on the bill, refolded it,
followed his friend. The band stopped playing as they sat
down at their table. Marcel ordered dinner with a charming
apology for its war-time paucity. He said:

'Do you like Spanish music?'

She said she did.

'I'm going to ask them to play something – something
special,' said Marcel. 'If they know it.'

He got up, walked over to the band platform. She thought
he had a graceful walk; that it was a pity he was so ill. Marcel, you should know, had valvular disease of the heart. It
was for this reason that the De Gaulle forces in England had
not been able to make use of his services. Possibly Marcel
had known that. He had also known that it was a thousand
to one that there was no one at Free French Headquarters
who would know that the real Marcel Du Puisse lay buried
in a deep ditch somewhere in France, and that Karl Walcz,
who carried his papers, had been put in by the enterprising
Herr Himmler to continue the being and tradition of that
Marcel Du Puisse who had died for France.

Free French Headquarters had not known that. Karl had
got away with that one. He was, however, unaware of the
long-reaching arm, the far-seeing eye, the long nose of Mr
Fenton, who existed in a third-floor office in Golden Square.
To Karl, Karl Walcz was dead. There lived only Marcel Du
Puisse. Therefore Karl was merely a memory to himself,
and, incidentally, to his own rather peculiar mind, it seemed
better to be Marcel than Karl, possibly safer. The chances
one took so far away from Herr Himmler were perhaps not
so great as those which existed when one worked in closer
proximity. For Herr Himmler had a habit of shooting his
own agents for the oddest reasons. For them the sudden

bullet or the concentration camp if they knew too little. For them the bullet if they knew too much. So that working close to S.S. Reichsführer Himmler one was in a perpetual mental turmoil as to whether one knew too little or too much.

Whereas one worked in England with a certain safety. One was safe from Herr Himmler anyhow, or the petty jealousy of some Gestapo sub-chief. One risked only being shot by the English, and that, of course, was a normal working chance.

Marcel said in attractive broken English to the band-leader: 'I expect a lot of people bother you to play tunes, but I wonder if you know a number called "Sweet Conga"?'

The leader grinned at his first violin.

'That's funny,' he said. 'What do you know about that, Harry?' He said to Marcel. 'We do know it. It's rather a joke you asking about it. I'll tell you why. A customer here asked us if we knew it. We said we didn't. It's a Spanish tune. We'd never heard of it. But he was crazy about this tune. He gave us a record of it, and we vamped it up for him.'

Marcel said: 'How extraordinary. I wish I could buy a record. It's a lovely tune. I'm very fond of it. Do you know where I could get one?'

The band-leader said: 'He *said* he bought one in London. He said he got it at Williams in Greek Street. I've got the number of it. I'll give it to you if you like.' He produced a notebook from his hip pocket, turned the pages. 'That's right,' he said, 'Williams – the gramophone shop in Greek Street. The number of the record is 41927 M.'

Marcel said: 'Thank you very much.'

The band-leader said: 'You're welcome. We'll play it for you in a minute.'

Marcel went away, but he did not immediately return to his table and the charming W.A.A.F. Instead he walked round the outer edge of the tables until he came to the spot where a diminutive page-boy was leaning against the wall. Marcel gave him half a crown and some instructions. Then he returned to his table, sat down, apologised for his absence, and began to talk about all sorts of things in his soft, delightful voice.

He was interrupted after a few minutes by the page-boy,

who said: 'You're wanted on the telephone, Mr Du Puisse. I think it's urgent.'

Marcel nodded. He asked to be excused. He followed the boy outside. He returned after five minutes. His face was grave. He said:

'Mary, my dear, a terrible thing has happened. My brother was injured last night. There was an air-raid on the south-east coast. I have just heard. I must go to him immediately. I know you will understand.'

She was concerned. She said: 'Of course, Marcel. I'm terribly sorry. Can I do anything?'

'Only stay here and have your dinner,' said Marcel. 'I'll arrange everything as I go out. They're going to play that tune "Sweet Conga" in a minute. You'll like it. Promise me when they're playing it you'll think of me. *Au revoir*, my dear. I must go at once to Georges.'

She smiled at him as he went away. To-night he seemed more attractive, more brave then ever.

Marcel got his hat and overcoat at the cloakroom, He went out into the street. He walked through the narrow passage that leads into Regent Street, crossed the street and went into the call-box near the end of Sackville Street. He took from his pocket the piece of paper on which he had written the number of the record that the band-leader had so obligingly given him – 41927 M. Karl smiled faintly to himself and dialled Mayfair 41927. He was thinking how surprised the band-leader would be if he knew.

Somebody answered. Marcel said:

'This is Marcel Du Puisse.'

The voice at the other end asked: 'How did you get the number?'

Marcel said: 'I got it from the Marigold Club. The band there is the only one in London that seems to know "Sweet Conga." They got it from a record. The record was bought by a gentleman at Williams, the gramophone shop, in Greek Street.'

The voice said: 'All right. Have you got a car?' Marcel said he had. There was a little more talk; then he hung up; went out into the street. It was raining, but he did not mind the rain.

It was a quarter to nine when he drove his little saloon car through the High Street at Hampstead, and not many minutes after that when he turned off a road on the other side of the Vale of Health into a deserted lane. He drove the automobile on to the grass verge, switched off the lights, immobilised the car like a good citizen. He walked ahead in the darkness, picking his way carefully over the wet ground. Fifty yards down the lane – a hundred yards from the road at the other end – was a car. Marcel looked in at the window. He said:

'Good-evening!'

The man inside said: 'Good-evening to you.'

Marcel produced a cigarette case and offered it. Then he got into the car. They sat smoking in the darkness, sheltering the glowing ends of their cigarettes in the palms of their hands.

Marcel said: 'What is it you want to know about – the invasion thing or the Marques thing?'

The other laughed in his throat. 'I don't deal with invasions,' he said. 'I am merely interested in Marques.'

Marcel said: 'I have a part of the story. Considered properly, it might mean something.' He settled back in the passenger seat. He went on:

'Helda went to a party – a party at a Mrs Jeanes in Charlotte Court near here in Hampstead. She's known Mrs Jeanes for some time. Mrs Jeanes is a fool. Helda used her place to meet people. It seems that during the party a woman called Mrs Mallary arrived – also a stupid type. With her was a man – a Belgian – Pierre Hellard. It seems that he and Helda became friendly during the course of the evening. That part I don't understand because, as you probably know, she wasn't like that.

'Anyhow, it seems that he and she spent the greater part of the evening talking together. I don't know what they talked about.' He shrugged his shoulders in the darkness. 'Possibly she thought she might use him for something. Later there arrived a friend of Hellard's – a man by the name of Singleton. Singleton was supposed to be in the business of making tanks.

'Towards the end of the party there was some little trouble

between Hellard and Singleton. Then Helda went away with the Belgian. She went to a flat in St John's Wood. That again, you will agree, is not like Helda. But she went. It seems that this flat belonged to Hellard. He did not use it very much and he loaned it to Singleton when he was not there.

'It also appears that Singleton, with some friends of his, all rather drunk, arrived at an inopportune moment. Singleton insulted Helda, and there was a dramatic scene in which Hellard produced a pistol which was supposed to be unloaded. Then Singleton knocked him down and as he fell the pistol went off and killed Helda.'

Marcel smiled cynically into the darkness.

'Of course there was an inquest,' he said. 'Of course there was a verdict of "Accidental Death." Hellard was censured by the Coroner for being careless about firearms. Afterwards he was fined forty shillings in a police court for being in possession of a pistol without a licence.'

The other man made a clucking noise with his tongue.

Marcel said: 'An extraordinarily inconvenient accident.'

The other man said: 'Nicely done. Rather artistic, don't you think, Du Puisse?' He went on: 'Do you know anything of this Hellard and this Singleton? Where are they now?'

Marcel said: 'They left for Lisbon, but they aren't Singleton and Hellard.' He smiled again. 'Now they're Kenneth Michaels and Guelvada.'

The other man began to laugh. He said:

'My God! Kane and Guelvada again, hein? Why is Guelvada using his own name this time?'

'He must,' said Marcel. 'He used to be a *courier*. He is known in Lisbon. They know him there as Guelvada. Is that all?'

'It will do,' said the other. 'I shall report that Helda has been liquidated. They will be very annoyed. There was no one quite like her. Someone else – an experienced woman – must be got over; there is one in Eire who might do. This means that I shall be away for a week or so. As for you, Walcz, you will stay here in London. The next time I want to contact you the name of the tune will be "Bravado Tango."

Ask for it in some night club on the west side of Regent Street. Don't use the Marigold in future.'

Marcel got out of the car. He said good-night. He went back to his car, started it, backed on to the road, drove towards Hampstead.

It was five-and-twenty past nine when he drove into the little garage in a side-turning off Haverstock Hill. He locked the garage doors, entered the small house by the back door. He was surprised to see as he walked along the passage that there was a light on in the sitting-room. He wondered if he had left it on. He thought that was careless.

When he opened the door he saw he had not been careless. There were two men sitting in the armchairs in front of the electric fire. Marcel raised his eyebrows. One of the men said:

'Mr Du Puisse ...? I am a police-officer. I'm arresting you under a section of the Defence of the Realm Act. ...'

He produced a warrant card. The other man said:

'Take that hand out of your pocket, Du Puisse. Don't try anything funny. The game's up.'

MacMurray was dozing in the outer room when the telephone jangled. He took the call. After a minute he said:

'Hold on.' He switched the line through to the other room. He said: 'Mr Fenton, there's somebody on the line wants to talk to you. He says it's a call you'll take. Do you want it?'

Fenton said: 'Yes ... put me through.' There was a pause. Fenton said: 'Hello ...'

Somebody said: 'This is "S" for Sammy. Du Puisse went to-night to the Marigold Club with a W.A.A.F. We've talked to her. She's quite nice. She met Du Puisse at a dance and rather fell for his line. She met him to-night and they went to dinner at the Club. He went to the band-leader and asked about a tune called "Sweet Conga." The band-leader there had got this tune from somebody else, who had given him the record of it. The band-leader gave Du Puisse the number of the record. It was 41927 M.

'This number means something. There's evidently some sort of contact through the playing of this tune. I've seen the record and the centre paper with the title has been printed and stuck on specially. Maybe the playing of the tune is a recognition signal for agents operating in the same town or something on those lines. When he left the Club – he told the W.A.A.F. he was going to see his brother, who'd been hurt – Du Puisse went to a telephone-box and made a call; then he went to Hampstead. He met a man near the Vale of Health – Villinger. They've both been arrested. They're not talking.'

Fenton said: 'Where did this come from?'

The voice at the other end said: 'The C.E. Section, Special Branch.'

Fenton said: 'All right ... thank you.' He hung up.

He walked over to the filing-cabinet. He opened two drawers – 'D' and 'V' and took a card from each. One was headed with the name of Marcel Du Puisse; the other William Villinger. Fenton put a little pencil cross against each name. Then he put the two cards in a filing-cabinet marked 'Z.' He put them in a folder that bore a label 'Disposed of.'

He locked the filing-cabinet. He went back to the desk, picked up the telephone, rang a number. He said:

'This is Fenton. Get a telephone message by the quickest possible means to "M" for Michael at the Estrada in Lisbon. Code it to give him this:

'*Attention to tune "Sweet Conga." Probably recognition or contact signal. Mary.*'

III

Kane and Guelvada went into the crowded restaurant. Kane thought the place could be described by a news-reel commentator as 'colourful.' Most of the men wore tuxedos and some of the women were exquisitely dressed, heavily bejewelled. Kane, looking round him as he walked, wondered how many or how few of them were the Aryan ladies of high birth and no morals to speak of who did a little 'on the side' for the Führer.

In any event a small percentage of people were immediately recognisable as either undercover, or open, agents for the German Government. There was the man who booked the propaganda 'shorts' for the Goebbels service – they gave you a free film of sporting events if you ran a few hundred feet of specially selected pro-Axis stuff. Near to him was the lady who was busily engaged in booking film 'technicians' for the new Berlin film company that had taken big offices a few weeks before. The fact that most of this lady's technicians had never been inside a film studio in their lives mattered to no one.

The place was hot. The tables set fairly well apart – probably an attempt on the part of the management to prevent everybody listening to everybody else – covered one side of the large room and one L-shaped end; on the other side was the band platform and the service doors. Round the edges of the tables – the edges nearest the wall – was an avenue of palms – the cover, according to Guelvada, from which peered the lovely eyes of countless black-velvet-gowned *frauleins*, continuously on duty on the chance of picking up something from someone who had dined not wisely but too well.

Over in the far corner, at a table set close to the turn in the palm avenue, Kane could see Mrs Lahn and her daughter, Griselda. He waved his hand.

Mrs Lahn greeted them with her usual cheerful smile. Looking at her, Kane thought she presented an excellent example of the type of American that he described to himself as 'tailor-made.' Everything about Mrs Lahn was just so. Even when she wore a feminine dinner frock, as she did now, it looked as if even it had been cut by a very good tailor. Her hair was beautifully waved; her fingers sparkled with rings.

She said: 'Good-evening to you both. Is this your first appearance to-day? Griselda and I were wondering what had happened to you.'

Kane said: 'That was very nice of you.'

Guelvada added: 'And it was nice of Griselda.'

Griselda smiled. She was an attractive girl of twenty-five – inclined to romance. She thought that both Kane and Guelvada were 'interesting.' She wondered about them. She had found, on the occasions when she had spoken to them, that they presented a change to the majority of other male guests in the hotel.

Mrs Lahn said: 'I hope we didn't disturb you – calling through to your suite – but we were a little bored. Griselda says she finds the men around this place a little heavy.'

Kane said: 'I expect she's curious about us.' He smiled at Griselda. 'I think she's very observant. I've seen those keen eyes of hers examining everybody.'

Mrs Lahn laughed. 'That's because she took a psychology course at college,' she said. 'She tries to typify people.'

Guelvada said to Griselda: 'And so you've been trying to typify us. Me – I think it's wonderful being typified. What do you think I am?'

Griselda rested her chin on her clasped hands. She looked serious for a moment. She said:

'I don't know, but I should say that you both had something to do with finance.'

'Excellent,' said Guelvada, 'almost true. I have *something* to do with finance. I am invariably struggling to keep my overdraft within reasonable bounds.'

Kane said: 'Don't tell me we look like Company promoters. ...'

Mrs Lahn said: 'Are there Company promoters in wartime?'

Griselda said: 'Well, anyway – I suppose it's rude to ask – but what exactly are you both? You're much too interesting to be anything that's normal.'

Kane smiled at her. He said:

'We're not really normal. At least I'm fairly normal, but Ernie here is practically only one step removed from the local asylum.' He lit a cigarette. 'However,' he went on, 'I'm quite prepared to satisfy your curiosity.' He smiled cheerfully. 'Ernie and I are a pair of well-known gangsters,' he said.

Griselda said: 'Are you? I'm afraid I don't believe that. If you were you wouldn't talk about it.'

'Quite,' said Kane. 'No, I'm afraid our occupation is much more prosaic. We work,' he went on, 'for the Ministry of Information. They've got an idea in England that the Germans are getting too much film propaganda here in Portugal. Too many German 'shorts' and things like that. We're going to try and put some English short films over here – you know, interesting little everyday features with a story behind them. I think people would like it.'

'I'm certain they would, said Mrs Lahn. 'There's much too much German propaganda on the cinemas here.'

Griselda said to Guelvada: 'How interesting! So you're a film man?'

Guelvada looked modest. 'Yes,' he said. 'And do you know, I was thinking that *you* are an absolute type! I wish I were back at my studios on the Hollywood coast. I think I could use a film face like yours.' He looked mischievously at Kane.

Griselda said: 'I expect you've met some very interesting people, haven't you?'

'Very,' said Guelvada, 'and I hope to meet a lot more.' He leaned across the table. 'Would you like to dance the Conga?' he asked.

'I should,' said Griselda. 'Isn't this a lovely tune?'

'*I* was thinking that too,' said Kane. 'It seems a favourite with the orchestra too. Upstairs in my room I could hear them playing it earlier. They played it again when we came in here. This is the third time.'

'I'm not surprised,' she said. 'It is nice, isn't it?'

She got up. Guelvada followed her to the dance floor. Mrs Lahn watched them go. She said to Kane:

'A war at her age is an unfortunate thing for a girl like Griselda. It upsets the normal course of her life.'

Kane nodded.

'Naturally,' he said. 'But she seems to be having a pretty good time.'

'Can you have a good time anywhere now?' asked Mrs Lahn. 'Everything's unsettled – everything's odd and wrong. You can't rely on anything. Normally one would be thinking of finding a husband for Griselda. But what man – what eligible man – is considering marriage in these days? I think we shall have to go back to America. I shall feel happier there.'

Kane grinned.

'You can't make a tour very easily these days, can you?' he said. 'That's why Lisbon's become a sort of playground. It's one of the few playgrounds left in the world – that and Miami Beach. And both of them are a little dangerous.'

She smiled.

'Of the two I think I prefer Miami,' she said. 'Don't you

find there is too much atmosphere in Lisbon, Mr Michaels?'

Kane said: 'There is an awful lot of atmosphere any-where, but naturally one notices it here more than anywhere else. This is about the only place where English, Americans, Germans, Frenchmen, Spaniards, and Italians can meet without being able to kill each other, except illegally, and the fact that they can't do it except illegally doesn't mean that they don't want to. I should think that's what makes the atmosphere rather strong.'

She nodded.

'I think you're right,' she said.

Kane said: 'If I were you I'd go back home and stay put.'

'That's what my husband thinks,' she replied. 'I had a cable from him yesterday saying we were to go home.' She smiled. 'Possibly he thinks Hitler's got his eye on Portugal as well as all the other places.' She looked round the room. 'It's an extraordinary war, isn't it?' she said. 'Look at this place ... crowded ... and it's after one o'clock in the morning. In Russia people are fighting each other to the death ... and in Libya. In France, Holland, Norway ... millions of people are unhappy, starving ... subjected to all sorts of oppression. ... What a topsy-turvy world it is.'

Kane shrugged.

'That's the way we wanted it,' he said. 'We asked for it – your country and mine – and we got it. Now we've got to do the best we can about it, and when it's over we've got to see it doesn't happen again.'

A page-boy came to the table. He said:

'Senor Michaels, there is a gentleman to see you. He has a message. He says it is urgent.'

'Thank you,' said Kane. He asked Mrs Lahn to excuse him, got up, followed the page-boy out into the lounge.

A short, broad-shouldered individual with a pleasant English face was waiting there. The page-boy went away.

Kane said: 'You have a message for me? I don't think I've seen you before, have I?'

'No, sir,' said the man. 'You're Mr Michaels, aren't you?'

Kane nodded.

'We had a message from London,' said the man. 'It came over the Consulate wire. It was for Mr Kenneth Michaels to be delivered personally here. Could you tell me who the message would be from, sir, just so that I know I'm talking to the right person.'

Kane said: 'I think the only person who would possibly want to send me a message through your Chief would be my Aunt Mary.'

'Thank you, sir,' said the man. He handed an envelope to Kane, said good-night; went away.

Kane put the envelope in his pocket; went up to his apartment. He opened the envelope, took out the message. He read:

> *'Be careful tune Sweet Conga probably*
> *recognition or contact signal Mary.'*

He lit a cigarette. He burned the piece of notepaper and the envelope over the waste-paper basket.

He sat down in the divan chair, cocked his leg over the arm, and waited for Guelvada.

The small Spanish clock on the mantelpiece began to make the jarring noise that indicated that it was about to strike. There was a pause. Both Kane and Guelvada looked at the clock to watch it strike. It had become a habit with them.

It struck. The three different notes, struck on a tiny bell, echoed through the room.

Guelvada looked fondly at the pineapple in his left hand. He took a knife from the sideboard and began to slice the pineapple into a cut-glass bowl. When he had done this he took a fruit masher and mashed up the pineapple. He spent quite a while mashing the pineapple, taking an almost loving care about the process.

Kane sat on the divan chair, one knee cocked over the arm. He was watching Guelvada.

He said: 'All right ... well ... we can talk, and we can go on talking, and where does it get us? Some time we've got to face the fact that Gallat hasn't turned up. He ought to have turned up. He ought to have been here an hour after the plane got in yesterday afternoon. He isn't here. Well ... where is he, and why? Sooner or later we've got to concern ourselves with the fact.'

Guelvada opened a bottle of curaçao. He poured half the bottle over the mashed pineapple. The sound of the liqueur

77

falling on the broken fruit and splashing against the sides of the glass bowl was attractive. Kane liked the sound.

Guelvada said: 'It is not for me to argue. You are the boss. If you say we should concern ourselves about this Gallat then I am concerned. I reek with anxiety. I declare that I sweat about the tardy Gallat. But having indulged in these sensations I pause for a moment, say, so what!'

He put down the bottle of curaçao and opened one of Bacardi rum. He poured four tablespoonfuls of Bacardi into the bowl, and added a bottle of fizzy lemonade. He picked up the bowl and began to shake up the mixture.

'Gallat should have been here yesterday,' said Kane. He stubbed out his cigarette and lit a fresh one. 'He isn't here. We've got to do something about it.'

Guelvada shrugged. 'But why?' he asked. 'Are we also wet nurses to the so charming Gallat?'

Kane said: 'Don't be a bloody fool, Ernie. What else can we do? We can't stick around and do nothing. Gallat knew whatever it was we've got to do here. He had some instructions ... written ones maybe. The odds are that somebody has knocked him off. This place stinks with German C.E. people looking for boyos like Gallat. They were probably on to him directly he got out at the airport. Waiting for him.'

Guelvada put down the cut-glass bowl and took up a cocktail shaker. He poured off the mixture into the shaker, emptied the remainder of the curaçao into it, put in a lot of ice and began to shake it with vigour.

'I agree,' he said. 'My dear Michael, I am invariably in agreement with you over everything. I have always said that you are the veritable embodiment of common sense. Very well, then – what, exactly, are we to do? Where do we begin to look for Mr Gallat? We do not even know what Mr Gallat looks like. He may be a young and handsome man or an old gentleman with a red beard. Supposing that we *knew* what he looked like. What then? Where do we go? Do we go and ask the police if they know anything of Mr Gallat? That, having regard to the piece you read out of the *Evening Standard*, might be unfortunate. We might be unlucky enough to strike the very police officer who is getting a little on the side from Herr Himmler. Probably they are waiting for us to do something like that. They would like nothing better than that we should disclose the fact that we are the individuals who are waiting for the delightful and absent Gallat.'

Guelvada poured two glasses of the mixture, put down the shaker, went over to Kane, handed him a glass.

Kane said: 'Am I supposed to drink this stuff? God ... it makes a terrible mixture.' He sniffed the contents of his glass. 'Although, I must say, it smells good.'

'Listen,' said Guelvada earnestly. 'When I was here seven years ago I became greatly in love with a woman. I don't think I told you about her. She was wonderful. She had everything that a woman should have, and she also had a lot of brains. She was the berries, that baby. ... Well, it seemed to me that life would be ill-spent without experiencing this delightful creature, but she was as cold as ice. She had a soul that was surrounded by icicles. I tried everything, *mon cher*, but she was utterly adamant. Then, one night I thought of this drink. I made some and persuaded her to drink it. I had some too. Immediately she forgot everything except that she loved me. It was quite delightful.' Guelvada sighed.

'The last I heard of her,' he said, 'was that she said she would kill me if ever she set eyes on me again. I believe she would, too. She was quite superb. ...'

He went to the sideboard for the cocktail shaker. He came back and refilled the glasses.

Kane asked: 'What did you talk to Griselda about, Ernie?'

Guelvada smiled amiably.

'Sweet nothings,' he said. 'That one is romantic, you know. For a girl of twenty-six or seven she is much too romantic. I allowed her to do most of the talking. I find that she is very interested in you.' He looked sideways at Kane.

'Why?' asked Kane.

Guelvada shrugged.

'That's what I would like to know,' he said. 'But she says that you are a type, that you have a very strong personality and that you might be very attractive.' He grinned. 'She was talking from the psychological angle, of course.'

'Of course,' said Kane.

'She's been studying male types at this hotel,' Guelvada went on. 'She doesn't think a lot of them. She says they are interesting but superficial. She wants to find what she calls some strong Portuguese types and study them.'

Kane grinned.

'She might find them a little too strong,' he said.

'That is what I suggested,' said Guelvada. 'I said, "Scratch a Portuguese and you will find practically anything – that you don't expect."'

Kane asked: 'And then ...?'

'And then the dance was over, so we returned to Mrs Lahn,' said Guelvada. 'You had gone ... I didn't know why ... and there was with her an old friend, an American who is here for a few days, an old gentleman with a little goatee beard and a black string tie to his dinner jacket. He looked like the picture of a Virginian Judge in the fifties. So I made my *adieux* and left them. Besides ... I was a little bored. I find it difficult to be with an attractive girl for very long and not make love to her. I prefer to drink under those circumstances.'

Kane said: 'I'll have another glass of that stuff. It's got a hell of a kick.'

There was a knock at the door. A hesitating knock. Kane looked at the door and nodded to Guelvada. As Guelvada walked towards the door, Kane slipped his hand into the breast of his coat. He kept it there.

Guelvada opened the door. Mrs Lahn stood outside.

'But come in, dear Mrs Lahn,' said Guelvada.

Mrs Lahn came into the room. She was worried obviously. Also, she was trying to make light of the fact. But it was apparent that something was bothering her. Kane, watching her, as he got up and indicated a chair, wondered what could have happened to cause Mrs Lahn to visit them at this time in the morning. His brain was working – very quickly. Kane's business made him suspicious. When things went wrong he trusted no one, confided in no one, suspected every one. Even Mrs Lahn. The non-appearance of Gallat had produced in Kane the wariness – the peculiar instinct – that Fenton admired so much. That small additional sense that had enabled Kane to handle the toughest, most sinister assignments for over two years – and to remain alive.

He said: 'Sit down, Mrs Lahn. What's wrong? And now you're here won't you have just a tiny drink?'

'She said: 'No, if you don't mind, I won't. I'm probably being awfully silly, but I'm worried about Griselda, and I don't know why. ...'

Guelvada raised his eyebrows. He looked the picture of concern. His concern did not prevent him, however, from pouring out two more drinks from the cocktail shaker.

Kane asked. 'What's happened to Griselda?'

'She's disappeared,' said Mrs Lahn. She said it in a manner intended to indicate that she was perfectly well aware of the fact that the idea that Griselda had *really* disappeared was fundamentally silly. But that she wanted someone else to confirm the fact.

Kane said quietly: 'Just how did she disappear?'

'Well ...' said Mrs Lahn. 'After you'd gone an old friend of mine appeared, and then Mr Guelvada here and Griselda, who had been dancing, came back to the table. Then Griselda went off and danced with a young man she's met here at the hotel once or twice. I was busy talking and I saw her in a vague sort of way on the dance floor, but I did not notice that she hadn't come back to the table. I suppose I thought she was still dancing. Then I went to the smoking-room to continue my conversation with my friend, and, when he went, I went to my suite. I expected to find Griselda there. But she wasn't there. I waited a little while, and then I went down to the lounge and dance floor, but I couldn't find her. Then I asked at the desk, and they said she went out about an hour before ... with a man ... a young man ...'

'Probably the young man that she was dancing with,' said Kane. 'I expect they went to look at the moon. Or perhaps Griselda was studying him – psychologically I mean.'

'No,' said Mrs Lahn. 'It wasn't that young man. It was another young man. The people at the desk didn't know him at all. They did not remember ever having seen him before. I wonder if I ought to telephone the police?'

Kane took out his cigarette case, offered it to Mrs Lahn; lit the cigarette she took and his own. He went back to his chair. When he sat down he put the case back into his pocket and then, quite casually, rubbed the back of his left hand with the palm of his right.

Guelvada got the signal. It meant: *'I'm going to try and schmooze her. Play up.'*

Kane said: 'Look, Mrs Lahn ... I hate breaking a confidence, but at the same time I don't like you worrying. I don't think you need trouble about Griselda. I think we know that she's all right, don't we, Ernie?'

Guelvada smiled amiably. He said with a little shrug:

'But, yes. ... I *think* we do.' He laughed softly. The laugh was decidedly comforting.

'What do you two know, that I don't know?' said Mrs Lahn. 'What's going on here?' She smiled at them. Her expression showed her obvious relief. 'And do you know, Mr Michaels,' she said, 'I think I *will* have a drink – a very little one – now that you two are so perfectly certain that Griselda is all right.'

Kane said: 'Ernie here has got the most marvellous drink. It's terrible to watch him make it, but the result is quite good. Have one ...?'

'Don't you believe anything he says, Mrs Lahn,' said Guelvada. 'He's jealous of me. He's jealous of my ability to make drinks and my understanding of women.'

She laughed.

'I don't know what you meant about not breaking a confidence,' she said to Kane, 'but is there some big secret on between you two and Griselda? How is it that you know where she is and I don't? Or is that a secret too?'

Kane said: 'Look ... you know Griselda likes to play at being a psychologist? Well, like most female amateurs, she's mainly concerned with *male* types. I have an idea that possibly she's a little bit interested in somebody. Don't you agree, Ernie?'

Ernie understood. He said:

'Yes! If you ask me, Mrs Lahn, I think you'll find this young and attractive man with whom Griselda disappeared is someone who is probably well known to you.' He looked poetic. 'Love's young dream ...' he continued, 'may have manifested itself to Griselda in Lisbon. Even psychologists have to fall sometimes.'

'I see,' said Mrs Lahn cheerfully. 'So Griselda's keen on somebody, is she? She's gone off in the moonlight. Well, I suppose that's all right. At any rate, it's all right if it's somebody I know ... although why Griselda should have kept it a secret ...'

Kane interrupted.

'I've got an idea that Griselda thinks you're inclined to laugh at some of her young men,' he said. 'Possibly she wants to be quite certain before she says anything to you about it.'

Mrs Lahn put down her empty glass. She stubbed out her cigarette in the ashtray on the table at her side. She said:

'Well, it's very late, and I'm going to bed.' She got up. 'I'm not going to worry about Griselda,' she went on, 'but it is a bit late, isn't it? Since you know so much about her, perhaps you can also tell me what time she'll be in?'

Kane said easily: 'I can tell you two things. She's not *very* far away and she won't be *very* long. My advice to you is to go off and get your beauty sleep – not that you need it. Tomorrow morning you'll find Griselda safely tucked up in her little bed, drinking her early morning tea.'

Mrs Lahn laughed.

'Well, I'll trust you,' she said, 'although I don't know why I should. So you guarantee Griselda *will* be back, do you?' She went over to the door. Guelvada held it open for her.

'Kane said: 'Yes, we guarantee that. Good-night to you, Mrs Lahn. If it's of any interest to you, we like you very much, don't we, Ernie?'

Guelvada said: 'You speak for yourself. Me – I go further than that. I adore Mrs Lahn passionately.'

She went down the passage laughing.

Guelvada closed the door. He returned to the sideboard, poured some Bacardi into a glass and drank it. He said:

'What is all this about the so sweet Griselda and our knowing where she is? I don't understand.'

Kane said: 'Listen, Ernie. ... You remember when we were sitting up here before we went down to have supper? Whenever the service door opened at the end of the corridor we could hear the band playing? You remember you said thay were playing a conga – you said it was a nice tune ... ?'

Guelvada nodded. 'I remember,' he said. 'So what?'

'When we went down to have supper with Mrs Lahn,' said Kane, 'when we went into the dance room, the band played the same tune. Isn't it rather odd for a band to play the same tune twice in so short a time? I've never known them do it here before.'

'Perhaps,' said Guelvada. 'But I still don't understand.'

'Maybe you don't,' said Kane. 'The third thing is that when you went off to dance with Griselda they played that tune again. In other words they played the same tune three times within half an hour. You go downstairs, find out the name of that tune.'

'Willingly,' said Guelvada. 'I'll do my best. Is it permitted to ask why?'

Kane nodded.

'Fenton got through,' he said. 'He got a telephone message through to the Embassy. One of the messengers came round here with it. There is a Spanish tune called "Sweet Conga." Fenton says it's some sort of contact signal for their people. Get it?'

'I've got it,' said Guelvada. He smiled. 'It looks as if things are beginning to get interesting, doesn't it?' he said. 'It would be amusing if the C.E. people had got on to us before we even knew what we were doing here.' He shrugged his shoulders; went out.

Kane lit a cigarette. He cocked one leg over the arm of the chair; smoked silently, blowing smoke rings towards the ceiling. He was still blowing smoke rings when Guelvada came back. Guelvada came into the room, closed the door behind him, stood with his back against it.

'*Mon cher* Michael, wonders will never cease! The name of the tune *was* "Sweet Conga" ...!'

Kane nodded. He looked depressed.

Guelvada went on: 'I don't know what it means to you – this tune, and Griselda and Mrs Lahn, and all the rest of it – but it doesn't mean anything particularly to me. Do you feel like explaining? If you do, I'll be very interested.'

Kane said: 'I want a drink – an old-fashioned whisky and soda.'

Guelvada went to the sideboard. 'I think it's an idea,' he

said. 'I'll have one too. I don't like whisky, but my brain always works better when I've had some.'

'*Your* brain?' said Kane acidly. 'I like that. Your brain never works. You're merely an automatic gangster. Somebody presses a button and you fog somebody.'

Guelvada began to pour out the whisky. Kane went on:

'I've told you about the message from Fenton; you know that tune was played three times to-night; you know Griselda's disappeared into thin air. But you don't know why ... and you talk about your brain!'

Guelvada sighed. He came over to Kane, a whisky and soda in his right hand.

'*Mon vieux*,' he said. 'I am not the brains department. You are the brains department. I do other things. I am merely a practical person who likes to do practical things in an artistic way. And I still don't understand.'

'All right,' said Kane. 'Well, you bring your practical mind to bear on this. Gallat should have been here yesterday. He should have come in on the afternoon plane. Well, he's not here, is he? But we know he came in on the afternoon plane. Therefore something happened to him, didn't it? You know damned well that if Gallat was supposed to contact us he'd have done it. Obviously he's working for Fenton, and people who work for Fenton do what they're told – unless something very drastic stops them. You understand that?'

'Very well,' said Guelvada. 'All right. ... Gallat got here and they've knocked him off. The German C.E. people have knocked him off.'

'That's all right,' said Kane. 'It is all right providing Gallat hasn't any written instructions on him. But it's a stone certainty that he has. If Gallat had come straight from England Fenton wouldn't have used *him* in order to send us instructions – he's got other means – quicker, safer means – as you know. Therefore the probability is that Gallat's come from somewhere else; that he's got something in writing – because it's *got* to be in writing – a list of names, one of the usual things, or something like that – things that can't be remembered easily. Things that Fenton couldn't get straight to me because they had to come from somewhere else.'

Guelvada nodded.

'I understand,' he said. 'Gallat's an American. Probably he came from America. He's probably one of Fenton's contacts in Washington.'

'Probably,' said Kane. 'Well, if they've got Gallat, they've got everything he had on him. But that isn't the point that's worrying me so much.'

'What is worrying you, Michael?' asked Guelvada.

'I'm worried about "Sweet Conga,"' said Kane. 'Look ... the first time they played that tune to-night was when we were up here talking. I imagine that they played it about the time that Mrs Lahn and Griselda went into the restaurant. Maybe that was the recognition signal. Somebody was to recognise Mrs Lahn and Griselda by the fact that that tune was played when they went into the room.'

'All right,' said Guelvada. 'Why did they want to recognise Mrs Lahn and Griselda, or either of them?'

'Because, you nut-head,' said Kane, 'Mrs Lahn and Griselda are the only two people in this hotel that we've talked to to any extent since we've been here.'

'My God!' said Guelvada. He began to grin. 'So they think that Mrs Lahn and Griselda ...'

'Exactly,' said Kane. 'They think that Mrs Lahn and Griselda are associated with us. Having established their identity for somebody who's sitting in the dance room by playing "Sweet Conga" when they come in, they play it again when *we* go in. That fixes *our* identity. There we all are. Mrs Lahn, Griselda, yourself and myself. Somebody in that room wanted to identify us. Well, they've done it. They know who we are. The tune was the signal.'

'Excellent,' said Guelvada. 'That looks like sense. I understand perfectly. But why does Griselda disappear?'

Kane lit another cigarette.

'Listen, hop-head. ... Supposing they've got Gallat? If they got Gallat they've got the list or the instructions or whatever it was he had on him. That's all right. Now the next thing they want to know is what we were going to do when we got those instructions. Whatever they intend to do with us it would still be useful for them to know what we were going to do. All right. So they want to make somebody

86

talk, don't they? And of we four people who would the easiest one be?'

Guelvada whistled.

'They're going to make her talk,' he said.

'Exactly,' said Kane.

'Not so good for Griselda,' said Guelvada. 'Especially as she doesn't know anything, and therefore she can't talk. Not so good ...! Me – I am extremely concerned for her.' He took out his cigarette case. 'You remember what they did to that woman at Soissons, Michael?' he said. He tapped his cigarette end on the case.

Kane said: 'I don't want to remember.'

Guelvada nodded.

'That's the trouble with you,' he said. 'You have a flair for forgetting unpleasant things. But for me – I always remember them ... every little thing and every bad thing that I have known them to do ... I make one big mathematical sum in my mind, and then ...'

'I know,' said Kane. 'And then when you've added it all up, whenever you get your chance, you get your own back in your own way.'

'Precisely,' said Guelvada. He finished his whisky.

'Now I understand,' he went on. 'Now I see why you smoothed down Mrs Lahn. Why you pretended that we knew where Griselda was ... you wanted to stop her. ...'

'I wanted to stop her shouting her head off all over this town, ringing police stations and hospitals,' said Kane. 'That wouldn't help us, as you know. If they've got Griselda, ringing police stations isn't going to help us. What we need is a mortuary.' He stretched out his long legs; folded his hands behind his head.

Guelvada mixed more whisky and soda. He leaned against the sideboard; began to drink the whisky. Every time he took a gulp he made a grimace as if he disliked it.

'What are you going to do, Michael?' he asked.

Kane said: 'I'm very sorry about Griselda – very sorry. But I ought to be concerned with Gallat. Gallat's our business. Griselda isn't. She's just unfortunate.'

Guelvada nodded. 'Agreed. But it's tough luck that because a young woman and her mother are nice to us and like to talk to us in an hotel, somebody should do something *not* nice to her.' He sighed. 'They'll probably be *very* unkind,' he concluded.

Kane lit another cigarette.

'Well, we've got something to start on,' he said.

Guelvada raised his eyebrows. 'Have we?' he asked.

Kane said: 'Listen, stupid. ... The band played "Sweet Conga" three times to-night. We know "Sweet Conga" is a contact signal. All right. Well, somebody told somebody to play it three times, didn't they?'

'My God!' said Guelvada. 'You mean the band-leader?'

'Precisely,' said Kane. 'I mean the band-leader. You go downstairs and do a little snooping. Find out where the band-leader lives. Have you got that?'

Guelvada nodded.

'Perfectly,' he said.

'While you are downstairs,' said Kane, 'you might take a look at the night porter. If he's the one who was on last night, he looks intelligent, as if he might listen to reason. Tell me what you think of him. Talk to him if necessary.'

'I'll talk to him,' said Guelvada, 'and when I've talked to him for a few moments I shall know all about him. I have only to talk to a man and I know *all* about him. I am very good indeed at judging people's characters.'

Kane grinned cynically.

'So you can do that *too*,' he said. He lit another cigarette.

Guelvada went away.

Kane, his leg still cocked over the arm of the chair, looked at the ceiling ruminatively and blew smoke rings. He was a trifle worried – as worried as he ever allowed himself to be, because people in Kane's profession are quick to realize that worry is non-constructive. It does not help – it merely blunts the instincts.

Kane was a little concerned with the situation. He wondered precisely how he was going to play this business.

He got up, went to the sideboard, poured himself another whisky and soda. In spite of the mixture of drinks during the evening, his brain felt clear and active. He made up his mind that *somehow* Gallat must be found. It was necessary.

A quarter of an hour afterwards Guelvada came back. He

said: 'I've found out about the band-leader. He's a Spaniard – a nice fellow. Everybody likes him. His name is Juan Roccas. I've got his address. He lives near the Rua Augusta. I think it would be a good idea if I went to see him. I go very well with Spaniards.'

Kane raised his eyebrows. He said:

'Is there anybody you don't go well with?'

Guelvada looked serious.

'Candidly, between you and me,' he said, 'I have not discovered *any one* yet – except perhaps the woman I was telling you about – the one I met here.' He smiled suddenly. 'And even then,' he said, 'things *might* have been all right if I'd played my cards with a little more finesse. In point of fact,' he went on brightly, 'in spite of the fact that she wished, at the end, to kill me, I think she was very very fond of me.'

Kane said: 'I see. They get so fond of you they want to kill you.'

Guelvada looked surprised.

'Why not?' he said. 'It should be obvious to any one that the businesses of love and hate are so near to each other that often it is impossible to separate them.'

There was silence for a few moments; then Kane asked:

'What was the night porter like?'

'The right sort of man,' said Guelvada. 'I don't know what you want him for, but he's still the right sort of man. He'd be right for anything.' He grinned. 'He's one of those people – you know ...'

Kane said: 'One of *what* people ...?'

'Well,' said Guelvada, 'he's not a bad-looking fellow. His clothes fit him very well; he's fastidious and neat. He's got tired bedroom eyes. He looks very experienced, which is natural, because to be a night porter in a place like this one must be experienced – very experienced. In fact,' he concluded, 'he is the sort of man who would, I think, do anything that was required providing somebody gave him some money.'

'All right,' said Kane. 'Well, I've got an idea. It may not work, but I'm going to try it, and in the meantime I want you to go and see this Spaniard Roccas. You find him. Maybe he's at home.'

'And maybe not,' said Guelvada. 'You know these bandleaders – when they finish work they go on somewhere else. They meet their friends. To them the night-time is their play-time. They sleep during the day.'

'Never mind,' said Kane. 'You find Roccas. When you've found him, find out why he played "Sweet Conga" three times to-night, but don't start anything, will you?'

'Meaning exactly what?' asked Guelvada.

Kane said: 'I want you for once to be tactful. I don't want you to threaten this man. I don't want you to be theatrical, or work out some wonderful act that is unnecessary and is going to have a lot of repercussions. Just be quiet and plausible. Work out a story that sounds reasonable. If someone asked him to play the tune, find out who it was. If you think he's working for the other side, you'll possibly discover the fact in conversation.'

'Possibly,' said Guelvada. 'And supposing he is, do I still have to be tactful?'

'Why not?' said Kane. 'Let's *try* tact in the first place. Remember I want to get out of here with a whole skin if I can.'

Guelvada nodded. 'Me too!' he said.

Kane looked at his watch.

'It's four o'clock,' he said. 'Try and get back here by five. And don't get involved in anything, Ernie.'

Guelvada said: 'I shall become involved in nothing. You may trust me implicitly.'

He went into the bedroom, got his hat; grinned at Kane as he passed through the drawing-room. Kane thought Guelvada looked happy. He wondered exactly what was going on in his mind.

Five minutes after Guelvada had gone, Kane got up. He went into his bedroom, opened a box of cigars, selected one, lit it. The cigar gave him an appearance of well-being, of ease, almost of complacency. He knew this. He took his hat and went downstairs to the lounge and looked about him. In the far corner, nearest the entrance of the hotel, was the night porter's glass box.

Kane walked over casually. He looked through the glass door at the night porter, who was sitting at a desk writing figures in a notebook. Kane looked at the man quickly. He agreed with Guelvada. The night porter looked possible.

Kane spoke in French. He said: 'I am in a little difficulty. I think you might be able to help me.'

The night porter got up. He was of middle height, slim, quite good-looking. Kane realised that when Guelvada had said that he had tired bedroom eyes he was for once understating the case.

He said in a pleasant voice: 'I am at your disposal. Anything that I can do to help ...'

Kane said: 'The position is as follows: Yesterday I have reason to believe that a friend of mine arrived at the airport by plane. He should have come here to see me. He has not arrived. I am wondering what's happened to him. At the same time I do not want to make inquiries that are too obvious. For instance, I do not want to go to the police or get hospitals checked or anything like that.'

The night porter said : 'Quite!'

'As a matter of fact,' Kane continued, 'it may be that my friend, before coming to see me, decided to call on someone – possibly he has lady friends here – I don't know. It occurred to me that you might know a police officer – a junior police officer – an intelligent, agreeable individual who might be inclined to help a little – in an unofficial way, of course.'

The night porter sat down. He closed his little notebook with a snap. He folded his hands together. He looked at Kane and smiled. He said:

'I understand, but you will realise that an inquiry like that is sometimes a little difficult, especially in these times ...' He shrugged his shoulders. 'Lisbon is a difficult place. ...'

Kane inhaled from his cigar. He blew the smoke slowly through his nostrils.

'Why?' he asked pleasantly.

'Consider,' said the night porter, 'all the time people are trying to find things out. Sometimes they are people who are interested in the German point of view; sometimes they are people who are interested in the English point of view, or the French. One is always in rather a difficult position, because, as you will understand, it would be unfortunate if I were to put you on to the wrong man.'

'Precisely,' said Kane. 'Shall we say that the individual I

would like to meet is one who might be more interested in the English point of view?'

The night porter smiled.

'I'm glad to hear you say that,' he said, 'because I am very much for the English. I dislike the Germans very much. So does my friend.' He took a piece of paper and wrote on it. 'Here is his address,' he said, 'his private address. He ought to be at home now. I'm certain of that. His name is Serilla. He is an assistant inspector – on the plain-clothes branch – and he is concerned with the movements of foreigners in Lisbon. He is very fond of the English, and,' he concluded with a small smile, 'is always prepared to listen to reason.'

'Excellent,' said Kane. He took out his pocket-book, extracted four or five notes, folded them, handed them to the night porter. 'I'm most grateful to you,' he said.

'And I to you, sir,' said the night porter. 'I am now and always at your service.'

Kane put the piece of paper into his pocket. He put on his hat and went out.

IV

Guelvada sat back in the corner of the taxicab. He smoked a cigarette. He felt quite contented. A discussion with the driver had informed him that there were two Rua Augustas – the one he knew in the Praça do Comercio and one in the Biarro Alto, almost on the edge of the Alcantara. Guelvada had told the driver to go to the second Rua Augusta because it seemed to him that the leader of an orchestra as well known as that which played at the Estrada would be more likely to live on the Biarro Alto.

Guelvada wondered whether the band-leader would be in and, if he were in, whether he would talk. He wondered what he would do if the band-leader was not inclined to talk. He began to smile a little. The cab stopped. The driver looked back through the open partition and said:

'I can't get you any nearer than this. The street is on the other side of those gardens. It will take only a minute to walk.'

Guelvada got out of the cab. He paid the man and began to walk through the gardens. It was a lovely night. The air was quite warm. A pleasant mixture of the scents of plants and flowers came to his nostrils. A delightful night, he thought, and a delightful neighbourhood.

On the other side of the gardens was an iron gate. He passed through this and found himself in a narrow winding street that ran uphill. The moonlight, gleaming on the white houses on each side of the roadway, on the gardens, the shrubs, the palms, created a picture of miniature fairyland. Guelvada thought it would be wonderful to live in a place like this, if it always looked like this and if there was nothing else to worry about ... and lots of attractive women.

He walked up the centre of the roadway. The street got narrower as he progressed, and towards the end, almost on the summit of the hill, it seemed that the balconies of the houses on each side of the roadway almost touched.

Guelvada examined the numbers on one or two of the houses; decided roughly the situation of the house he sought, increased his pace. It was the house before the last on the top of the hill. There was a delightful garden in the front, and a flight of stone steps flanked by stone balustrades ran steeply up to a front door set back in a pillared porch. Guelvada stood looking at the house, thinking that whoever had planned this house had an eye for beauty. The place looked romantic, mysterious. Guelvada considered that it was the sort of house that a leader of a well-known orchestra might desire to possess.

He went quickly up the steps. There was an iron bell-pull on the right of the door. He pulled it. From inside the house came the musical clanging of a bell. Guelvada threw his cigarette stub away and waited. Two or three minutes passed but no one came. He thought it would be annoying if the band-leader had not returned home, was not going to return home. He realised that there was no time to be lost, that unless the missing Gallat were found quickly he might as well not be found at all.

Another minute passed. Guelvada lit a fresh cigarette, began to walk down the steps towards the roadway. He had descended four of the steps, when with a shrug of the shoulder he turned back and gave the bell a final pull just on chance. He leaned against the pillar on the left of the doorway. In front of him, through the space between two houses on the opposite side of the narrow road, he could see a vista of gardens sloping downwards away from him, and somewhere at the bottom of it a small white house with a flat roof, standing out like an island in a sea of green vegetation.

Surprised, Guelvada took the cigarette from between his lips, flicked it expertly into the roadway. He remembered that house.

He forgot for the moment about Kane, about Gallat, about the band-leader. His mind went sailing back to the time when he was a *courier* in Lisbon, when he had been in the habit of going to that house a dozen times a week. He smiled when he thought of the woman who lived in it.

From inside the house behind him came the sound of slow footsteps. Guelvada dismissed his dreams, turned to the doorway. After a moment it opened. A woman, discreetly garbed in black, looking like a housekeeper, stood in the doorway. Her expression was a mixture of inquiry and annoyance. She held a lamp in her hand.

Guelvada took off his hat. He said in excellent Portuguese that he was greatly depressed at having to disturb her at this hour of the morning, but it was a matter of the utmost urgency, and was Senhor Roccas at home, because it was of the greatest importance that he, Guelvada, should see him. The woman shrugged her shoulders.

'Senhor Roccas is not at home,' she said. 'He seldom returns before the middle of the day. He sleeps in the afternoon.'

Guelvada nodded.

'Thank you, Senhora,' he said. He looked at her whimsically. He was smiling. Under the influence of his gaze, the rather hard features of the woman softened a little. Guelvada said:

'Might it be possible for you to tell me where he is? I have said it is most urgent that I should see him.'

There was a pause. Then she asked diffidently:

'Are you from the police, Senhor?'

Guelvada thought very quickly; then without hesitation he said:

'I regret to inform you that I am, Senhora.'

94

She shrugged her shoulders, a little sadly, he thought.

'I thought it would be like that, Senhor,' she said. 'I told him it would have been better for him to have gone at once to the police bureau, to have told him all the circumstances of the accident. I said that if the man died I was certain there would be trouble of some sort.'

Guelvada nodded sagely. It seemed to him that Roccas had knocked somebody down and not reported the accident. Excellent. He said: 'How sorry I am, Senhora, that your worst fears are justified. The unfortunate man is dead. So that you will realise how necessary it is that I should see Senhor Roccas quickly ... for his own sake.'

She said: 'Would you care to step inside? Please come in and be seated. Perhaps you will drink a glass of wine, Senhor ...? I will do my best to help you.'

Guelvada, murmuring the appropriate things, followed her. He was thinking that the housekeeper was in a flat spin, that she was torn between a desire to help her employer, yet did not want to say too much. Guelvada followed the oil lamp as it proceeded down the corridor. At the end she opened a door, switched on the light. He followed her into a well-furnished, comfortable room. She went to a sideboard, returned after a moment bringing a bottle and a glass on a silver tray. Guelvada sat in an easy-chair and sipped the wine. It was very good. He said:

'I think it would be as well if you were quite frank with me. You realise that it will not serve Senhor Roccas' interests if the police are kept waiting any longer about this business. I should not like to have to report to my superiors that I was unable to find him.'

She sat in front of him, her hands folded primly. She said:

'Senhor, I am in a difficult position. I know where Senhor Roccas is, yet I am wondering whether he would prefer me to disclose the information even to you, or whether it should remain a secret.'

Guelvada said: 'It would appear that a woman is concerned, Senhora. If that is so, set your mind at rest. The police are not concerned with Senhor Roccas' private affairs. They are concerned merely that he should make an immediate statement on this unfortunate accident. Whatever you may disclose to me I shall treat with the greatest discretion.'

She nodded.

'Very well, Senhor,' she said. 'When you have finished your wine, if you will come with me, I will show you.'

A few minutes later Guelvada followed her to the porch. She stood by his side looking across the narrow roadway. She pointed to the opening between the houses. She said:

'Senhor, do you see that white house with the red roof – the one standing half-way down the hill – the one surrounded by evergreens and shrubs?'

Guelvada nodded. He was saying to himself: 'My God! This is funny ... so that's where Roccas is ...! Well ... well ... well! Isn't life amusing?'

'Senhor Roccas is there,' she continued. 'When he finishes at the Estrada, sometimes he goes to supper. But always afterwards he goes there to see a ... a friend of his.'

Guelvada nodded.

'And he comes back to lunch next day, I suppose,' he said, 'and goes to bed in the afternoon. Is that right?'

He looked at her whimsically. He was remembering when he used to go to that house, to stay for lunch, to come home and sleep in the afternoon. He sighed. Those were the days. ...

'That is correct, Senhor,' she said.

Guelvada put on his hat. He lit a cigarette.

'Have no fear, Senhora,' he said. 'I shall handle this matter with the greatest delicacy – the greatest tact. You may rest assured that Senhor Roccas will be more than pleased that you have divulged to me his whereabouts. May God be with you, Senhora. ...'

Guelvada tripped blithely down the steps, into the roadway. She stood on the top step, a sombre figure in black, watching him, thinking that there was something strangely attractive about this police officer, who appeared so suddenly at four-thirty in the morning. She wondered why the police should be so interested in the Roccas accident – so interested that they should investigate it at this early hour. She shrugged her shoulders. She went inside the house, shut the door behind her.

Guelvada turned right half-way down the steep roadway, and walked through a narrow stone-paved passage towards the hill where the white house was. He was thinking that life was very amusing. He was thinking that it would be even more amusing if the inmate of the white house was the one that he had known. In any event it seemed safe for him to proceed.

He threw away his cigarette stub, lit a fresh one, began to walk slowly. He was walking slowly because it was necessary for him to formulate a plan of campaign. Guelvada liked plans of campaign. It was a habit of his to plan out everything he was going to do, and then when the time came, to do something quite different. One might say that he almost took pleasure in deluding himself.

But *this* plan of campaign was necessary – most necessary. Guelvada thought out all its possible ramifications; then, a smile on his countenance, his hat on one side of his head, he hastened his footsteps.

Kane walked across the Praça do Comercio. He was thinking about the police officer, Serilla. He was wondering what Serilla would be like. Kane did not mind very much what he was like. It was a practice of his to walk blindfold into a situation, to allow the situation to develop until something tangible showed – something that one could take hold of. In any event something would happen with Serilla.

If the night porter at the hotel had been speaking the truth when he had suggested that both he and the police officer were pro-British, then the situation was all right, because Serilla would help. He would want to help if his sympathies were with the British. He would certainly want to help, especially if those sympathies were assisted with some money. But supposing his sympathies were not with the British; supposing the night porter had been pulling a fast one; supposing that even now he was on the telephone to Serilla, warning him that the mysterious Mr Kenneth Michaels was on his way to see him. Well, what did it matter? Serilla was either going to help or to obstruct. If he helped, all well and good. If he tried to obstruct, the process would be obvious, and Kane would have to think of something else.

In any event, he must do something. He must make an attempt to find Gallat one way or another – through the band-leader Roccas – through this police officer, Serilla – through somebody – they *must* find Gallat.

Kane began to think about Guelvada. He hoped Ernie was not going to make a fool of himself. He hoped Ernie would play this in the way he had been told to play it, if such a process were possible. Kane began to grin. Ernie was a type, he thought, and what a type! A man with a single purpose – that purpose being disguised all the time under a whimsical character that was not as superficial as it seemed; that process being interrupted by the continuous ramifications brought into Guelvada's operations because of his desire to be artistic, not to mention sundry episodes in which women had played a leading part.

Yet Kane knew perfectly well that of all the operatives that he had met in different parts of the world since he had been engaged in his present business, there was no one he would have in Ernie's place. Guelvada was difficult but unique.

He turned into one of the narrow streets on the far side of the Praça do Comercio. The moonlight, casting grotesque shadows over white pavements, made the street appear to be even longer that it was. He thought that life was rather like that street – patches of moonlight and shadow – and mostly shadow.

Half-way down he came to the apartment house where Serilla lived. He went inside, found the electric lift, ascended to the third floor. He walked along the corridor, tapped gently on the door of the flat.

It was opened quickly. It was opened by a suave, thin-faced individual, in a violet velvet dressing-gown and a gold-fringed scarf, who smiled and said: 'My name is Serilla. Senhor Michaels ...?' He spoke in French.

Kane said: 'I'm glad to meet you. I suppose the night porter at the Estrada telephoned you?'

'Yes,' said Serilla. 'Come this way, if you please.'

Kane hung his hat on the rack in the hallway, followed the police officer into the sitting-room. He sat down in the chair indicated by Serilla, who offered him a cigarette.

Kane said: 'You're very kind, Senhor Serilla. Did the man at the Estrada give you any ideas as to my business?'

'No,' said Serilla. 'He did not. But he said it was a matter with which I should probably sympathise.'

Kane said: 'You are very charming.'

They smiled amiably at each other.

'Senhor, you are, I think, English?' said Serilla. 'To-day, as you know, Lisbon is a city almost torn between the contending parties of this war. Here one is either pro-German or pro-Allies. There is no true neutrality, and most of the things that happen in this city have something to do with one or the other of those parties. If it will comfort you, I should like to tell you that my sympathies are entirely with your country. More, if it is possible for me to help you, I shall be glad to do so.'

'Excellent,' said Kane. He took his note-case from the breast-pocket of his coat, took out a packet of banknotes, folded them casually, put them back again. He returned the case to his pocket. Then he looked at Serilla, who was standing in front of the fireplace smiling placidly. Kane said:

'My trouble is a very simple one. Yesterday a friend of mine – an American by the name of Gallat, who had come to Lisbon to meet me on confidential business – arrived at the airport. I have not seen or heard of him since. It is most essential that I should find out where he is. If you can assist me I shall be more than grateful.'

Serilla said: 'I shall be very glad to assist you. Luckily I think I *can* assist you. You see, my business at the moment is to keep a fatherly eye on different nationals who come into Lisbon by air; to know more or less something about them; to see that they do not indulge in activities which might repercuss badly on Portuguese so-called "neutrality." It is perhaps lucky for you that I am in charge of the secret police at the airport, because, for instance, my colleague who looks after the railway stations is definitely pro-Nazi.' Serilla smiled at Kane, as if that was a good joke.

Kane grinned. 'I *am* lucky,' he said.

'Of course,' Serilla went on, 'many strange things happen in Lisbon to-day. There are disappearances – there are even killings. But what can you expect? Normally our city is a peaceful place, but with all these strange people here, all trying to find out things, all trying to do things ...' He shrugged his shoulders. 'Practically every empty shop in the town is taken by the Germans,' he said. 'Even if they only fill the windows with German magazines and newspapers. They think they are helping their country to win the war. Sometimes it is almost amusing ... almost ....'

Kane said: 'Don't you think there is a good chance of somebody having killed Gallat?'

'I don't know,' Serilla answered. 'But I might make some guesses. Before I do guess I should like to ask you some questions. First of all, what was the business of your friend – Senhor Gallat? Was he a business man?'

There was a pause. Kane thought quickly. Time was the essence of the contract. He had to hurry, and you had to take a chance sometimes. Why not now? In any event *something* would happen. He said casually:

'Senhor Serilla, I am going to show you my confidence in you. I am going to put myself in your hands.'

'I assure you,' said the police officer, 'you will not regret the process.'

'First of all,' said Kane, 'because I do not see why you should be disturbed at this unearthly hour of the morning, and because I do not see why I should take advantage of your kindness of heart, I would ask you to accept this small gift as a token of my esteem.'

He took out his case, folded together four high-denomination Portuguese notes, held them out to Serilla. Serilla made a charming bow. He put out a long, thin hand, took the money.

'I am most grateful, Senhor,' he said. 'I am at your service. I am yours to command.'

Kane said: 'I am here on confidential business. My friend Gallat had come a long way to see me for a conference. My movements in the near future are entirely dependent on that conference.'

Serilla said; 'Do you think that any one – some friends of the Nazis – might be interested in your business with your friend, Senhor Michaels? It is possible ... is that not so?'

Kane said: 'Yes ... I should think it might be possible.'

The police officer thought for a moment; then he said:

'I will make my guess. I do not think it probable that

anything *very* drastic has happened to Senhor Gallat. But it should not be very difficult for me to find out. It is half-past four now. I think I will dress, go to my office, and make some inquiries.' He smiled at Kane. 'You see,' he continued, 'we have a note of all the Nazi agents who might be inclined to make themselves objectionable. It is not difficult to find out what they have been doing during the last forty-eight hours. I'm going to suggest to you, Senhor, that you telephone me in an hour's time at the number which I shall give you – say between half-past five and a quarter to six. I hope to be able to give you some information.'

Kane got up. 'I am more than grateful to you,' he said.

They shook hands. Serilla came to the door of the apartment with Kane. He picked up a pad from the table in the hallway, wrote on it, tore off the piece of paper, handed it to Kane. He said: 'Here is the telephone number. Do not worry, Senhor. I am certain that everything will be all right. My friends think I am a very *efficient* police officer.'

Kane said: 'I hope I shall think so too.'

'You will,' said Serilla with conviction. 'Telephone me in an hour's time. I feel I shall have news for you. Good-bye, Senhor. ...'

Kane walked slowly back to the Estrada, thinking about Serilla.

The assistant-inspector had been sure of himself. Perhaps *too* sure, thought Kane. Lisbon was a big place, and an hour was not a long time to ascertain the whereabouts of a man who had somehow managed to disappear for over twenty-four hours.

The fact that Serilla was so certain that he could discover, through his contacts with Nazi agents, whether someone had been interested in disposing of Gallat, did not reassure Kane. First of all, if any one *had* got Gallat it would be the German *contre-espionage* people, and they were not likely to advertise their presence. Serilla, with the best will in the world, might know and inquire of the more obvious Nazi agents of one sort and another who functioned in Lisbon, but he would certainly not know the C.E. people. *Contre-espionage* details worked secretly, as secretly as Kane and Guelvada worked. The very fact that their presence and work were known to a police officer of Serilla's rank would automatically merit their removal to some place where they were *not* known.

On the other hand the night porter at the Estrada might be playing on the other side. He might be in the pay of the Germans – dozens of hotel assistants in Lisbon were – and he might have put Kane on to Serilla because the police officer was also working for the Nazis. ...

Why not? Kane smiled cynically in the darkness. Well, if this was so, Serilla was going to do something about it. He would have established the fact that Kane was Gallat's contact in Lisbon, and the people who were paying him would be content to leave the situation where it was. They would want to know more about Kane. They would want to dispose of Kane was well as Gallat. Of that there was no doubt. Kane had no delusions about the thoroughness of the Nazi C.E. people. He had experienced it on previous occasions. He knew all about it. He also knew that any Nazi who could prove that he had liquidated Kane or Guelvada, or both of them, would be well in line for an Iron Cross, or, at any rate, a second-class Order of the German Eagle. Kane realised that he might easily have walked into a trap that he had carefully set – for himself.

But even that had been done before. More than once, during the past two years, Kane had deliberately walked into traps – and out again. And never empty-handed. Of course, you could do that once too often. ... But you had to try things. If they came off the results were amusing. If they did not the results might be even more exciting. Too exciting.

He turned into the Avenida. It was deserted except for an occasional taxi that sped across its wide expanse, accentuating its spaciousness, making the stillness of the night more obvious.

He looked at his wrist-watch. It was five minutes to five. He began to think about Guelvada. He wondered what Ernie was doing, whether he had had any luck. If he had he would probably have telephoned the hotel and been annoyed because Kane was not there.

He hoped Guelvada would not start anything serious. But you never knew with Ernie. His temperament would run away with him at the oddest moments, and he would do the strangest, most risky things. Yet sometimes they seemed to pan out all right ... sometimes.

He turned into the Estrada. As he walked across the lounge he glanced at the night-porter's office. Kane could see the man, through the glass door, sitting at the desk, writing. He sauntered over. The night porter smiled. He said:

'I hope you were successful, Senhor.'

Kane said: 'I think so. I appreciate your help. I think your friend Serilla will be able to assist me.'

The man smiled. Kane saw that he had excellent teeth. They were so white they almost gleamed in the half-light of the desk lamp.

'There was a telephone call for you, Senhor,' said the night porter. 'The caller would leave no message. I said you were out and expected you back shortly.'

Kane said thanks, and walked over to the lift. So there *had* been a telephone call. That would be Guelvada. He had called because he was on to something. He and Kane had an old rule that you never telephone to report *non*-progress, but only when *something* had happened.

So Ernie was on to something. Perhaps the band-leader, Roccas, had known something. Perhaps he had been able to talk.

Kane stopped the lift at his floor, got out; walked along to his suite and entered the sitting-room. He switched on the light, glanced quickly about the place; walked over to the sideboard and poured a drink. Carrying the glass in his hand, he walked into his own and Guelvada's bedrooms, looking around, whistling softly to himself.

He locked the bedroom doors that led out on to corridors. Then he returned to the sitting-room. He went over to the door, opened it, looked out into the main passageway, closed the door, locked it. He sat down on the big settee and took out the pistol from its soft leather holster under his left arm. He took off the safety catch, pulled back the ejector, released it, pushing a cartridge into the barrel in the process, put on the safety catch, replaced the pistol in its holster.

He put his feet up on the end of the settee. He closed his

eyes. He reminded himself that he wanted to wake up at five-thirty exactly. He went to sleep.

v

Guelvada pushed open the tall wrought-iron Spanish gates that guarded the narrow drive, bordered by evergreens, that led up to the white house with the red roof.

The business of opening the gate, closing it quietly behind him, and walking quickly towards the house was a reminiscent business. It brought all sorts of things back to Guelvada. Mainly it brought back delightful memories of Marandal.

He looked at his watch. It was just five o'clock. Guelvada sighed. A sigh that came from the heart. How often, about this time, with his heart beating – possibly a little quicker, had he walked up this same winding carriage-way knowing that, just inside the closed door, waiting, wearing that delightful confection of black lace that was so discreetly revealing, would be Marandal.

Delightful Marandal. ... There were very few women anywhere in the world like her. And now there was no Marandal. One came to this delightful place, this so charming *casino*, surrounded by sweet flowers and verdant plants, merely for the purpose of trying to bluff information out of the leader of an orchestra.

Quite obviously she would not be there. Because quite obviously Marandal would never be able to bring herself to consent to an *affaire* with the leader of an orchestra. This seemed quite certain to Guelvada. The fact that she had consented to an *affaire* with him when he was merely a *courier* could not discount the fact. Guelvada as a *courier* was, of course, still Guelvada. Nothing else should matter to any woman.

But it would be strange – and delightful nevertheless – if she *were* there. Already Guelvada was wondering how he could switch this business so that he had an excuse for discovering if Marandal was still the lady of the house. But a sudden sense of caution warned him. Kane would be merciless if, in the pursuit of an old *amour*, the endeavour to

104

recapture something delightful that one had considered to be gone for ever, he were to 'start something.' He realised that too often, in the pursuit of his business with Kane, he had stopped by the wayside in order to 'start something.'

He began to think about Marandal ... the unique Marandal. The Marandal of that so superb figure, that sweet and affectionate smile, those lovely arms, that delightfully incongruous fair head that belied her Portuguese father and Andalusian mother; that Marandal of the temper unequalled in both hemispheres and all Guelvada's wide experience of women.

She had said that if she saw him again she would kill him. She had told a mutual friend – knowing that at some time the news would reach Guelvada – that whenever she saw him, whatever the circumstances, she would kill him. Guelvada admitted to himself that she had good reason. For Marandal, giving everything, still retained a fierce Andalusian pride that baulked bitterly at the infamy that Guelvada had put upon her. The infamy of having *two* other mistresses at the time that she considered him entirely hers.

Pondering on the matter, Guelvada concluded that she would keep her word. Definitely, he thought, she would want to kill him. Certainly she would attempt to kill him. Stopping to light a cigarette, smiling whilst he did it, he thought that death at the hands of Marandal might be rather sweet, inasmuch as one was perfectly certain that, at the moment she struck, her heart would go out with the blow, and she would fling herself upon his prostrate body, showering kisses on his nearly cold lips.

A delightful picture. ... Guelvada grinned happily.

The drive curved suddenly, and before him, with the same sense of surprise, he saw the white door with the door-knocker in the shape of a black Spanish stiletto ... the door-knocker that he himself had bought and presented to the house.

Guelvada sighed. With that sigh went the delightful pictures of the past, came the more practical business of the moment. He seized the knocker and achieved a rat-tat-tat that shattered the stillness of the early morning. Then, his cigarette hanging from one end of his mouth, his body relaxed, he waited.

Soon there was the sound of steps. Guelvada could hear the chain clanking as it was taken off the door. The door opened. On the other side, framed in the subdued light of the hallway door, stood Roccas, the band-leader.

He was smoking a cigarette. He was wearing a well-fitting dinner-jacket, and a diamond ring glittered on the little finger of his left hand. His soft white *percale* shirt and double collar were immaculate, and his black bow was of watered silk. A concise, neat figure of a man, with small hands and feet that were almost too small.

He smiled gently at Guelvada as if it were a matter of course that people knocked on the door so peremptorily at five o'clock in the morning. He said softly in Portuguese:

'What can I do for you, Senhor?'

Guelvada said brusquely: 'Senhor Roccas, I regret to disturb you at this hour. I have already been to your house, and from there was directed here by your housekeeper. I would like to talk to you for a moment.'

Roccas looked behind him towards the passage. Then he said:

'Will you forgive me if I do not ask you to enter. It is a mild night and perhaps we could walk for a few moments in the garden. I shall be happy to assist you in any way I can.'

'That will be excellent,' said Guelvada. He stood on one side as Roccas pulled the door to, but did not entirely close it. They walked out of the little pillared porch and round the right-hand side of the house, where there was a well-kept lawn. Out of the corner of his eye Guelvada could see the chink of light peeping out from the curtains of the drawing-room.

Roccas said: 'I am at your service.'

They began to walk along the paved pathway that bisected the lawn and curved round the far end of the house. They walked slowly, appreciating the beauty of the moonlight.

Guelvada said: 'Senhor Roccas, this will seem a very foolish thing to you, but to me it is important. To-night I was dancing at the Estrada. I was with some friends, and a bet was made. I will not tell you the exact terms of the bet, but I stand to lose heavily about it. The bet concerned the playing of a *conga* by your band. The name was "Sweet Conga." I think I am right in saying that you played this tune three times in the course of half an hour. I would be most grateful to you if you would tell me why this tune was played by your orchestra so many times in such a short space. I hazarded a guess as to the reason and, if I am right, I win my bet. If I am wrong, I lose it. The sum of money is considerable.'

Roccas smiled amiably.

'How amusing,' he said. There was a little pause, then:

'Tell me, are you from the Police Bureau?' he asked.

Guelvada thought quickly. Obviously the housekeeper at Roccas' house had telephoned. Obviously she had told Roccas to expect a visit from a police officer.

'And did you merely wish to see me about the playing of this *conga?*' asked Roccas. 'Was there no other matter?'

Guelvada realised that he must chance it.

'You are right, Senhor,' he said. 'I am from the police. Also I had intended to discuss another matter with you. *After* you had satisfied my curiosity about the *conga.*'

Roccas took out a very thin gold cigarette case. His initials were set on the inside in tiny seed pearls. He offered it to Guelvada. They took cigarettes; Roccas lit them with a gold lighter. He said:

'Would it be convenient to discuss the other matter before we talk about "Sweet Conga"?'

Guelvada thought quickly. He did not like the question. He answered almost at once:

'But certainly, if you wish it. It is necessary, as you know, that you should make a statement, as soon as may be, about the accident. Normally, I should have waited until to-morrow morning before seeing you about that, but as it was necessary to settle this bet about the *conga* before ten o'clock to-morrow morning, I thought I would come and see you at once.'

'Quite,' said Roccas. He was smiling amiably. 'What statement did you wish – about the accident, I mean?' he asked.

Guelvada shrugged his shoulders.

'The usual thing,' he answered. 'When one has a car smash, one makes a statement about it. Isn't that so?'

'I see,' said Roccas. 'Just the ordinary statement that one

107

makes to the police? I understand. Well, Senhor, do not worry about it. Later, after I have had a little rest, I will go down to the police bureau. I will make the statement you require. Is that in order?'

'Perfectly,' said Guelvada. He drew on his cigarette. He wished that he did not feel quite so uncomfortable. The skin at the back of his neck was beginning to stiffen a little. He did not like this Roccas. He did not like the ease with which the band-leader dealt with the matter of the car accident. The idea came to Guelvada that Roccas was playing with him. He did not like the idea.

By now they had walked right round the house; were on the lawn on the other side, walking back towards the narrow carriage drive. Guelvada found the silence oppressive. He finished his cigarette quickly; threw the stub into a rhododendron bush.

Roccas said: 'This is a delightful house, do you not think, Senhor? And at this time in the morning, with the moon shining, everything looks quite superb. On your way up the carriage-drive you did not, I suppose, notice the little summer house?'

'No,' said Guelvada, 'I did not.'

Roccas said: 'We will walk along there. I would like to show it to you. The owner of this house has an eye for beauty, and whilst the outside of the summer house is like any other summer house in any other garden, the inside is decorated and furnished entirely in the Chinese antique. I would think,' said Roccas, looking sideways at Guelvada, 'that in spite of your very practical profession as a police officer, you would be interested in the artistic.'

Guelvada smiled. He said: 'You are a good judge of character, Senhor. I am most artistically inclined.'

He was beginning to feel better. He had ceased to be afraid of Roccas. Now Guelvada considered Roccas to be an enemy. Quite obviously, the band-leader was playing with him; quite obviously stalling for time. Very well. ...

They walked down the winding driveway. Twenty-five yards down, Roccas indicated a little side turning, so narrow that the heavy green plants on each side almost touched. They walked along the pathway for a minute; then came to a little clearing. In this clearing, raised on wooden tiers a few feet above the ground, a balcony all round it and steps leading up to a doorway, was the summer house.

Guelvada said: 'What a delightful place. How I should like to own such a place.' He was thinking of the hundred times he had sat in the summer house and talked to Marandal; the hundred times he had admired the Chinese interior.

Roccas led the way up the wooden steps. He pushed open the door and went in. He switched on a light; stood waiting for the other to enter. Guelvada went in. He stood in the middle of the floor on the thick Chinese carpet. He gave an exclamation of delight.

'This place is quite wonderful,' he said.

Roccas closed the door.

Guelvada took off his hat with his right hand. He stood with both hands behind his back holding the hat, looking about him, his eyes wide with interest.

But his fingers were busy. Inside the lining of his soft hat was the flat handle of a Swedish knife – one of those knives with a button at one end which, being pressed, expels four inches of blade concealed in the handle. Guelvada experienced a sense of comfort as he felt the blade shoot out.

Roccas said: 'Senhor, I am very interested in your question about the *conga*. I think I would like to give you my answer in these pleasant surroundings, where we are not likely to be observed.' He took his right hand out of the pocket of the dinner-jacket. In it was a very small automatic pistol.

Guelvada said: 'It seems that your answer is of a very practical nature.'

Roccas smiled.

'Precisely,' he said. 'You see, it was unfortunate about that accident, because in any event it would be unnecessary for me to make a statement about it. That, my friend, was your great mistake.'

Guelvada nodded lugubriously.

'That's what I thought,' he said.

Roccas went on: 'I regret, of course, that it is necessary that I should kill you, but by now you will realise that your death is a necessity.'

He stood some five feet from Guelvada, his right hand, pistol in it, hanging down by his side. He was smiling pleasantly.

Guelvada said: 'Senhor, believe me, I recognise the necessity from your point of view, but before this killing process begins, may I be allowed to put one very small point to you? It will not take more than a minute.'

'Certainly,' said Roccas. "But please see that it does not take longer than that."

Guelvada said: 'Here it is. ...'

He brought his left hand from behind his back in a melo-dramatic gesture. In one movement, he dropped the hat, brought his hand right round, flicked his wrist upwards and forwards. The point of the knife hit Roccas just above the Adam's apple. The blade penetrated its complete four inches.

Guelvada said: 'I have always been very expert with a knife. I learnt that art in your country, Senhor.'

Roccas was on his knees on the carpet, the pistol fallen from his hand. He knelt, his body supported on his two hands held before him, waving his head from side to side. As he fell sideways, he tore at the hilt of the knife. He lay for a few seconds, writhing. It was not a pleasant sight.

Guelvada picked up his hat. He stood in the centre of the floor, looking at the band-leader. He stood there for two or three minutes. Then he moved forward, picked up the knife, wiped the blade on the inside of Roccas' dinner-coat, pushed it back into the handle, replaced the handle in his hat. He went out of the summer house, closing the door quietly behind him. Then he descended the steps slowly.

Kane awoke the second before the clock on the mantel-piece chimed the half-hour. He put his legs on to the floor, sat running his fingers through his hair. He felt tired; his mouth was dry from too much smoking. He took the piece of paper that Serilla had given him, walked to the telephone, called the number. A few seconds afterwards, he heard Serilla's voice.

Kane said: 'This is Michaels. I am ringing as arranged. Am I lucky or unlucky?'

The police officer said: 'I told you I was efficient, Senhor. You are lucky. Your friend, Gallat, is all right. You need not worry about him. Unfortunately there was some question about his passport. He had left the airport and was on his way, no doubt to your hotel, when he was stopped by one of the police patrols that operate from the airport. However, I may say that the situation is now in order.'

Kane said: 'Thank you very much. Could you tell me where I can get at Gallat?'

'But certainly,' Serilla answered. 'My information at the present moment is that he is busily engaged in sleeping off a little too much liquor. It seems that Senhor Gallat, like so many of his compatriots, is fond of rye whisky. However, he is staying at No. 46 Rua Ambrosio. That is on the other side of the Avenida from your hotel, Senhor. It would take you a few minutes in a taxi, if you can get one, or fifteen minutes to walk.'

Kane said: 'Thanks. I will walk. I'll be there in fifteen minutes. I hope to see you to-morrow, Senhor. I think you have been more than kind.'

Serilla said: 'I shall always be glad to see you. I shall be at my office at the police bureau all day to-morrow, if you care to drop in. Good-bye, Senhor.'

Kane hung up. He went into the bedroom, took a writing pad from the drawer of his dressing-table. He wrote a note to Guelvada:

'*Dear Ernie,*

'*Since you've been out I've made a contact through the night porter here - a police officer name of Serilla. He says he knows where Gallat is, and that everything's in order. I'm going to see Gallat now at No. 46 Rua Ambrosio, off the Avenida.*

'*This may be all right or it may not. Perhaps Serilla's got something on ice for me, but if he has, and I don't show up again, then it will mean that he knows who's got Gallat and is playing in with them. It will also mean that the night porter here is on that side too. In any event there will be a situation that you can deal with, even if you have to get very tough with Serilla, and, in the event of my not showing up, I hope you'll be very tough indeed. You can be as artistic as you like!*

'*So long, Ernie.*'

Kane folded the note. He put it in an envelope, went into Guelvada's bedroom, removed the pillows and the bolster from the bed, slipped the envelope half-way down the bed beneath the top sheet. He replaced the bolster and the pillows. He went back to the sitting-room, poured himself a small whisky and soda, put on his hat, lit a cigarette and went out.

VI

Guelvada pushed open the white door. He was very glad that Roccas had not quite closed it. Of course, if the door had been closed then he could have used the artistic knocker. But that process would not have been pleasing.

Guelvada stood in the softly-lit hall. He closed the door behind him. He thought of all the times he had entered thus. And he was mildly excited. As excited as it was possible for him to be.

He felt rather like a small child that opens the door of a dark cellar and expects someone to jump out from a corner.

It was, of course, quite impossible that Marandal should be in the house. Why should she? Marandal was a bird of passage. She would not have stayed in Lisbon all these years. But then, against that, she might have returned for the war. Lisbon would be the place to which she would return. It was as much her home as any place could expect to be for a person of the temperament of Marandal.

Well then, if she had returned to Lisbon, it was not impossible that she should be here. And, supposing she was here, then what of Roccas?

Guelvada could not *see* Marandal with Roccas. He could not believe that she could be interested in Roccas. Marandal – who had so many men to choose from – what should she have to do with Roccas? Unless. ...!

Guelvada began to smile. Things were beginning to take shape in his mind. He ran his tongue over his lips – a habit of his when he was pleased. He had an idea. Definitely a most artistic idea.

The idea presupposed that he was right in his guess about Marandal and Roccas. But even if he were wrong it would not matter. He could still play it that way. He could still succeed. And it might be amusing.

He walked quietly along the passage that ran from the hallway to the rear of the house. Half-way down there was a door. It was the door of the room from which the gleam of light had showed itself when he had been walking with Roccas – the late Roccas – on the lawn at the side of the house. It was the room that Marandal had always used for her own place of retreat.

Guelvada opened the door. He stepped into the room and closed the door behind him softly. He stood with his back to the door looking at Marandal.

He began to smile. He moved away from the door – two or three steps towards the centre of the room. Then he stopped and, still smiling as if in quiet enjoyment of the scene, he continued to gaze at Marandal.

She was, of course, quite superb. She was more beautiful than ever, he thought. Ravishing would be a better word than beautiful, because in addition to beauty she possessed an extreme quality of allure.

She was playing patience at a rosewood table. Guelvada considered that it was characteristic of Marandal to be playing Spanish patience on a rosewood table at five-thirty in the morning. Yet, because she was doing it, it seemed the ordinary and natural thing to do.

Everything about her was quite perfect. She sat sideways towards Guelvada, and her profile, against the light of the rose-shaded standard lamp, set behind the table, showed to extreme advantage. The curve of her back, the grace of the leg and ankle, the easy, supple movements of her hand, wrist and fingers, as she held the cards, were not lost upon him. He was busy trying to find a word in any language that he knew which would describe the beauty, the strange attraction, of Marandal.

She was wearing a pink lace negligée lined with pink georgette. There were tiny blue velvet buttons to fasten it down the front. There was a wide blue velvet sash fastened at the waist, and the small and exquisite foot nearest him, peeping out from the folds of the lace gown, was shod in a blue velvet sandal with a thin gold edge.

113

Marandal wore a high Spanish comb in her fair hair, and behind it, with its soft folds draping her shoulders, was caught a pink lace mantilla. The wide, unlined lace sleeves of the negligée showed the white, rounded arms beneath, and were caught at the wrist with blue velvet ribbons.

All this had taken a matter of seconds, and in that matter of seconds she had dropped the card on the table as she saw him. She did not drop the card in any gesture of fear or excitement. She dropped it casually and quite deliberately. She opened her fingers and allowed the card to fall on the table.

She looked at Guelvada as he stood there in the centre of the room, relaxed and smiling, in exactly the same manner and with the same intense curiosity as she might have looked at the devil had he suddenly appeared.

Then, as quickly as a flash of lighting, she moved. She flung the table away from her. It crashed against a painted firescreen, into the fireplace. An ornament, shaken from a precarious position on the edge of a cabinet, fell to the ground, smashed into a dozen pieces.

Marandal was on her feet. As she spun away from the chair on which she had been seated, her right hand, outflung, fell upon an unlit electric table lamp, an amber globe set in an old china vase. Her fingers closed round it and she flung it, with excellent aim.

The vase hit Guelvada fairly on the side of the face, just beneath the cheek bone. It cannoned off and fell against the door. A thin stream of blood began to run down Guelvada's cheek, down his neck and on to his soft, white collar.

He did not move. Nor did he move as Marandal followed the vase. She almost flung herself away from the chair and at him. One hand, laden with rings, slashed across his face, tearing a corner of his lip; the fingers of the other, grasping at the front of his collar and black evening bow, tore them away from his shirt; then grasping at the front of the shirt, tore that too. Guelvada, standing like a smiling statue, dishevelled, bleeding, but entirely unperturbed, allowed himself to consider that Marandal was still strong in the wrist.

The hand that had hit his face was raised again. This time it descended in a back-handed manner from the opposite direction. The sharp ring that had cut his lip now made worse the original cut from the vase. The fingers at his shirt front detached themselves, and the forefinger, its long well-manicured nail stained a pearly pink, was pointed at his eye with the definite intention of gouging out that valuable organ. As Marandal, making a not unattractive hissing noise between her teeth, jabbed with the long forefinger, Guelvada moved his head slightly. Not sufficient to spoil the artistic stillness with which he had met the attack, but sufficiently to deflect the finger from his eye to the space between his eyes. The sharp nail penetrated, making a neat clean cut. A little trickle of blood now ran down Guelvada's nose to join with the other small rivulets from other wounds.

Marandal began to speak. The words hissed from her mouth, taking form as they came out. The soft huskiness of her voice – always attractive, thought Guelvada – lost nothing from the temper that possessed her.

She dropped her hands, turned her head, looking for the nearest weapon with which to continue the attack.

'Sweet Jesu ...' hissed Marandal, ... 'beloved saints aid me!' She told the saints mentioned, in no undecided manner, exactly what she desired to do to Guelvada. She spoke in Spanish, and he considered that Spanish was the language for her purpose. Its easy sibilancy formed a perfect lingual background for the quite unprintable sentiments which Marandal was expressing so fluently.

Her eye lit on a Moroccan sword that hung upon the wall above the fireplace. So did Guelvada's. But before she could move in that direction he had put up his hands and seized her by the wrists.

Marandal began to writhe. Her slender wrists were held in Guelvada's steel fingers. He had held her thus on former occasions when they had decided to disagree about something, and she knew that it was impossible to escape. She did the next best thing.

Surrendering her wrists, she drew back her right foot and kicked Guelvada hard upon the shin, forgetting in the process that there was no toe-cap to her velvet sandal. Guelvada's shin was harder than Marandal's toes, and she fared the worse in this effort. So, twisting sideways, she tried to kick backwards with the heel of her sandal, but this attempt also failed, for Guelvada, deftly putting his foot forward, swept her ankles from under her and she slipped, hanging precariously by her wrists which Guelvada held breast high.

He began to speak. He spoke quickly and softly in Spanish. He intended his voice to be attractive, and it was. It held a note of deep sorrow, almost of anguish.

'Sweet chicken,' said Guelvada, 'do not struggle in case you hurt yourself. I understand your feelings. Believe me when I tell you, core of my heart, that if it were not for your own sake I would permit you to do the most unmentionable things to me. Any hurt from your hands is more than a pleasure. And I do not have to implore you to believe that this is indeed the truth. You must be well aware that I would know that to return here to you would be equivalent to signing my own death warrant. I know perfectly well that you desire nothing better than to kill me by the slowest and most painful methods. And I realise that I deserve such a fate. But your own reason will tell you that I have either returned because I prefer death at your hands to the business of living without you, or for some reason that must, of necessity, be so important that it might even be worth your while to listen to it.'

This speech Guelvada considered to be quite good. First of all it was flattering, and secondly it was intended to arouse Marandal's curiosity.

It succeeded. Marandal, allowing the whole of her weight to hang from Guelvada's wrists, looked up at him with violet eyes which, whilst still blazing with anger, showed additional gleam of interest.

Guelvada sighed. He thought that only she could look attractive in the peculiar position in which she was suspended.

She said: 'Let me go.'

'But certainly,' said Guelvada. He released her wrists suddenly, and she fell with a crash to the floor.

'Scum of the Belgian gutters,' she said. 'I did not mean that.'

'I'm sorry,' said Guelvada. 'You asked to be let go and I obeyed.' He helped her to her feet.

They stood in the centre of the room facing each other.

'I will tell you what you are,' said Marandal. She told him. Her description embraced the proclivities and atmospherics, all rather peculiar and non-biological, attaining his birth. She went on at length, expressing the most extraordinary desires as to what might happen to any children that he might have in the future, and to any woman stupid enough to be associated with him. Guelvada listened amiably. He did not interrupt. He had the gift of patience.

After a while Marandal finished, more for the want of breath than for any other reason. She stood, her hands hanging down by her sides, her breast heaving, a picture of outraged womanhood.

Guelvada said: 'Marandal, I ask you to listen to me for a few moments. I promise you that when I have finished talking you will at least be grateful that I risked your justifiable anger to come back here and to warn you.'

'So you came to warn me,' said Marandal. 'Is that all? What can *you* warn *me* about?'

Guelvada shrugged his shoulders. He looked at the floor. His face assumed that peculiar expression of contriteness and humility that he could adopt at will. The effect was possibly heightened by the damage done to his countenance.

He said: 'Ever since I left Lisbon and you, I have been miserable. Any other woman who has come into my life has simply served as a comparison in your favour. For years I have realised that there is for me only one woman in the world – you – a woman I was fool enough to lose. But in any event I had to see you. It was necessary – not for my sake but for yours.'

She went to the couch by the fireplace. She sat down. She said:

'Ernest, you have always been quite impossible. At the moment you present a fearsome sight. Whatever you have to say to me must wait until you have washed your face. The bathroom is in the same place.'

Guelvada bowed his head. He went slowly from the room. When his back was turned towards her, he permitted a slow smile to appear on his lips. At any rate he had won *this* round.

117

He switched on the light in the bathroom, shut the door softly behind him, washed carefully, and then, taking his time, lit a cigarette. *Now* he was certain that his idea had been right. Juan Roccas had been working for the Nazis, and Marandal had been helping him. This would account for the association. The drama and sensation of the business would have appealed to Marandal. That was the obvious explanation.

Therefore she would believe him. If he suggested that it was known that she was working with Roccas; if he said that knowing that fact he had come to warn her and, because it was necessary for her safety, killed Roccas, she would believe it. She must believe it. Events would have proved to her the truth of Guelvada's carefully thought-out lies. He grinned. Life was like that. Events which were facts and which ought to prove truth seldom did. He felt quite pleased with the situation, but realised that he must handle it carefully.

When he returned to the drawing-room, Marandal was draped effectively on the sofa. She had arranged herself so that her figure showed to the best advantage and so that a charming foot and ankle protruded adequately from the negligée. This was not lost on Guelvada. Marandal, he thought, was still interested in the effect she could have on him. Possibly she was sufficiently scared to be prepared to forgive and forget. He decided to chance everything on one stroke.

He drew up a chair and sat down by her. He looked at her with eyes that shone with admiration. Just for a moment. Then a most serious expression came over his face. He took out his cigarette case, offered it to her, lit their cigarettes and began to talk. He said earnestly:

'I am here because I still adore you. Marandal, I ask you to believe that before I say any more. Do you?'

She inhaled cigarette smoke. She smiled at him. She said:

'Ernest, I know you to be the best liar in Europe. I will listen to what you have to say before I believe anything.'

Guelvada nodded.

'All right,' he said. 'Well, first of all I would like to tell you that not very long ago I killed Roccas – in the summer-house. I am afraid that there is rather a mess on the carpet. But it had to happen.'

'My God! ...' Marandal was almost affected. She looked at Guelvada with interest. 'So you have killed Juan Roccas ... Why?'

'I did it for your sake,' said Guelvada. 'It was necessary for your safety.'

'Why?' demanded Marandal. She sat up straight.

Guelvada proceeded with caution. He shrugged his shoulders.

'You know what Roccas was doing?' he said. 'You know the people he was working for. ... Well ... ?' He shrugged his shoulders again.

Marandal was interested. She puffed her cigarette and looked at the ceiling. Guelvada considered that she was playing for time, endeavouring to discover just how much he knew.

She said: 'Supposing I do. I still don't understand, Ernest, why it should be necessary for you to kill him in order to protect me. Perhaps you would be good enough to explain?'

Guelvada smiled.

'You are very winsome, my tiny heart of a lettuce,' he said softly. 'But I suppose that it never occurred to you that it was dangerous to be associated, *in any way*, with such an indifferent person as Roccas, a band-leader. I suppose it never occurred to your trustful nature that the gentleman might be playing both ends at once; that he might be professing to work for certain people and, at the same time, selling them out to the enemy?'

Marandal threw her cigarette end into the fireplace. She watched it smouldering. She asked:

'And who would be the enemy?'

Guelvada grinned.

'Myself ... for instance, and others. ...'

Marandal nodded. She understood. She said:

'So you are working for the British. Is that it?'

Guelvada shook his head.

'I was,' he said. 'But now it seems that I am working for you. This killing of Roccas will put me in bad with the British. Now they will be finished with me. But I *had* to do it for your sake. ... Roccas was working for the Nazis – you knew that. You were helping him. What you did not know was that he was selling you all out to the British at the same time. Playing both ends against the middle. That would be like Roccas. ...'

He sat back in his chair and looked at her with a smile, delighted with this last lie, which fitted into the scheme so excellently.

Marandal shot bolt upright on the settee.

'Santa Maria ...' she said softly. She put her hands behind her head and lay back on the sofa. Guelvada thought she looked very nice like that. 'That pig. ... But are you sure?'

'If I were not sure why should I kill him?' asked Guelvada. 'I came here to Lisbon for the express purpose of settling accounts with Senhor Roccas, for the express purpose of confronting him with proofs of his double dealing.' Guelvada stopped speaking in order that he might think for a second. Having thought he decided to take another chance.

'I came here with orders merely to frighten Roccas,' he continued. 'And *that* was not a difficult process. He scares easily. Then he talked a little and I realised quickly that you were in this thing with him. Your face came before me. Your sublime features and figure appeared in a cloud of loving memories, and I knew that I must kill him for your sake.' Guelvada shrugged his shoulders. 'I did it immediately without a thought,' he said. 'Naturally ... it was for you.'

Marandal looked serious.

'You had better tell me everything, Ernest,' she said. 'It seems that we both must be quite frank with each other. It will pay us both.'

'Precisely,' agreed Guelvada. He smiled at her fondly. 'I will make a bargain with you, my once and always beloved,' he said. 'I propose to tell you everything, and in return you shall be entirely frank with me. After you have done this I shall tell you how I propose to save you from an extremely undesirable fate.'

Marandal nodded. She sighed heavily. Guelvada wondered just how far Marandal was 'in' with Roccas and his associates – whoever they might be. Probably pretty far in, he thought. She was not one for half-measures, and it would

120

be like her to involve herself in any sort of business that promised a certain amount of sensation and possibly drama – provided the drama did not touch *her* too closely.

She said: 'Possibly I have been a little foolish. But tell me about Roccas. Are you not in great danger, having killed him? How do you propose to explain his death? How did you kill him?'

'I threw a knife at him,' said Guelvada cheerfully. 'You remember the other one that I did like that ... ?'

She nodded. 'That little knife,' she murmured. 'You are good with that. But tell me ... ?'

'I killed Roccas in self-defence,' said Guelvada. 'I accused him of having taken money from the British, of having worked for the British and at the same time taking money and working for the Nazis here. I told him that that was all very well for him, but that for him to involve you in such a messy business was foul and unforgivable. I said that I would confront him with you and tell you in his presence how he had very nearly achieved your complete ruin. This I think was too much for him. He pulled out a pistol, but I was ready for him ...'

Guelvada drew deeply on his cigarette.

'His death will not matter a great deal,' he went on. 'When I go I will remove his body and leave it, concealed, in the gardens at the back of his house. I shall allow the fact that he was working for the British to become known to the Nazis here – the people who were paying him. Well ... *they* are not going to worry about him. The British will no longer worry about him because he is dead. But they will worry about *you*. You are associated with him. They will plan to do something unpleasant to you ... something to stop further operations on your part.'

She nodded again. 'That sounds reasonable, Ernest,' she said. 'Also it is plausible. Tell me more.'

Guelvada stubbed out his cigarette on the sole of his shoe and placed the butt carefully in an ash tray. Now he decided to go the whole hog. Marandal was prepared to believe anything; to be as scared as it was possible for her to be scared. Very well. He proceeded glibly:

'For some time the British have suspected Roccas,' he said.

121

'He has been taking money from them for a year. He was supposed to report to them on what the Nazi *contre-espionage* people were doing here. He was supposed to look after British agents operating in Lisbon. He was supposed to act as a letter-box. In fact he was supposed to do all sorts of things.

'But he was not clever. One or two British agents have disappeared after they have arrived in Lisbon. Several important pieces of information entrusted to Roccas have leaked out. One piece of information – spoof information – given only to him, was all round the place in a few days. That was the last straw. A trap was laid for him.'

Marandal sat up. She clasped her beautiful hands round her knees and looked at Guelvada with interest.

'One of the most successful – probably *the* most successful British agent – myself – was chosen to deal with this delicate situation,' said Guelvada modestly. 'I came here to the Estrada with a colleague – one Kenneth Michaels – and we were supposed to contact an agent – an American – named Gallat. Information about this was allowed to leak out. Probably it reached Roccas – or someone associated with him – as it was supposed to do. What was the result? Although Gallat arrived at the airport some thirty-six hours ago he has disappeared. I suspect Roccas.'

Guelvada leaned forward. He fixed Marandal with a most serious look.

'But worse is to come,' he continued. 'It has been known that there was a connection between you and Roccas of some sort. It has been known that some police officers here are working for the Nazis. Why, even the English papers talk about the Nazis and the Lisbon police. Every one knows it. Roccas is a Spaniard. So are you. Spain is supposed to be neutral. So is Portugal. Very well. The American Government are going to want to know all about Gallat. They and the British are going to make plenty of trouble over this. They are going to demand the arrest of Roccas, yourself, and a dozen other people. They are going to demand the immediate production of Gallat. Then they are going to show that Roccas had been attempting to sell information to any one who will buy it. After that, you can trust the Nazis to take care of the situation. They will go after every one connected

122

with Roccas. They will be after you, my sweet chicken. They will cut your throat without a second thought. You see? Imagine how I have feared for you. Everybody is going to detest you. The British will suspect you. The Nazis will suspect you. The police here, who are trying to play hand in glove with every one, will suspect you. In any event you may rely on the Nazis cutting your throat. They always do in such cases.'

Marandal nodded unhappily.

'I believe you, Ernest,' she said. 'Now I know you are telling the truth. What you have told me matches with what I know. It seems that I need your help. I should not like to be involved in any trouble, and I should dislike greatly to have my throat cut by Nazis. It would not be interesting.'

Guelvada nodded.

'Tell me all,' he said. 'Trust me to find a way out of this. On occasions like this I am extremely brilliant.'

Marandal said: 'When you spoke of the American, Gallat, I knew you were telling the truth and that you knew what was happening.'

'Quite,' said Guelvada. He lit another cigarette. After all, he thought, everything was perfectly simple if you lied hard enough. He thought that the story he had told Marandal, invented about Roccas on the spur of the moment, was good. Apparently it was *so* good that it was near enough to the truth to scare Marandal. Guelvada thought his technique was good. He hoped it would continue to be good, for, if he failed, the idea of facing Kane, endeavouring to explain this and that, would not be at all comfortable. Kane could be very tough.

Marandal said: 'I am worried. I need your help, Ernest. I believe you when you say that you came back here to help me. It seems that Roccas has been working for both sides and that I may easily be caught up in this trouble. Either the British will make a great deal of trouble for me or else the Nazis will cut my throat. In any event it will be very unpleasant.'

'I shall be able to deal with *any* situation,' said Guelvada casually, 'providing you tell me exactly what has happened. And you must be quick. There is no time to lose.'

'It was known that Gallat was to arrive at the airport,' said Marandal. 'Serilla, a police officer who is in charge of the airport, knew this. Gallat was kept at the customs office at the airport, on some pretext, until it was dark, and then allowed to leave. A hired car was placed at his disposal. Some distance from the airport, the driver stopped the car and said that there was trouble with the engine. He got out. Almost immediately, Roccas, who had been waiting in a side street, drove his car into Gallat's car. The American was badly injured.'

Marandal shrugged her shoulders.

'Roccas got out of his car. There is no doubt that he would have finished off Gallat and hurried away, but at this moment a car driven by a young man appeared. It seems that the young man was a medical student at the Santa Anna Hospital. He did what he could for the injured man and sent for an ambulance. So Roccas was foiled. He could do nothing. He could not even search the unfortunate Gallat.'

Guelvada nodded. 'Very pretty,' he said. 'All very amateur. ... Continue, my heart. ...'

'Roccas went off and informed Serilla, who said that Gallat must be moved as soon as possible. They did not intend that he should have an opportunity to talk. And so it was arranged. The American was moved to a private nursing home kept by a pro-Nazi friend of Serilla's. ...'

Guelvada interrupted.

'And where is the nursing home?' he asked.

'No. 46 Rua Ambrosia,' said Marandal. 'Well. ... Gallat was moved there and they discovered that they had nothing to bother about, because he had been unconscious since the accident and he was dying.

'I see,' said Guelvada. He smiled a little. It was now quite obvious why Roccas had intended to liquidate him immediately the subject of the accident had been mentioned. Roccas had known that no one from the police would be interested, officially, in that accident.

He said: 'A delightful plot, my best beloved, even if a little uncouth. Please continue ... I am more than interested.'

'In the meantime,' continued Marandal, 'something else had happened. It seems that your associate, Michaels, was interested in the whereabouts of Gallat. He spoke to the night porter at the Estrada Hotel. The night porter is a friend of Serilla, the police officer.'

Guelvada began to smile again.

'Ho! ho!' he said. 'So the night porter at the Estrada is a friend of Senhor Serilla's? Your story becomes more interesting at every moment, my heart of a rose.'

Marandal went on: 'The night porter sent Senhor Michaels to Serilla. Serilla played for time. He told Senhor Michaels to telephone him at five-thirty, when he thought he might have information about the missing Gallat. Serilla was going to tell him when he telephoned where Gallat is.'

'I see,' said Guelvada. 'And how did you know this?'

'Serilla telephoned through here,' answered Marandal, 'immediately after Michaels had been to see him.'

'I see,' said Guelvada. 'And how did the late Roccas take that information?'

Marandal stretched. She yawned a little.

'He was rather pleased,' she said. 'You see, Serilla had everything arranged. When Michaels arrived at the nursing home he would discover that Senhor Gallat was dead, for I regret to tell you that he died early this morning. After which Serilla proposed to arrest Michaels. ...'

Guelvada began to laugh.

'On a charge of murdering Gallat. Marvellous! That would be what Serilla would do. Is it not so?'

'Yes,' said Marandal. 'He was to be charged with the murder of Gallat. You see,' she continued, 'it was quite obvious that the friends of Gallat who had sent him to Lisbon would not be in a position to ask for information about his death, and both Serilla and Roccas considered that no one would be interested in what happened to Michaels. Why should they? Both these gentlemen were engaged in activities which *officially* concerned no one.'

Guelvada nodded.

'Quite,' he said. 'So Michaels is arrested. That disposes of the death of Gallat. And then Michaels is sentenced and disappears, or possibly he dies in prison before trial ... I know. ... These things have happened before.'

He looked at his watch. It was twenty past six. Marandal yawned again prettily. She said:

'I did not like it at all – being mixed up in all this business. It perturbs me.'

'I understand that very well,' said Guelvada. 'But do not worry, my chicken, I shall now proceed to make arrangements for your safety. Listen to me ...'

He leaned forward in his chair. He spoke earnestly.

'You have made a grave mistake, my dear,' he said. 'The mistake of trying to be on two sides at once. That is a dangerous process, because it means that one has no friends at all. I propose to alter it.'

'How?' asked Marandal.

'Officially, and for the purpose of getting you out of Lisbon, which I think is going to be a dangerous place for you to be in, you will come on to our side. You will write a complete statement telling all you know about this plot against Gallat and Michaels. You will give it to me. This statement will enable me to prove to our people that you are being frank with us, that you are doing everything you can to help, and on the strength of that,' said Guelvada, 'I shall get you an American *visa* here which will enable you to leave with safety.'

'In fact,' he went on, 'I see no reason why you should not leave to-morrow morning and go to America. That, I think, would be the safest place for you.'

Marandal nodded.

'I think so too,' she said. 'But are you certain that if I write this statement you will be able to arrange all that?'

'I am more than certain,' said Guelvada. 'I promise it. Write the statement, my sweet.'

'Very well,' said Marandal. 'But you must tell me what I am to write. I am not very good at composition. Also, if I am to go to America I think I should like you to come too. I feel a sudden renewal of love for you, Ernest. You have killed Juan for me. I think it possible that I might easily adore you some more.'

'Beloved ...' murmured Guelvada, 'of course I shall accompany you to America. That was my idea. In any event it is the best place to be in. Now, are you ready?'

126

He began to dictate the statement.

A church clock struck the quarter after seven as Guelvada pressed the doorbell at the apartment of Senhor Serilla. He waited patiently, a cigarette hanging from the corner of his mouth. He was not even perturbed when the door was not answered promptly. He imagined that Serilla would be in bed sleeping after his nocturnal activities.

Guelvada shifted the cigarette to the other side of his mouth. He considered that fate was sometimes very kind. He thought that it had been kind to him. He was proceeding with this line of thought when the door opened. The police officer, in pyjamas and dressing-gown, his gold-fringed scarf about his neck, stood looking at Guelvada inquiringly.

'Senhor Serilla,' said Guelvada. 'I regret very much to have to disturb you at this hour. I should like to talk to you for a few minutes.'

'It would be a pleasure,' said Serilla courteously. 'But are you sure it is business that cannot wait until I go to my office in a few hours from now?'

'No,' said Guelvada. 'My business is very urgent.'

Serilla looked down. He saw that Guelvada's hand was in his right pocket, and that some hard object within that pocket was pointing at his stomach. He sighed.

He said: 'I am at your service, Senhor.' He turned and led the way towards the sitting-room.

Guelvada followed him, closing the apartment door softly behind him. Serilla went to the fireplace. He stood, his back to it, his hands clasped behind his back, looking at Guelvada. Guelvada said:

'Senhor Serilla, all of us with the best intentions in the world occasionally make grave mistakes.'

Serilla nodded. 'That may be so, Senhor,' he said. 'Even the cleverest men have been known to err.'

'Precisely,' said Guelvada. 'And I take it, Senhor, that you are a clever man and that you have erred?' His voice became metallic. 'Listen ...' he said. 'The man Gallat is dead. He cannot be brought back to life. And that is that. But still the fact inconveniences me. Also you have inconvenienced me in other ways, Senhor. You have erred greatly. These errors must be put right. Otherwise,' Guelvada went on, producing the automatic pistol from his right-hand coat pocket, 'I propose to kill you without further ado. And if I do kill you, Senhor, I shall shoot you through the stomach. This, I am told, is a very painful process.' He smiled at Serilla.

The police-officer said: 'Anything I can do, Senhor ...'

Guelvada said: 'Let me be quite frank with you. I have obtained a signed statement from the Senhora Marandal D'Alvarez. She has said everything that there is to be said. She gave me the statement in order that I should arrange that her passport might be *visaed*, so that she might go to America, where she thinks she will be safe. I imagine,' said Guelvada primly, 'that she will endeavour to take a plane to-morrow morning.'

'Quite,' said Serilla.

'The point that interests me more than anything else,' continued Guelvada smilingly, 'is that I understand that a friend of mine – Senhor Michaels – has been arrested on a trumped-up charge of killing Gallat. You will arrange to do something about that immediately, Senhor. You will telephone the police. You will give orders that Senhor Michaels is to be released at once. What do you say, Senhor?'

Serilla smiled amiably. He said:

'There is no doubt, Senhor – I have not the honour of knowing your name – that there has been a grave miscarriage of justice. I hasten to put it right.'

He went to the telephone. When he had finished, Guelvada said:

'Now I think we might smoke a cigarette, Senhor. I have no doubt we shall find some pleasant subjects to converse about. We shall do that until such time as Senhor Michaels telephones me here, as you have arranged, to tell me that he is safely back at the Estrada, after which I shall, with the greatest regrets and thanks for your hospitality, take my leave.'

Serilla said: 'I am at your service, Senhor.'

'But I should like you to know,' Guelvada continued, 'that if either Senhor Michaels or myself is troubled should we remain in Lisbon, the sealed package which I have left with the British Consulate General this morning, and which contains the statement by the Senhora D'Alvarez, will be opened. That might make a lot of trouble for you, Senhor.'

Serilla shrugged his shoulders.

'Believe me,' he said, 'I am your friend. I shall make it my business to see that nothing of any sort happens either to yourself or Senhor Michaels that is not pleasant.'

'Excellent,' said Guelvada. He took out his cigarette case, offered it to Serilla. They sat, one on each side of the fire-place, smoking.

At a quarter to eight the telephone rang. Serilla answered it. He looked over his shoulder at Guelvada.

'It is your friend, Senhor,' he said.

Guelvada poured himself out coffee. He had eaten well. He approved his breakfast. He lit a cigarette, relaxed in his chair.

Kane said: 'Whoever it was ran into Gallat meant to finish him off. But they couldn't because of the medical student turning up. This student had Gallat moved to the hospital. After a bit the police arrived and searched Gallat's clothes and baggage. But they couldn't find anything. They went off hoping that when they'd got him moved to the nursing home in the Rua Ambrosia they'd be able to make him talk.'

Guelvada nodded. 'Naturally,' he said.

'When they'd gone,' Kane continued, 'Gallat recovered consciousness for a few minutes. He was too clever to mention my name, but he asked the medical student to go out and get any American citizen he could find quickly. The medical student, who was a good boy, came round to the Estrada. He knew he'd find more Americans there than any-where else. And who do you think he found?'

'I can guess,' said Guelvada. 'He found Griselda.'

'Right,' said Kane. 'That was the explanation of the mys-terious young man who went off with Griselda. She saw Gallat and he gave her the instructions he had for us. They were photographed in miniature, hidden in his hair. The damned fools never thought of looking there when they were searching.'

Guelvada said: 'You know, Michael, women can be use-ful sometimes. ...'

5 – D.D.

'Yes,' agreed Kane. 'Sometimes. ...' He looked at his watch.

'We must get packed,' he said. 'We've got to get out of here. I'll tell you about it on our way to the airport.'

Guelvada began to grin.

'So we are going to the airport,' he murmured. 'That should be amusing. ...'

He got up, went into his bedroom, started to pack. He threw away his cigarette, began to sing a Portuguese love song.

Marandal came into the Customs Office at the airport. She looked entrancing. She wore a black coat and skirt and a very smart tailored hat in black velvet. A porter came behind with her bags.

Guelvada said to Kane: 'Excuse me for a moment, Michael.' He walked towards Marandal.

She said: 'I am here, Ernest. I have decided to trust you once more.'

Guelvada said: 'Core of my heart, whatever may or may not happen you may assure yourself always of my entire devotion. I love you with a passion that is quite amazing.'

Out of the corner of his eye he saw Serilla and two other men crossing the wide floor.

He said: 'Excuse me, beloved, whilst I get some cigarettes.' He went away.

Serilla and the two men took Marandal into the small office. They handcuffed her. Then they took her to the car outside.

Guelvada came back to Kane. Kane said:

'Who was the woman that Serilla just knocked off?' He looked suspiciously at Guelvada. 'You haven't been up to anything stupid with that woman, have you, Ernie?' he asked.

Guelvada shook his head.

'Nothing that matters,' he said. 'But nothing at all. One day I will tell you about it. I think she has got in bad with the police here. And they will hold her for a few days and then let her go. Which is not a very pleasant thing ...'

'Why?' asked Kane. He began to walk towards the tarmac.

Guelvada shrugged.

'Nothing,' he said casually. 'But she doesn't like me ... not a lot. ...' He grinned. 'And that is annoying. Because I am very fond of that woman. She has great charm. And if she gets the chance she will certainly kill me one day.'

Kane laughed.

'There are a lot of women would like to kill you, Ernie,' he said. 'By the way, how did you know what Serilla planned to do last night?'

Guelvada grinned.

'When I left you I met a man I used to know,' he said casually. 'He told me that Serilla was bad medicine. I hung around until I saw them take you away from the nursing home and then I went to his flat and persuaded him.'

'Yes?' said Kane. 'So that was it.' He looked at Guelvada sideways. 'What were you doing all the rest of the time?' he asked.

Guelvada shrugged.

'I was talking to that woman I told you about,' he said. 'The one I knew years ago. The one who wanted to kill me.'

'I see,' said Kane. 'And she doesn't want to kill you now ... hey?'

Guelvada smiled. 'You never know with women,' he said. They walked across to the airplane.

CHAPTER III

YOU CAN ALWAYS DUCK

I

SEITZEN stood looking out of the window. Outside the rain descended in sheets. The grass patch between the cottage and the woods was soaked, the shrubs broken and bedraggled. The sound of the steam whistle of a train rumbling in the direction of Dublin made the twilight even more dolorous.

Seitzen murmured: 'This is one hell of a country when it rains.'

He turned from the window. He was short, squat, heavy. The raincoat he was wearing seemed too large for him. The sleeves almost covered his hands. His face was round and his jowls hung almost over his collar. He wore horn-rimmed spectacles. He looked studious and unpleasant.

Hiltsch, who was sitting at the table writing, said:

'It looks bad when it's *not* raining. Everywhere looks bad to me.' He smiled ruefully. 'It's going to look much worse in a minute.'

Seitzen raised his eyebrows.

'Yes?' he said. 'Why? What are you afraid of?'

'The same thing as you are —' said Hiltsch, 'Hildebrand!'

Seitzen said impatiently: 'I don't understand this business about being afraid of Hildebrand.'

'Don't you?' said Hiltsch.

He shrugged his shoulders, laid down his pen. He tilted his chair back, and put his feet on the desk. He regarded his well-cut shoes with his head on one side.

Seitzen turned back to the window. He was annoyed. You couldn't talk to Hiltsch. And if you did talk, it didn't do any good. He fumbled for a cigarette with pudgy fingers.

Hiltsch began to whistle softly to himself. He was good-looking in a way. He looked like a young imitation of a *boulevardier* of the fifties – except that he was clean shaven. His middle-brown hair was wavy and his skin good. He was tall, slim and well-dressed. At one time he had been a Group Leader in the S.A. with hopes of getting a good job in the S.S. That was a long time ago.

The trouble with Seitzen, thought Hiltsch, is that he is yellow. As yellow as hell. What a hell of a fellow to work with – and on a job like this one. Why, if they wanted a difficult job done, didn't they give you good material to work with.

He began to speak quickly and softly in German.

'You are either a liar or a damn fool, Seitzen,' he said. 'I've never met anybody yet who wasn't afraid of Hildebrand. Have you ever heard of Columbia House?'

Seitzen nodded. 'Yes,' he said. 'Well?'

'Hildebrand used to run Columbia House,' said Hiltsch.

132

'That was the time when he was running the 12th Berlin Group. They used to take suspects to Columbia for questioning. Some of them thought they were tough, but they always talked. Hildebrand has got more and better ways of making people talk than anybody I know.' He lit a cigarette. I saw him do something to an old Jew one night with a fire-hose ... you can't imagine how damned slowly the old boy died. Hildebrand certainly has imagination.'

Seitzen said: 'Very likely. But I still don't see why *we* have to be afraid of Hildebrand – in Eire.'

Hiltsch lit a cigarette.

'That makes a hell of a lot of difference – whether it's Berlin or Eire or anywhere else. Have you ever known a keen Party Member – a *real* Party Member – worry about his methods because he was in a foreign country? He simply takes a little more care, that's all.'

Seitzen sat down. His raincoat flopped open. When he sat his paunch hung down almost over his thighs. Behind his horn-rimmed spectacles his cruel little pig's eyes twinkled brightly. He said: 'Well, I'm not scared. I have always done my job the best I could.'

Hiltsch said: 'You're scared all right. So am I. So would anybody else be.' He got up, walked over to the window, stood looking out, smoking. He went on: 'Hildebrand's not coming here to ask us how we are, or to give us the Führer's kind regards. Wherever he goes, there is trouble for somebody. His visit here means trouble for us.' He sighed heavily.

'It was good in the old days,' he said. 'When Adolf Hitler was not such a God Almighty, and even used to find time to talk to S.A. Group Leaders. I remember him coming across to me one night and clapping me on the back. That was a few days after the Bremen thing, when I led the twenty-fourth *Standarte* and kicked hell out of those bloody dock Communists. Those were the days. And I wasn't happy. I wanted promotion. I took the devil's own chances to get it. Goddam it, I even burgled the British Embassy – and got away with it – and all because I wanted promotion. Well ... I got it, and here I am ... God help me. ...' He began to laugh as if it were a good joke.

Seitzen said: 'I wonder what Hildebrand wants to see us about.'

From the other side of the house, where the country road wound in a curve towards the woods, came the sound of a car stopping.

Hiltsch said with a grin: 'We shall soon know.'

He turned; walked out of the room towards the hallway. In a minute Hildebrand came into the room. He was very tall, very slim, very well-dressed. His complexion was good. He was clean-shaven. He seemed quite a good-humoured individual. He stood just inside the doorway, his soft brown felt hat held in long sensitive fingers. He said very softly:

'*Heil Hitler!*' When he said it he half-smiled, showing his white teeth.

Seitzen got up. Both he and Hiltsch, standing by the side of the doorway, said: '*Heil Hitler!*'

Hildebrand came into the room. He sat down by the table. He put his hand inside his coat and produced a large gold cigarette case. He opened it, laid it on the table; indicated it with a long finger. His attitude was easy, pleasant and amiable.

'Sit down,' he said, 'and smoke.'

The two men sat down at the table, Hiltsch opposite Hildebrand, Seitzen on his right. Hildebrand looked at them – first at Hiltsch – then at Seitzen. He said:

'I have come over here because I think you need to re-organise a little. Don't you think you do?' His voice was incisive, metallic, but not unpleasant. Only his eyes were unpleasant. They were very hard.

Hiltsch said: 'You ought to know it's getting very difficult to work over here. The damned English get more cautious every day, and the Irish are a sick headache. They're being *very* natural. During the last twelve weeks it has been awfully difficult to get anybody out at all.'

Hildebrand nodded. He said to Seitzen: 'What do you think?'

Seitzen said: 'It's not easy. I agree with Hiltsch. But still I think we've done fairly well, don't you?'

Hildebrand looked at him. He smiled. He said:

'Do you?'

134

There was a silence. Hiltsch said: 'Look, why not get it over with? There is some trouble, isn't there?'

Hildebrand nodded.

'Oh, yes,' he said. 'There's some trouble, and there's going to be some more trouble in a minute. There's going to be some trouble for you.' He spat the words out of his mouth. His eyes were mere slits.

Hiltsch looked at the table. He found it difficult to look at Hildebrand. Seitzen's right hand fumbled with a loose thread in the cloth of his trousers.

Hildebrand went on: 'I can stand most things, but I don't like being a joke. There are two other people who do not like being jokes either. One is called Heydrich and the other is Himmler. I have been on the mat. Having been there, I'm putting you there. Understand this: I don't want talk – I don't want excuses. I want action.'

Hiltsch put out his hand to take a cigarette from the gold case. He lit it. He said: 'What's the trouble about?'

Hildebrand said: 'The trouble is about Kane.'

Hiltsch nodded.

'I thought so,' he said. 'Kane and Guelvada?'

Hildebrand shrugged.

'Guelvada does not matter,' he said. 'Guelvada is merely an opportunist with an over-developed sense of the dramatic. Take Kane away and Guelvada would help to cut his own throat in six weeks. Guelvada by himself is nothing. The trouble is Kane.'

Hiltsch said: 'I gathered that. But exactly how? What's Kane been doing?'

Hildebrand raised his eyebrows.

'What has he been doing?' he said. 'You ask me that? What in the name of God are you and Seitzen here for? You mean what hasn't he been doing?' He leaned forward over the table. 'For your information, gentlemen,' he said, 'during the last nine months no less than twenty-seven of our most important agents in different parts of the world have been liquidated. Sixteen of them, including Helda Marques, operated from your group. Most of them have been liquidated after they have been jockeyed into a position in which they *could* be removed. There are a lot of other things, too

135

numerous to be mentioned, apart from that. Well, you're nearest to them. You have ample opportunites for getting at them. We think it's time you did something about it.'

Hiltsch said: 'I don't think you understand how difficult the position is for us, Karl. We are in the dark. I agree with you that most of our people who have been liquidated have come from this group. Well ... what do you expect? As you say, we're nearest, and so we do the most work. The fact that our people were killed doesn't help us. And, believe me, nearly all of them – including Helda Marques – were *killed*. Not one of them was taken by the English and shot officially. After Helda was killed, and we found out how it was done and who did it, I sent two of our smartest people over with instructions to worry about nothing but that cursed pair. They were arrested and shot. Since then we have had no news. And I can't work unless I have information.'

Hildebrand said: 'It's your business to have information. It's your business to keep your contact lines open ...'

'God Almighty!' snarled Hiltsch. 'Keep my contact lines open. ... I like that. For God's sake! Listen, Karl, do you think these bloody English are fools? *You* may think they are. *I* don't. England is about the easiest country in the world for an agent to go into, and the goddamned hardest to get out of. One might even think that they encouraged people to come in just to get themselves picked up and shot. And look at our Army people. Look at the lunatic things they do. They send half-trained soldiers, who can speak English, with little radio sets and attaché cases, and packets of English banknotes. My God! The last one was picked up on a railway station trying to read the time table. He had four hundred pounds in notes, a radio set, a pistol, and a sausage. I've been awake for nights on end trying to work out what he had the sausage for. I suppose it was in case he got hungry in the night. ... But what do you think the sausage was? It was a sausage that is only made in Leipzig. ... If the fool had been successful and got somewhere, and some Englishmen had looked in his attaché case and seen that sausage the game would have been up. Even an Englishman would have known by the smell that the sausage came from Germany. ... Can't you see how difficult all this amateur

136

business on the part of the Army branch makes things for us?'

Hildebrand said: 'It is your business to overcome difficulties. You must try something new.'

Hiltsch said: 'Listen, Karl, it's all very well talking like that. We've tried everything.'

Seitzen broke in: 'We've got a very good man on the job now,' he said. 'Hillmer – one of our best men.'

Hildebrand nodded. One side of his mouth was twisted up in a cynical smile. 'So?' he said. 'You have a good man on the job – Hillmer! Tell me about Hillmer.'

Seitzen said: 'Kane is in London. We learned that. I sent Hillmer out of here three weeks ago. He won't come back here unless he has done what he set out to do.' He put his hands flat on the table in front of him. His little eyes bespoke a certain self-satisfaction.

'*So!*' repeated Hildebrand. 'We are to rely on Hillmer? I wonder would it interest you two gentlemen to know that five days ago the unfortunate Hillmer had an accident? Perhaps you will remember it was a foggy night. He managed to fall over a railway siding near Euston in the fog. A train ran over him. ...' He paused for a moment. 'That makes twenty-eight,' he said. 'Thus exits Hillmer.'

He got up, walked towards the window; kicked petulantly against the leg of a chair.

'I can imagine the accursed Guelvada – for I'll bet it was he – standing at the top of that railway embankment waiting for the train to go over your *clever* agent Hillmer. The Hillmer type makes me sick. ...'

Hiltsch tilted his chair backwards. His eyes were focussed on the middle of Hildebrand's back. They looked nasty, those eyes, thought Seitzen. He wondered if Hiltsch hated Hildebrand as much as he did. Hiltsch said: 'Look, Karl. I know you're not satisfied. Neither are we. All right. Now you tell me something. ... If you were me what would you do?'

Hildebrand turned abruptly; began to laugh. When he laughed he drew his lips back over his teeth. He looked rather like a snarling dog. He said:

'I'm going to tell you what you are going to do. I think it is time that you and this fellow here stirred your lazy stumps.

I'm giving you a direct order. You get out of here. Go over to England and get Kane. If you don't I'm going to recall you both.' He took a cigarette from the case on the table. 'You know what that means?' he said.

Hiltsch said: 'That's all right. But you still haven't answered my question. I wonder if you realise the difficulties of going after people like Kane and Guelvada.'

'Why should there be extreme difficulties about Kane and Guelvada any more than anyone else?' asked Hildebrand.

Hiltsch got up. He put his hands in his pockets; began to walk about the room. Seitzen watched Hiltsch and Hildebrand in turn. His eyes went from one to the other. After a moment Hiltsch said: 'They've got an odd way of working. They don't do anything that's conventional. They don't use any of the old systems.'

'My God!' said Hildebrand. 'Are you telling me that the British are beginning to use imagination?'

Hiltsch said: 'Karl, I've never had any delusions about the British. Once they take the gloves off – once they forget to play cricket – to be English gentlemen – they are the toughest things on earth.' He sighed. 'The trouble with Kane is he doesn't play cricket.'

Hildebrand said: 'So much the easier.' He drew on his cigarette. 'Possibly,' he went on, 'you have heard of Achilles who had a weak spot? Well, this Kane will have one. No man is perfect. Every man leaves himself open in some place. Usually with a man it's a woman.'

Seitzen said: 'Exactly. That's always been a theory of mine. But here is a case in which it doesn't work. As far as Kane is concerned there is no woman.'

Hildebrand turned towards Seitzen. His glance was almost vicious in its intensity. He said:

'Seitzen, you're a damned fool. You are one of those fools who is never right. I think if the English were to cut your throat or push you in front of a train in a fog, or do something else to you, I'd be positively relieved. In any event,' he said, 'if they don't do it, I shall, sooner or later.'

Hiltsch said: 'You suggested something just now. You suggested that ...'

'That there was a woman,' said Hildebrand. 'There is.

She is an actress in London. Kane sees her. He's fond of her. I don't know very much about her; whether she's working for him; whether she's merely his mistress. I don't know ... but there's something.'

Hiltsch stopped walking. He said:

'Now you've got something, Karl. I told you a man like Kane by himself is very difficult, but if he's fond of this woman maybe we can get at him through her.' He turned to Seitzen. 'You remember what we did in that other thing ...' he said, 'through that blonde woman ...?'

Hildebrand interrupted.

'Do we have to discuss things that are redundant?' he said. 'Let us concentrate on this business. ... The woman's name is Valetta Fallon.'

He came back to the table and sat down.

'I'm coming back here in three weeks,' he went on. 'I want to know that this matter has been dealt with. If it has not been dealt with, it would be better if I did not see either of you again. It would be better if the English got you. Unless you get results. And if I do see you, I shall recall you, and, by God, things will go hard with you in Germany. You understand?'

'Perfectly,' said Hiltsch.

Hildebrand shut the gold cigarette case with a snap.

'Very well,' he said. 'I look forward to seeing you in three weeks' time – to hear good news. Good-evening, gentlemen.'

He went out. They heard the car start outside. Seitzen said: 'I wonder why we stand for this sort of thing.'

Hiltsch began to laugh.

'That's the joke,' he said. 'You tell me what we can do about it. We're like people who have pushed a cart down a hill and jumped into it just as it gets going. We started it, but we can't stop it. We're caught up in something. We've got to go on. Our only hope is that the cart will one day arrive on the road at the bottom of the hill and stop of its own volition, so that we can get out.'

Seitzen sighed again. 'This is going to be tough,' he said.

Hiltsch shrugged.

'I don't know,' he said. 'You've been lucky and so have I. I've been in a dozen things when I never expected to get out, but I've got out. This Kane has been lucky too. But no man's luck lasts for ever.'

Seitzen said: 'That's an idea. Perhaps we're going to be his bad luck.'

Hiltsch said: 'We've got to be his bad luck. Hildebrand's made it pretty clear, hasn't he? If Heydrich's interested in this business, you can bet your shirt on one thing. It's Kane or us, and I hope it's not going to be us.' He took out his cigarette case, lit a cigarette.

Seitzen said: 'I wish that damned rain would stop. That pattering outside is driving me crazy.'

Hiltsch looked at him. He was grinning. He said:

'For a man who's supposed to be a first-class operative with a Gestapo training, you've got an odd set of nerves. Be careful they don't go back on you.'

Seitzen said: 'I'm not certain that they're not going back on me. And what about you? You don't feel as good as you did eighteen months ago, do you? You felt pretty good when you were leading that *Standarte* in Bremen. That was all right. That was really honest-to-goodness straight fighting. It's pretty easy to cut people's throats when you're top dog, but this is a different business. I tell you quite frankly the idea of going into England now, when those cursed British are getting so hot on everything, doesn't appeal to me. Does it to you?'

Hiltsch shrugged his shoulders.

'Candidly, no!' he said. 'But what do we do? We're between the devil and the deep sea. The deep sea is the British and the devil is Hildebrand. If we're recalled, we'll be for it. They'll probably send us to the Russian front. They'll freeze some of that fat off you, Seitzen. ...' He heaved a semi-humorous sigh. 'I am afraid there's no way out for us,' he said. 'We've just got to go on, unless. ...'

Seitzen said softly: 'Unless what ...?'

Hiltsch drew on his cigarette. He opened his mouth and exhaled a large volume of smoke.

'There is one way out,' he said. 'But you and I are good Party members. We wouldn't even consider it.'

Seitzen said: 'I can't consider anything unless I know what it is. What is it?'

140

Hiltsch drew on his cigarette again. There was a pause; then: 'If we went to England and sold out to the British,' he said, 'we'd be all right.' He laughed. 'My God, would we give them some information!'

Seitzen said: 'Yes ... and when they'd got it, they'd probably shoot us.'

'No,' said Hiltsch, 'they wouldn't do that. They'd keep us on ice. They'd want to refer to us about all sorts of things. They'd stick us into a gaol somewhere; keep us till the end of the war, using us as reference books from time to time. At the end of the war, if we'd behaved ourselves and told them what they wanted, they'd let us go. They do things like that.'

Seitzen said: 'It's an idea. ... But you wouldn't consider a thing like that, would you?'

Hiltsch said: 'I don't know. Why shouldn't I consider a thing like that? If we go on as we're going, we're going to be for it anyway. I don't fancy this Kane business. Somebody's going to get us – either the British or, if we fail, Hildebrand. In any event we haven't a long time to go. This way at least we'd be certain of going on living. ... That is, if you want to go on living?'

Seitzen said: 'Naturally I like life.' He looked at Hiltsch for a long time; then he said: 'Are you serious about this, Hiltsch?'

Hiltsch nodded. 'I am if you are,' he said. 'We've got to make up our minds quickly. Shall we do it?'

'By God ...' said Seitzen, 'let's do it. Let's throw our hands in. I'm sick of being treated like a dog by that –'

'So am I,' said Hiltsch. 'Well, this is where we get even with him.'

Seitzen grinned a little ruefully. 'Well, if we do it,' he said, 'I hope the English win. It would be funny if the Führer took London and got us after all, wouldn't it?'

'Don't kid yourself. The English will win all right,' said Hiltsch. 'They always do. It's a habit. We've started to lose already. Look at this Russian business. ...'

Seitzen said: 'Give me a cigarette, Hiltsch.' His fingers were trembling a little as he took the cigarette. 'How are we going to do this?' he said.

141

'That's easy,' said Hiltsch. 'We shall pretend to work in the usual way. Hildebrand will expect that. In two or three days' time you'll get out of here and go to England. We shall use the usual process. We shall do that in case Karl is still hanging about here to see how soon we get working. You get there; you go to Liverpool to the usual place. I shall join you two or three days afterwards, coming by the other route. The rest's easy. We go to London. We walk into Scotland Yard; we say, "Good-morning, we're two German Secret Service agents who have been operating a group from Eire for the last nine months. We wish to give ourselves up."'

He threw his cigarette stub into the fire.

'Of course,' he went on, 'they won't believe us at first. They'll think we're mad. But we shall be able to prove what we say. Once they realise just how much we know, and of what use we can be, we shall be safe enough.' He laughed. 'I shall only ask one favour of them. When I'm safely in prison,' said Hiltsch, 'I shall ask permission to send a rude telegram, through Sweden, to Karl. He will be very annoyed.'

Seitzen said seriously: 'He will be mad with rage if we talk. The whole of the organisation that he's built up here, in France, in Holland, and in England, will be broken down. If he ever gets his hands on us he'd kill us by inches.'

Hiltsch shook his head. 'No,' he said, 'he'd do it by quarter inches. ... But don't worry. He'll never get us.'

Seitzen nodded. He got up from the chair. He said:

'Then it's agreed.' He put out his hand. Hiltsch took it.

'It's agreed, Seitzen,' he said. 'You and I have always worked together. Whatever we may have done, we've never let each other down. We will see this thing through together. We will be two people who will continue to live.'

'That suits me,' said Seitzen. 'Well ... I'm going to bed.'

Hiltsch nodded.

'I shall take a walk,' he said, 'rain or no rain. I need exercise, and I have some thinking to do. You will leave here, say the day after to-morrow, and I shall be with you three or four days after that. Be ready for that.'

'All right,' said Seitzen. 'Good-night.'

He went out. Hiltsch heard him walking up the stairs.

After a little while Hiltsch went into the hallway. He put

142

on a raincoat and a soft hat. He opened the door and regarded the wet blackness without. The air smelt of rain. He opened his nostrils appreciatively.

He was thinking about Seitzen and the arrangements they had just concluded. Life was damned funny, thought Hiltsch.

He walked down the wet earthen pathway on to the dirt road. The mud squelched beneath his well-polished shoes.

He thought, regretfully, that he should have changed them before he came out.

He walked along the road that led towards the village. On the way he began to think about the old days in Munich and Bremen. The brave old days when National Socialism was a word to conjure with and to be a Party member meant something. Hiltsch wondered if those days would ever come again. He thought not. Nothing ever happened twice. One had an experience and that was the end of it. Life was like a love affair. It was all right when things were good, but it was no use trying to resuscitate anything. You couldn't – even if you wanted to. Especially friendships with men and *affaires* with women. When they were dead they were dead, and that was that.

He stopped to light a cigarette, shielding the flame of his lighter with his cupped hand. The hand was strong, well-shaped – a practical hand. But then Hiltsch was a practical man – definitely practical. If you wanted to work for Karl Hildebrand and succeed, you had to be practical, and a dozen other things too. ...

He turned off the road and took the pathway that ran, through the plantation, behind the house. He experienced a certain feeling of satisfaction in pushing through the wet tree branches, in feeling the heavy drops of rain fall on his face.

Now he was behind the house and near it. He moved quietly and easily, treading carefully. As he came round the far side of the house he looked up towards Seitzen's window, noted that no crack of light showed through the tear in the dark curtain.

He flicked away his cigarette stub, moved towards the garage – a shed on the right of the house. He unlocked and opened the doors deftly in the darkness, got into the car, started it up, backed slowly out. As he turned on to the dirt road he looked up again at Seitzen's window. He shrugged his shoulders. Seitzen would be asleep. Nerves or no nerves, the fat Wurtemburger slept like a pig immediately his head touched the pillow.

Hiltsch drove slowly down the dirt road until he came to the intersection. He swung right, switched on his parking lights, headed for Dublin. He put his foot down hard on the accelerator.

He began to sing softly to himself – a Nazi marching song – one of the songs they used to sing in the good old days with the twenty-fourth *Standarte* in Bremen.

Hildebrand looked up and smiled as Hiltsch came into the room. He was wearing a black velvet dressing-gown with dark blue cords. He looked distinguished. He fitted into the tastefully-furnished background of the room with its rows of bookshelves.

He said: 'I did not expect to see you so soon, Rupprecht. Your drive into Dublin must have been uncomfortable.'

Hiltsch helped himself to a cigarette from the silver box on the table. He lit it with satisfaction. His face, in the flame of the lighter, was poised and equable.

He said: 'I like sometimes to be uncomfortable, Karl. When one is uncomfortable it means that one appreciates the next comfort that arrives. I am a sensualist. I specialise in sensations.'

Hildebrand laughed.

'You are a damned old Nazi trooper, Rupprecht,' he said. 'But I like you.' He got up, stood in front of the glowing fire. 'Well,' he went on, 'why are you here? Something has happened? Something good? You look almost pleased with yourself.'

Hiltsch dropped into the big brown leather armchair.

'It is as I thought,' he said. 'Seitzen is rotten. He has had enough. He is prepared to sell out. He desires to go on living. He agreed with me that we had not much chance of continuing to live going on as we were. He agreed that we were between the devil and the deep sea – that is between you and the English.' He laughed.

Hildebrand said: 'So ...! Well, you always thought that

144

Seitzen would crack. Anyhow you will allow that I gave you a good opening to-night.'

Hiltsch nodded. 'I thought you were working up for me to try Seitzen out,' he said. 'I got to work on him immediately you had gone. He fell for it.'

Hildebrand's face was serious.

'You know, Rupprecht,' he said, 'there is too much cracking on the part of our operatives. I have had several cases. Sometimes they have been good Nazis but unable to stand the strain. They have shot themselves or drowned themselves. But nobody – to my knowledge – at least, no real Party member, has ever thought of selling out to the enemy – except Seitzen.'

'He didn't think of it, *I* did,' said Hiltsch with a grin.

The other shrugged. 'He liked the idea,' he said. 'It is the same thing.' He lit a cigarette. 'And now ... ?'

Hiltsch said: 'I shall do it on my own. I shall leave the day after to-morrow. I shall go to Liverpool and work from there. I gather you have a contact for me in London?'

'Yes?' smiled Hildebrand. 'And how did you gather that? It was clever of you.'

'It wasn't,' said Hiltsch. 'You had to find out about that woman of Kane's from somewhere. It isn't easy to get that sort of stuff.'

'You are right,' said Hildebrand. 'It is not easy. Yes, Rupprecht. ... I have two contacts for you. Two very good people. The very best people. I assure you they are not Seitzens. And then I am going to give you another one to take with you. ...'

Hiltsch grunted: 'I don't want another one. I don't want any of your goddamned novices pushed on to me for training. I am not a training school. Besides they are always so stupid. They bungle.'

Hildebrand held up his hand.

'Not this one,' he said, 'I assure you. This one is good. Very good. He has been brought up in the right way. Direct into the *Jugend*, then a year in the Labour Front – in the field and on administration, then a year with the Party. Then a little toughening process.' He smiled evilly. 'You know ... six months in the concentration camp at Haltz being nice to Jews, and another six months under me in the Investigation Room at Columbia House. He is amazing.'

He drew on his cigarette with pleasure.

'After that a period of diplomatic training and languages,' he went on. 'He speaks five. He speaks languages nearly as well as you or I. And he is calm. I have seen him kill a man with a rubber truncheon as casually as one kills a fly. Also ... and this is important ... the women love him. He looks like that too ... even if he isn't like it.'

Hiltsch looked up.

'So!' he said. 'He isn't like it, hey?'

Hildebrand said: 'No ... he doesn't like women – much. I think that's a good thing.'

Hiltsch grunted.

He said: 'My God ...! He must be marvellous. You'd better not let the Führer see him. He might be jealous. When can I see this paragon?'

'You can see him now,' said Hildebrand. He walked to the other side of the fireplace and pressed a bell. Then he stood in front of the fire, looking towards the door.

Hiltsch screwed round in his chair as the door opened. A young man came into the room. An amazing young man. He was five feet ten inches in height, and he moved with a controlled grace that indicated perfect training. He was slim. When he walked he put his feet on the ground like a cat.

His face was long and oval. His complexion perfect. His skin was as beautiful as a woman's; yet there was nothing effeminate in his appearance. He was blonde, and the wave in his hair, receding and fading out over the nape of his neck, gave him the appearance of a film star above the eyes.

His eyes were blue – rather light blue. When Hiltsch saw the eyes he knew the boy was a killer.

He felt for his cigarette case.

Hildebrand said: 'Rupprecht, this is Kurt Nielek. He will work with you. Kurt ... this is Rupprecht Hiltsch, once leader of the twenty-fourth Bremen *Standarte* – one of our most trusted people.'

Nielek raised his right arm from the elbow. He said: '*Heil Hitler!*'

Hiltsch said: '*Heil Hitler!*' They shook hands.

Hildebrand watched them. He said:

'You two will be good together. Your enthusiasm and energy, Kurt, tempered with the sage experience, caution and knowledge of Rupprecht. ...'

He walked over to the oak cupboard let into the bookshelves by the door, opened it, took out a bottle and three glasses. 'This champagne came from Soissons,' he said. 'I had sixty dozen. The owner had no further use for it – after we'd finished with him. Let us drink.'

The wine frothed into the glasses.

Hiltsch and Nielek faced each other. They said '*Sieg Heil*!' They drank.

It was raining hard. The rain beat down on the top of the car, and the tyres made a continuous splashing noise. As they went on, the road became worse. The automobile bumped and the springs protested. Once or twice, over bad holes in the road, Hiltsch, who was a first-class driver, had trouble in keeping the wheel steady. Nielek said softly: 'This Seitzen, he is, I suppose, the gross type – the type that runs to seed quickly – that becomes tired?'

Hiltsch shrugged his shoulders in the darkness. He was thinking that during the whole time of the journey back Nielek had never moved. He had sat quite still in the passenger seat beside Hiltsch, his hands folded in front of him, his legs stretched and relaxed. Excellent control, thought Hiltsch, perfect relaxation, the result of good physical training and condition. He wondered if Nielek's mind was as flexible and fit as his body.

'Seitzen is the result of circumstances,' said Hiltsch. 'Circumstances and women – the wrong sort of women – and beer – especially beer. It is almost impossible to drink great quantities of beer – as he does – and remain mentally alert. His brain is soaked in Pilsner and every other sort. Also his women are inclined to be gross and beefy – which is enervating. Also he is a sadist. But the fact that he has a brain that delights in certain twists, and therefore occasionally stirs itself, does not overcome his other disabilities.'

He took his cigarette out of his mouth and peered through the windscreen. They were on the dirt road now, and it was very dark.

'He joined the Party when it was well established,' Hiltsch went on. 'And then he was much slimmer than he is now. He was enthusiastic too. He became very fond of some woman who used to serve in a *Bierstube*. And it was perhaps unfortunate that his Group Leader also fancied her. The woman preferred Seitzen, which annoyed the Group Leader, and he had the woman arrested on suspicion and sent to Columbia House. He undertook her examination personally, and I bet she had a hell of a time. She was sent to a concentration camp afterwards and died. All this did not please Seitzen very much. He became broody and took to drinking. But he had not lost all his keenness.'

Nielek said: 'That sort of business should be stamped out. When Party members begin to disagree over women and use the organisation for their own purposes – as Seitzen's Leader did, well ... that is not good. I would never allow that sort of thing if I were in charge.'

Hiltsch grinned. 'You'd have a hell of a job stopping people using the organisation for their own purposes – especially where women are concerned. It doesn't hurt to give people their heads sometimes. After all, power is power, and if a woman won't listen to reason in the ordinary way and a man is sufficiently important to be able to fake a charge against her and *make* her listen to reason, he wouldn't be human if he didn't try it – would he?' He looked sideways at his companion.

Nielek said: 'I am not particularly interested in women.'

'No,' said Hiltsch. 'I didn't think you were.'

Nielek said: 'Tell me some more about Seitzen, please.'

'He went into administration,' said Hiltsch, 'and that finished him off. While he had to run around and use his muscles, there was hope for him, but when they sent him to *Jugend* administration and he had nothing to do but sit at a desk and sign papers he got fat and sleazy. Sometimes I used to go and see him. Every night was a thick night for Seitzen, and when he arrived at his office in the morning he looked like the wrath of God. But he did his job. He was promoted. He went to Labour Front Headquarters for a year on the financial side. Then, as you probably know, there was a general Party shake up, and all the Berlin people who had been sitting on their backsides in offices were pushed out to do active jobs. Seitzen asked to go to Intelligence. He asked to go to Intelligence because he thought that he might be put in one of the Army Sections. He'd done a course in that department. But they didn't fall for it. They sent him to one of the Gestapo sub-sectors, and he had a lousy time for six or seven months running around doing liaison work with the Police, and Party Secret Service squads. He didn't like that a bit. Then he volunteered for special employment because he thought anything would be good for a change. He got it. He was posted to Hildebrand's Special Section, and he's been there ever since.'

Nielek nodded. 'Hildebrand doesn't like him?' he asked.

Hiltsch grunted. 'Hildebrand doesn't like or dislike anybody,' he said. 'He's damned efficient and he wants results. He's done well ... damned well. Naturally, he wants keen people working under him. Enthusiastic people. He knows that if people don't have some sort of enthusiasm for the type of work we do they're no good to any one.'

'He thinks a lot of you,' said Nielek. 'He says the nicest things about you.'

'Why shouldn't he?' said Hiltsch. 'I've taken some goddam chances since I've been working with him and he knows it.'

'You like taking chances, don't you?' said Nielek.

'No ... not particularly.' Hiltsch threw his cigarette stub out of the half-opened window. 'But this type of work fascinates me. It's like gambling. You're wondering all the time just how long you're going to get away with it. Another thing is that it's worth while in one way. You take big chances, of course, but so does a fellow fighting in the Army. Look at the time the men on the Russian front are having, for instance. But when we've won this war – as we shall do this year – those of us who get through will be in line for big jobs. We shall be sitting pretty on our backsides in the occupied countries. We shall be safe. We shall have the pick of everything.

The dirt road narrowed. Hiltsch slowed down. He drove very carefully. Presently they came to the cross roads.

'The cottage is a few hundred yards away,' said Hiltsch. 'We'll put the car up. Seitzen is asleep. He sleeps like a pig.

We'll have a drink – I have some good hock – and I want to change my shoes. They're a little wet. After that we'll go and talk to Seitzen.'

Hiltsch made up the fire. He put on the pieces of coal deftly and without noise. He had taken off his shoes and was wearing a pair of felt slippers lined with dark fur. A woman in Potsdam had made them for him. Every time Hiltsch put on the slippers he remembered the woman. She was big and blonde and she had very blue eyes. She liked to eat and drink, and more than anything else she liked Hiltsch. She liked him so much that he had asked her why, and she had tried to explain and failed. And every time he put on the slippers he wondered about her. She had told him that he had the ability to 'ring the bell' as far as she was concerned more than any man she had ever met in her life before. Hiltsch was not quite certain what she meant by 'ringing the bell.' He had an idea, but was not sure. Usually, when he took the slippers off before going to bed at night, he would make up his mind to ask her to explain more clearly if and when he saw her again.

The fire began to burn brightly. Hiltsch went to the sideboard, took out a slender bottle of hock and two glasses. He poured out the golden wine and handed a glass to Nielek.

Nielek was standing on one side of the fire. He took the glass in his right hand. They said '*Sieg Heil!*' and drank.

Nielek said: 'This wine is good. There is no wine like hock. I seldom drink, but when I do I drink hock. It tastes clean.'

'All our German drinks are good,' said Hiltsch. He refilled the glasses. 'And our food and everything else. The British are the only other people who eat and drink really well. The rest of the world eats trash and drinks wine that tastes like vinegar.'

He put his empty glass down on the table. He said to Nielek:

'Are you ready for our friend?'

'Quite,' said Nielek. Hiltsch noticed that he was entirely relaxed. His lips were relaxed and his shoulders and body. His eyes did not alter. They were light blue and hard. Their colour seemed metallic.

Hiltsch led the way out of the room and across the hallway. He went up the stairs that curved round and met the short passage at the top. He stopped at the second door, opened it, flicked on the electric light. He stood to one side of the door so that Nielek could enter. Facing the door was the bed. Seitzen was asleep in it. His bulk seemed greater under the bedclothes. Hiltsch thought again that Seitzen slept like a Wurtemburg pig – which was what he was.

Nielek stood just inside the door, which he had closed behind him. His hands hung straight down by his sides. He was looking at Seitzen. On his face was an expression of faint disgust.

Hiltsch said abruptly: 'Wake up, Seitzen. I want to talk to you.' He walked to the side of the bed and shook Seitzen's shoulder.

Seitzen awoke. He opened his eyes and looked vaguely round the room. Then he ran his tongue over his lips. After a moment he focused his gaze on the figure of Nielek. He frowned. Then he rubbed his eyes with the backs of his hands and slowly sat up in bed. He sat up, his hands clasped on the coverlet before him, looking first at Hiltsch and then at Nielek.

He said: 'What the devil is all this about, Hiltsch? What has happened?' He yawned.

Hiltsch said: 'Nothing of importance. Wipe the sleep out of your eyes and listen.' His voice was hard.

Seitzen looked at him for a moment. Then:

'Well ... I'm listening. What is this? And who is this?' He indicated Nielek.

Hiltsch said: 'This is S.S. Group Leader Kurt Nielek. Together we constitute a Special Court Martial under the power conferred upon us by Herr Reichsführer Himmler through Special Section Director Karl Hildebrand.'

Seitzen said: 'For God's sake ...!'

'You are accused and found guilty of the crime of treachery against the Führer and the Reich. You are found guilty of traitorous intent to the Party. You are found guilty of treachery to your comrades of the S.A. You are found guilty of treachery against the Special Section. Under power

151

conferred upon me by Special Section Director Karl Hildebrand I sentence you to death.'

Seitzen looked at Hiltsch with wide eyes. Hiltsch took out his cigarette case and selected a cigarette. Nielek put his hand inside the breast of his double-breasted jacket.

Seitzen said in a croaking voice: 'This is some joke, Hiltsch. You would not do a thing ...'

Hiltsch said: 'Get out of bed.' His voice was almost disinterested.

There was a pistol in Nielek's hand. It was a short-barrel Mauser automatic with a flat wooden butt, taking eight cartridges – the special weapon, fitted with a two-inch silencer, light, compact and of high velocity, designed by Heydrich and supplied to all Secret Service operatives. It hung straight down by Nielek's side in fingers that were perfectly flexed.

Seitzen did not move. Nielek said in a soft voice:

'It would be better to do this somewhere else. One might make quite a mess in here.'

'Precisely,' said Hiltsch. 'The bathroom is next door. Get out of bed, Seitzen.'

Seitzen began to rock himself to and fro. He made a peculiar groaning noise.

Nielek said: 'Please hold this.' He held out the pistol to Hiltsch, who took it.

Nielek moved easily towards the bed. He leaned towards Seitzen. He put out his left hand and took Seitzen by the shoulder. With his right hand he pressed easily on Seitzen's right wrist.

Seitzen screamed. Beads of sweat appeared on his forehead.

Nielek said coolly: 'That is *ju-jitsu*, Seitzen. It can hurt even more. Please come very quietly. I do not wish to be too unpleasant.'

Seitzen flopped heavily out of the bed. Still holding him by the shoulder and wrist, Nielek pushed him out of the bedroom along the passage. Hiltsch opened the door of the bathroom. Seitzen stumbled across the room to the opposite wall. Then he turned and faced them.

He looked foolish and stupid. His blue and white striped pyjamas hung round his large belly in loose folds. He ran his tongue over his lips. He was trying to talk.

Nielek put out his hand. He took the automatic pistol from Hiltsch, who was leaning up against the wall by the side of the door, drawing easily on his cigarette.

Nielek said: 'Get into the bath, Seitzen. Please do as I say. If you do, it will be much easier for you.'

Seitzen opened his mouth. His eyes were riveted on Nielek. They were wide and staring. Some unintelligible sounds came from him. He stood pressing himself backwards against the wall.

Nielek said: 'Very well ... you force me to be unpleasant. So ...' He shot Seitzen in the stomach.

Seitzen gasped. His face twisted. He slumped sideways, holding his hands to his abdomen. He began to make a peculiar whining noise.

Hiltsch smoked his cigarette. His eyes were on Nielek.

Nielek fired again. The bullet knocked Seitzen, who was hanging over the bath, into it. The bullet went through Seitzen's chest and smacked against the other side of the iron bath.

Nielek fired again – this time through the head.

Hiltsch stubbed out his cigarette against the end of the bath. Nielek was stooping down, picking up the ejected cartridge-cases. When he had collected the three empty cases he slipped them into his side-pocket. He said to Hiltsch: 'It will be necessary to make some arrangements about the late Seitzen.'

Hiltsch nodded. He said:

'You can dig a hole behind the garage. The earth is very soft and it will not take long. And let me give you a tip. There is no necessity to use three bullets on a man. It is much easier to shoot them from behind, through the back of the head. You should have finished Seitzen as he walked into the bathroom, so that he would have fallen into the bath at the first shot.'

'Thank you,' said Nielek politely. 'I thought of that, but I intended him to stand in the bath. When he would not, I was a little angry. I preferred to shoot him in the stomach first.' He smiled at Hiltsch. 'He was such a gross person,' he said, as if in explanation.

Hiltsch shrugged.

'It doesn't matter,' he said. 'You will find a pick and spade in the garage. I will give you the key. You'd better get down to four feet. When you've done that, let me know and I'll help you move him. He'd better be wrapped in a mackintosh. I shall be at work downstairs.'

'I understand,' said Nielek. He went downstairs.

Hiltsch switched off the light and closed the door softly.

II

Valetta Fallon watched Standen as he poured out the drinks. She admired the certainty with which his long fingers held the glasses, the definite movements of his arm. From where she was sitting on the settee she could see the reflection from the shaded light of the standard lamp on his fair hair. She liked the way he wore his clothes. They were good clothes, sufficiently old, well-cut. And he looked just as well in uniform – but in a different way. She had only seen him on one occasion in battle dress, and then she had been intrigued with his air of vitality, of manliness. Now, in plain clothes, he appeared graceful, almost elegant. Definitely she liked Standen. She made up her mind on that point.

He turned and came towards her, carrying a glass in each hand. He put the glasses down on the table at her elbow.

'You know, he said, 'there is something very attractive about war.'

She raised her eyebrows.

'Do you think so? What ...?' she asked.

He sat down.

'I don't mean that there is anything *really* attractive about war itself,' he said, 'but there's something awfully attractive about the atmospherics of war. I can't exactly describe what I mean. I wonder if you understand ...?'

'Perhaps you mean it affects people?' said Valetta. 'I think sometimes it makes them more human in spite of all the misery it brings to some people.'

He grinned at her. He had a delightfully boyish grin, she thought. 'It makes people more than human,' he said. 'Quite often it makes them quite delightful. Consider *us*.'

Valetta laughed. She felt happy. The idea came to her that she was always happy when she was with Standen. He possessed the ability to make her forget the cares and worries of everyday existence. That she thought, was because life was an adventure to him – an amusing, exciting adventure.

'That's the fourth time you've said "Consider us" this evening,' she said.

'Is it?' said Standen. 'Well, that's how I'm thinking. Consider us. I met you exactly eight days ago. I feel I've known you for years. Normally you and I would have had little to talk about, possibly nothing in common. You certainly wouldn't have been interested in the sort of man I was before this war.'

'What sort of man were you?' asked Valetta.

'Oh, not very good,' he said. 'Not very interested in anything – rather weak-kneed.'

Valetta said: 'I don't believe you. Weak-kneed people don't do the job you're doing. They couldn't.'

'Oh, that,' he said. 'That's a joke too. If anybody had told me two years ago that I should be with a Commando I'd have had a fit. I should probably have died of fright.'

She said: 'I don't believe that. ... The child is always father to the man.'

'Not on your life,' said Standen. '*This* child wasn't father to *this* man. Not if you'd known the sort of child I was. But it's funny – the Commando thing I mean. When the war started I went into the Army. I volunteered quickly because I thought I was in love with a girl. I wanted her to think a lot of me. But when I'd been in the Army three months I realised I *wasn't* in love with her, but I was *still* in the Army.'

'And so you weren't in love with the girl any longer ... but you were still in love with the Army?' smiled Valetta. 'Tell me, what sort of girl was she, Edward? Was she a nice girl?'

Standen laughed. 'Exactly what is a "nice" girl?' he said. 'Oh, I suppose she was all right as girls go, and I imagine I was attracted to her because I hadn't had a great deal of experience of women. I hadn't any standards of comparison. How could I have? I'd never met you. ...'

'Dear ... dear ...' said Valetta. 'Are you trying to tell me that I'm now your standard of comparison for the women you meet? I don't know that I like that. ...'

'You ought to,' said Standen.

She changed the subject. She said:

'You like the Army, don't you, Edward – and more than anything you like the Commando? That type of fighting suits your temperament.' She took a cigarette from the box at her elbow and lit it. She looked at him through the smoke.

'Yes,' he said, 'I do like it. I suppose I like the life because it's such a change from anything I've ever known before. It's grand fun. Do you know, Valetta, you may not believe this, but even when I've been very frightened I've still enjoyed it?'

Valetta asked: 'When are you going back?'

'My leave's up in four days' time,' said Standen. 'I shall be sent off somewhere. Then my adventures will start again. I'm excited about that. I've never got over the excitement of not knowing what sort of job one's going to be detailed for next.'

Valetta's eyes shone a little. She said:

'I think you're rather nice, Edward. You're definitely my idea of a Commando Captain. I think you look the part too.'

'That's good news,' said Standen. 'But I was saying ... however exciting things are going to be, the most exciting thing has been you. I think you're the most marvellous person. I do really. ... And I do hope you won't mind my being so enthusiastic about you.'

'I like it,' said Valetta. 'What woman wouldn't? But I really didn't know I was so exciting.'

Standen said: 'Valetta, you're the most exciting woman I've ever met – superbly exciting. Everything about you is right. I like the way you look and move ... and talk. The two or three times I've seen you have made this leave the most wonderful thing that's ever happened in my life.'

Valetta said: 'You cover me with confusion. You're not going to propose or anything, are you?' She laughed softly.

Standen said: 'The joke is I am. Does that surprise you?'

'Oh, dear,' said Valetta. 'It does. ... Candidly, I was a little bit afraid of it. I hoped it wouldn't happen. I didn't want it to happen.'

Standen grinned a little wryly. 'Why not?' he asked.

She said: 'I like you, Edward. I like your type. When you were getting the drinks just now I was looking at you and thinking that you were definitely a rather delightful man.

Also I'm old-fashioned enough to believe that it's still possible – even in these hectic days – for a woman to have men friends. I was almost beginning to think of you as a friend. I wanted that idea to continue. I didn't want it spoilt.'

'I see,' said Standen. He was still smiling. 'And you don't see me as the rejected suitor? You can't visualise me as the sort of man who could possibly be a friend after he'd been turned down as a husband?'

'No,' said Valetta, 'I can't. I don't think you're the type of man who'd want to hang around after a woman had said no.'

Standen said: 'So I haven't a chance? You know, I've been thinking a lot about us for the last three or four days. I think we'd make a good couple. Of course I may get knocked out in this war – that's a chance everybody takes – but even so it would have been worth while. Another thing is that if I were knocked out you'd be all right. Believe it or not, I'm not at all a poor man – not by any standard. I know that hasn't a lot to do with it, but it counts. Why won't you marry me, Valetta?'

She said: 'I don't know. I don't *want* to marry anybody. But I think, Edward, that if I did want to marry someone, it would be a man like you.'

'Valetta, it isn't true that you don't want to be married,' said Standen seriously. 'You're obviously a woman who should be married. You're obviously a woman who wants to be married. Don't tell me you're not bored with this business of going to the theatre every night, living the sort of life that a popular actress like you leads in war time. ... Oh, I've no doubt you're doing a lot of good, bringing a lot of fun and gaiety into the lives of the troops and all that. ... But your real job is being married. Incidentally,' he went on, 'I think I'd make a good husband. I'm not certain, but I think I should.'

She put her hand on his.

'I think you would too, Edward,' she said. 'But, as you would say, it's no soap! The answer is definitely no.'

'All right,' said Standen. 'The answer is no. I think that calls for another drink. May I have one?'

She nodded. He poured himself out a whisky and soda. He came back and stood by the settee, looking down at her.

'All this tells me that you are in love,' he said. 'When a woman's mind is made up as quickly as yours is; when she says no with such definite assurance, there is only one answer. She is in love with somebody else. I'm interested. Tell me about it. I want to know about my rival. I promise I won't even be jealous.'

Valetta said: 'I'm not certain that I am in love. I worry about it. I think I am.' She sighed. 'It would be so much easier to be in love with someone like you, Edward,' she said. 'You're a solid sort of person in your way, my Commando Captain.'

He shrugged his shoulders. 'So it's like that, is it, Valetta?' he said. 'You're very much in love with him and are not certain if he loves you, hey? Not a good proposition. ...'

Valetta smiled. She said: 'You know quite a bit about women and love and things, don't you, in spite of that lack of experience you were telling me about. You're very quick in the uptake – very perceptive. Really, Edward, I imagine you've had a great deal of experience.'

'It doesn't take a great deal of experience,' said Standen, 'to see that you're both uncertain and unhappy about this business of *thinking* you're in love. It's pretty obvious that a woman who only *thinks* she is in love is dealing with a very uncertain proposition – the uncertain proposition being the man she isn't sure about. I think my guess isn't such a bad one. You're very much in love with him and are not certain if he loves you. Well. ... that tells me a certain amount about him.'

'Does it?' said Valetta. 'Tell me, Edward.' She was still smiling at him.

'It tells me that he's either a damned fool or an outsider. Both of those things are unforgivable in connection with a woman like you. And he must be one of those things. Either he hasn't realised that you're in love with him, and if he's as stupid as that he doesn't deserve consideration, or else he *has* realised it and just isn't doing anything about it. He's content to leave you hanging around while he either makes up his mind or doesn't. In this case he's an outsider. The thing that makes me angry about women is that they stand for such situations. Well ... am I somewhere near the truth?'

She nodded. 'That's about the strength of the position, Edward,' she said. 'I suppose you would think it's not a good one. Unfortunately one can't make bargains about love.'

'But you're not certain about it, are you? You don't know if you are in love. You only think you're in love.'

Valetta said: 'I'm not quite certain what love is, but if it is continuously worrying about somebody, being unhappy about them, wishing things could be different, wanting to be with them, being miserable because one knows so little about them; then I'm in love.'

'It certainly sounds like it,' said Standen. 'What a louse he must be to make you feel like that.'

Valetta said: 'I don't think he's a louse, Edward. He may be, of course – I don't know. I don't know anything very much about him except that I have a very strong idea that he needs me sometimes.'

'Damn nice of him!' said Standen. 'He sounds to me like a twirp of the first water. What is he – one of those lounge lizards that just hang around on the chance of getting something for nothing?'

'No,' said Valetta. 'He's not a lounge lizard – certainly not that. He's very tough, Edward ... very, very tough. One feels that about him. But there are some terribly nice things about him too. One's always discovering new little things when one thinks of him.'

He said, a little brusquely: 'I think it's a pity you don't know more about him.' He grinned. 'I suppose you don't even know his name ... or do you? Has he been generous enough to tell you that?'

'Don't be silly, Edward,' she said.

'I'm sorry, Valetta,' he said contritely. 'That was a damned silly remark. But then I'm jealous. And you've got to admit that I'm entitled to be jealous.'

'Are you?' asked Valetta. 'Why?'

'I'm prepared to devote the rest of my life to you,' said Standen. 'I'm prepared to give you everything I've got. I want you to be my wife. I can't pay you a higher compliment, can I? Very well ... all these things count as nothing because you think you're in love with a man about whom you know nothing. A man who obviously doesn't even trust you enough to tell you about himself, a man who may be – for all you know – a crook or something as bad.'

He walked over to the fireplace, stood with his back to it.

'After all, Valetta, I love you,' he said. 'I'd do anything in the world for you. I'd make the most graceful exit for any rival who was worth while, but it's rather terrible for a man who loves you as much as I do to hear that you're fearfully keen on this strange unknown quantity "X." Perhaps you don't know this fellow *at all*; perhaps you only *think* you know something about him.'

'I know quite a lot about him in some ways,' said Valetta.

There was a little pause; then he asked:

'Do I know this paragon? Maybe I've run across him somewhere or other – in a club or somewhere. Who is he?'

Valetta said: 'His name's Kane – Michael Kane. Does that mean anything to you?'

'Not a thing,' he said. 'But it could mean something. I could find out.'

She said: 'I wouldn't worry if I were you, Edward. I think it's always better to leave things as they are.'

'I don't agree,' he said. 'I think sometimes a situation should be forced. I'd like to find out all about this Michael Kane. I don't see why you should buy a pig in a poke.'

She laughed. 'The idea of Michael being a pig in a poke is definitely amusing,' she said.

He moved towards her. She could see he was irritated.

'I think it's a fearful thing,' he said, 'but it seems to me that all you really nice women always manage to fall for some damned outsider. ... Oh, I'm not talking about this Kane merchant – I'm generalising.'

'I know,' she said. 'You were generalising, but you meant him. He's not a damned outsider, Edward.'

'Maybe not,' he said. 'But you'll agree he sounds like one.'

She said: 'No, he's certainly not an outsider in any way. I'm absolutely certain of that.'

'I think you're illogical,' said Standen. 'Here is a man of whom you know nothing, and yet you're absolutely certain about him. How can you know *anything* about him?'

'My dear Edward,' said Valetta, 'a woman is forced to rely greatly on her instinct.' She looked at him. 'I'm perfectly certain,' she said, 'that I do know a lot about Michael. If I hadn't sensed something good about him, I should never have allowed to happen the things that *have* happened.'

Standen closed his teeth with a click.

'I see,' he said. He finished his drink. 'He is a lucky one, isn't he?' His voice was bitter.

Valetta said: 'I'm sorry if I have made you unhappy, Edward. I didn't mean to.'

He did not answer for a moment; then suddenly:

'Forgive me, Valetta. I'm a pig,' he said. 'I'm even worse than your friend Michael.' He put out his hand.

'Good-bye, my dear, he said. 'Anyhow it's been exciting knowing you. I shall think of you an awful lot.'

'Shan't I see you any more, Edward?' Valetta asked.

He said: 'I'm not certain. It depends on you. Perhaps one of these fine days you may discover a sign of the cloven hoof in Michael. I don't want to seem unfair, but he sounds like that sort of person to me. If you do, write to me, care of the War Office – I shall get your letter – and as soon as I get a chance I'll come and see you.' He smiled boyishly. His face lit up. 'I never give up hope,' he said.

Valetta said: 'It's nice of you to go on hoping, even if you know the gilt has been taken off the gingerbread, Edward.'

He shrugged his shoulders. For a moment he looked serious. She wondered what he was going to say. Then he grinned.

'Let's face a fact,' he said. 'Some pieces of gingerbread don't need gilt or rather they are so superbly gilded that the gilt could never really be removed. You're *that* sort of gingerbread. See? *Au revoir*, my dear.'

He went out. After the front door had closed, Valetta sat up on the settee. Suddenly, for no reason that she could think of, she began to cry.

III

Valetta stood by the door of her dressing-room. She wondered why she did not snap the light off. An idea persisted that there was something she had forgotten.

She looked at her reflection in the mirror on the opposite

6 – D.D.

wall. She was wearing an attractive black coat and skirt, a small tailored hat with a veil. She remembered Standen had said that she was beautiful. He had said that there was nothing that an attractive, alluring woman should have that she had not. She smiled a little cynically. Even if it were true – if she were like that – it did not, as the Americans say, seem to be 'getting her any place'.

She realised that during the last few days she had been thinking about Standen. Not so much about *him*, perhaps, as the things he had said. She could not put into definite thought the effect of what he had said. In fact she had begun to doubt. Herself and, more importantly, Kane. She did not like that.

Standen had been logical. The fact that there was a certain jealousy behind his attitude did not alter the truth of what he had said. After all, a man who wants to marry a woman, to give her everything he can, to make a life job of her, is entitled to be annoyed with an individual who was as casual as Kane.

Was Kane casual? Valetta realised that she did not know the answer to that one. How could she? To know if Kane were really casual about her she would have to know all about him. His background, his work, everything. And she knew nothing. And she had been content to know nothing.

Her fur coat lay on the chair by the side of her make-up table. She had forgotten to put it on, and it was a cold night. She wondered about the frame of mind of a woman who could forget to put on her fur coat on a cold night. She smiled, a little bitterly. Perhaps she was losing her grip, or was it that Standen and the things that he had said were disturbing her?

She walked across the dressing room, picked up the fur coat, put it on. When she turned back to the door she gave a start; sat down suddenly in the chair in front of her make-up table. Kane was standing in the doorway.

Valetta said: 'This *is* a surprise!'

Kane said: 'I hope it's not an unpleasant one.' He came into the room, closed the door softly behind him; stood leaning against it, looking at her. 'The old boy who guards the stage-door had gone out for a moment,' he said. 'I slipped past and I managed to find my way here on my own. Are you glad to see me?'

She said: 'Of course, Michael. I'm delighted. You know that. Where have you been?'

Immediately the question was out of her mouth she knew that she had done something extraordinary – something she had never *seriously* done before. She had asked Kane a question – one that he might not want to answer. She wondered why she had done that. Again a picture of Standen flashed across her mind.

Kane said: 'Oh, I've been around. Now I'm back for a little while.'

'So I see,' said Valetta. 'Have you been in London long?'

Kane shook his head. 'No,' he said. 'I arrived about an hour ago. I haven't wasted much time, have I?'

She picked up the cigarette box from the dressing-table, lit two cigarettes, threw one to him. He caught it deftly.

She said: 'No, you haven't wasted much time, Michael. That indicates that immediately you had the chance you came to see me, which must mean, I suppose, that I'm important. Correct?'

Kane inhaled tobacco smoke. He drew the smoke down into his lungs. He exhaled it slowly through pursed lips. The process took quite a while.

He said: 'Absolutely and entirely correct. I consider you to be very important. Now, having determined that fact, where do we go from there, Valetta? Or do we stop there?'

She said: 'I don't know that I want to stop there, Michael. because having determined that I'm important, aren't there some other things we ought to determine?'

Kane raised one eyebrow. 'Such as?' he asked.

'Such as our relative importance to each other,' Valetta said. 'You know, Michael, it's not much fun for a woman being important just at those times when a man decides she shall be. Women are awfully selfish. They like to be important *all* the time.'

'That's all right,' said Kane. 'I think you're important *all* the time too. Satisfied?'

Valetta said a little acidly: 'No, I'm not.' She turned

round on her chair, looked straight at Kane. She said rather coldly: 'Do you believe in facing facts, Michael?'

He nodded.

'If it's *possible* to face a fact,' he said, 'I think the easiest thing to do is to face it and get it over with, no matter how unpleasant it may be. By the way, what is all this leading up to?'

He looked at her a little whimsically. She thought that she loved the way his mouth twitched at one corner. In her heart she wanted to put her arms round his neck and kiss him. But she did not do that. Some spasm of bad temper seemed to possess her. She said:

'It's leading up to this: I've been thinking about you. I've been thinking that I ought to know more about you; that if you're really fond of me – as I believe you are – and if you know that I'm fond of you – as you must know I am – you ought to *want* to tell me more about yourself. After all –'

Kane interrupted. He was still smiling.

'What you really mean, Valetta, is that if a woman sleeps with a man she is entitled to know everything about him. I don't agree. I don't think that.'

Valetta said: 'You must be the only person in the world who doesn't.'

Kane said: 'My delightful infant, are you going to tell me that you sleep with me simply because you want to know about me ... or for some other reason? Don't delude yourself. People sleep with each other for one very good and old-fashioned reason ... they want to sleep with each other. There aren't – or shouldn't be – any strings to the process.'

She said: 'That's a matter of opinion.'

Kane drew on his cigarette. She found herself thinking that he had excellent control. Ever since he had come into the room, closed the door and leaned against it, he had not moved. Only his face and the arm and hand holding the cigarette had moved.

Kane said: 'That's my opinion.'

'Because it's your opinion that doesn't mean that it's absolutely final, does it?' said Valetta. 'I suppose I ought to be entitled to a viewpoint of my own, Michael.'

'Why not? Of course you're entitled to your own opinion,'

Kane smiled. 'I shouldn't be very interested in you, Valetta, if you were a person who hadn't opinions of her own. But what is all this leading to? Why don't you tell me what's on your mind?'

He moved away from the door and sat down on a chair near her make-up table. She looked at him. She thought he looked amiable and friendly.

She said: 'I don't know that it's leading to anything, Michael. But I think you'll agree that it is very natural for me to think about us sometimes, to think about us seriously, and then to think about me in connection with us.' She looked at him quickly. 'I suppose,' she said, 'that sometimes you think about *you* in connection with us, don't you ... or don't you?'

Kane grinned. 'I don't,' he said. 'I suppose now you're going to tell me that I ought to?'

'I'm not going to tell you what you ought or ought not to do,' said Valetta. 'But it occurred to me that some time perhaps you might have wondered what was going to happen about us. You might even have wanted something to happen.'

Kane was still smiling. He took his cigarette out of his mouth, held it between his fingers and regarded the glowing end for a moment. Then he said:

'If I were of a suspicious nature, Valetta, I might even think you were trying to force me into a proposal of marriage.'

She flushed. 'That's ridiculous,' she said. 'I've never heard you make such a stupid remark, Michael.'

Kane said: 'Just a moment ... let's examine this. ... Quite suddenly, for reasons best known to yourself, you're wondering whether I have been thinking about us; whether I have been thinking about our future. Now, it seems to me, from your point of view, that could only mean one thing – marriage. Quite obvious you're annoyed with me because I haven't been thinking about our future. Why should I?'

Valetta said quietly: 'I believe now you're merely trying to sound very tough. You tell me something ... why shouldn't you?'

'I counter that with ... why should I?' said Kane. 'And honestly, Valetta, why should I? Here is a delightful and charming woman – the most delightful and charming woman I've ever met in my life. For some reason or other this delightful woman is very kind to me on such occasions as I appear from out of the blue. Well, you tell me why I should want anything else.'

Valetta said: 'That might be very good from your point of view, and I must say it sounds as if you appreciate me. ...' She threw him a sudden smile. 'But has it occurred to you that it might not be everything *I* want?'

'It's occurring to me now,' said Kane. 'Quite obviously it isn't everything that you want, so there must be something wrong with the situation, and that is that you think we ought to be married.'

Valetta said: 'Nonsense! You're putting me in a false position all the time. You're trying to make it appear that I want you to propose to me. I'm not doing anything of the sort.'

He grinned. She thought that only he could look as nicely mischievous as he did.

'All right,' he said. 'Then it's agreed that you're not trying to make me propose to you. It's agreed that you don't want me to propose to you. In other words, you're telling me that under no circumstances would you consider marriage with a man like me.'

'I'm not trying to tell you anything of the sort,' said Valetta. She was realising that it was quite hopeless to deal with Kane. That he would slip out of any verbal situation.

He said: 'Just what are you trying to tell me?'

Valetta was aware of two distinct feelings – first a feeling of irritation in that Kane was putting her in a false position, and secondly that he was being quite logical and that she was making a fool of herself. After all, no one could make her do anything she didn't want to do. She realised that she'd been quite content with the situation until Standen had appeared. She shrugged her shoulders.

'You're an awfully difficult person to talk to, aren't you, Michael?' she said.

'I think you've only just discovered that,' he said. 'I think I know what the trouble is, Valetta.'

'Oh, so you know that too, do you?' she said. 'Perhaps you'll tell me what it is. I should like to know.'

'Just as if you didn't know,' he said. 'The trouble is this: For some reason you've developed a curiosity about me. You think, quite rightly, that you've been very good to me, and that, therefore, you ought to know all about me. Every woman who's in love with a man thinks she ought to know all about him.'

Valetta raised her eyebrows. 'So you know I'm in love with you?' she said. Her voice sounded a little angry.

Kane laughed softly. His eyes were twinkling.

'Of course you are,' he said. 'Very much in love with me. You must be.'

'Why must I be?' said Valetta.

Kane drew on his cigarette. He was looking at her through half-closed eyelids. 'My dear girl, you're not the sort of woman who goes to bed with a man unless she does love him. Or are you trying to tell me that you are?'

Valetta said: 'I think you're impossible.'

'So do I,' said Kane. 'Very often I think I'm impossible. But I'm damned logical. And after all,' he went on, 'if a man knows he's impossible, his only hope is to be logical. Then his impossibility won't matter so much.

He lit a cigarette.

'Now can I ask *you* a question?' he asked.

'Of course you can,' said Valetta, 'only if you ask me a question *I* shall try and answer it.'

'That's sweet of you,' said Kane. 'Well ... you tell me why you've suddenly developed this curiosity. What's the matter?'

'Nothing's the matter,' said Valetta. 'And there isn't any particular reason why I should suddenly develop a curiosity.'

'Oh, yes, there is,' said Kane. 'I could even make some guesses.'

Valetta raised her eyebrows.

'Could you?' she said. 'Well, guess on. ...'

Kane said: 'When a woman as intelligent as you, Valetta, is content to string along with an odd, unworthy sort of person like I am for a considerable time, and not ask any questions, it is because she is prepared to trust her instinct and take a man at his face value; when of a sudden she stops taking that man at his face value it is because a doubt has arisen in her mind. Well, as the doubt hasn't existed before, you'll agree that it is reasonable for me to think that it's been put there. And I should say the most likely person to put it there would be a man.'

Kane inhaled deeply; then he went on: 'And why not? I've been wondering why you haven't decided to marry someone – some really nice sort of person. You will one day.'

Valetta said: 'Michael, I think you're a beast. There are moments when I hate you.'

Kane grinned. He said:

'I'm very glad that there are moments when you don't. But why do you hate me ... because I am logical?'

'I don't hate you because you're logical,' said Valetta. 'I get fearfully angry with you because you have the ability to sort of stand on one side and watch you and me quite disinterestedly. When I asked you to-night if you ever considered yourself in connection with us, I knew what the answer was. You never did. There's a you that I shall never even know ... something that's quite independent – quite apart from the you that I do know. That's right, isn't it?'

Kane said: 'I don't know. But arising out of all this serious conversation there is one fearfully important question I want to ask you, Valetta. A great deal depends on it. So be careful how you answer.' He leaned towards her. He looked thoroughly dramatic. She wondered what was coming.

'Well, what's the question?' she asked.

'The question is this,' said Kane. 'Will you have supper with me?'

She got up. 'You're quite hopeless, Michael,' she said. 'The answer is ... damn you ... yes!'

IV

Hiltsch walked briskly down the street. He wore a dark grey overcoat, a bowler hat, woollen gloves. He carried a rolled umbrella. He looked like any fairly well-to-do middle-class Englishman. When he came to Thistle Street – a narrow street leading off the main road – he turned down, walked slowly along. He halted under a blued-out street lamp. He lit a cigarette, shielding the flame in his cupped hands, but not so much that the light could not reflect on his face.

Nielek came out of the shadows of the doorway in which he had been standing. He said:

'Why, it's Alleyn ... how are you?'

'Not too bad,' said Hiltsch. 'Working hard and not very much amusement. But it's the same for everybody.'

They began to walk down Thistle Street. After a moment Nielek said: 'How do we do it?'

Hiltsch said: 'This is the system I always use. Remember it. The café is in the middle of the next turning on the left, but you will leave me before we get to the turning. I shall go into the café. You will walk back to the bus stop, and go into the telephone box there. In about ten minutes' time, telephone through to the café and ask for me. Here is the number.' He gave Nielek a slip of paper. 'If I tell you to come along, come. But if they say I'm not there or that I'm there and have asked them to ask you to come along, get out quickly. That will mean that I've been picked up.'

'All right,' said Nielek.

They walked on for a few minutes; then Hiltsch said:

'Well, goodnight, Thomson. It's been nice seeing you.'

He turned off to the left. Nielek crossed to the other side of the road, began to walk back towards the bus stop. Hiltsch walked into the café. It was the usual sort of Tudor café, with imitation oak panelling, that one finds in any large provincial city. When Hiltsch went in, his eyes swept round a large room, taking in everything. His glance was apparently casual, but it missed nothing.

On the other side of the café was a young man in a blue suit. He was smoking a cigarette, and when Hiltsch entered he began to smoke it in a way that would seem odd if you were looking for it. He put the cigarette into his mouth with his right hand, puffed at it; then took it out with his left; then put it back into his mouth with his right.

Hiltsch began to smile. He walked straight across.

He said: 'Hello, Standen. How are you?'

Standen looked up. 'I'm very fit, Alleyn,' he said. 'Sit down. There are several things I want to talk to you about.'

Hiltsch sat down. He said quietly: 'Well, how is it?'

Standen said: 'It's all right. I've no reason to believe that anything at all is wrong.'

Hiltsch said: 'You look well enough. Hildebrand told me you'd been over here eight months. Have you been clever or lucky?'

Standen shrugged. He smiled cheerfully, and offered Hiltsch his cigarette case. To any casual onlooker they were having a pleasant conversation.

Standen said: 'Perhaps a bit of each, but you must remember that I was trained over here. I know this country pretty well. I know the people. It makes it a lot easier.'

Hiltsch said: 'Yes, it must do. It's some months since I was over here, and then I wasn't here for long.'

Standen said: 'I don't want to be here for more than another twenty minutes. There is some work I want to do tonight. Where is the other one?'

'He'll be ringing through here in seven or eight minutes' time,' said Hiltsch. 'To know if it's all right for him to come along.'

'What's he like?' asked Standen.

'He's new – but good,' Hiltsch answered. 'He's been well trained. His name's Nielek, but on this job he is Edward Thomson.'

'I see,' said Standen. 'So he's Edward Thomson. ... I've got all the other details about your English personalities. I'll go over them to-night.'

The waitress came over. Hiltsch ordered tea. He wise-cracked with the girl, and she went off thinking that it was good to meet a cheerful customer sometimes. A few minutes later she came back. She said: 'Are you Mr Alleyn? There's a gentleman named Thomson on the telephone. He described you and said he'd like to speak to you.'

'Thank you very much,' said Hiltsch.

He went into the telephone box by the pay desk. When he returned he said to Standen:

'That was Thomson. He'll be here in a few minutes.' He sighed. 'This is a bit different from the old days, isn't it?' he said.

Standen shrugged.

'I prefer it,' he said with a grin. 'Excitement suits me, and dodging these cursed English is exciting enough. They have very nearly got me twice. They know I'm here, but they don't know who I am, and they don't know where I am. So at the moment the odds are on me.'

He lit another cigarette. Hiltsch said:

'Well, I like the old days better, but I don't mind this.'

'I don't mind anything,' Standen said. 'It's not much good minding, is it?'

Nielek came in. He came straight over to the table. Hiltsch asked the waitress to bring another cup. When the tea had been brought and poured out, Standen said quietly:

'There are two things that we have to try to do, gentlemen. They are both important, but one is more important than the other. It is this: The first thing that we have to do at any cost and at any risk to ourselves is to find out the head-quarters of the organisation for which Kane works. That headquarters is supremely well organised. It is recognised that a great portion of Kane's success has been due to the information with which he is supplied by that organisation. We have to try and find out who is the key man. If we can get that information back to Hildebrand, we shall have done a good job.

'The second part of our work is the removal of Kane.' He smiled. 'Possibly the two things will march together.'

Hiltsch said: 'Have you got a definite plan, Standen? Karl said something about a woman in whom Kane was very interested – a woman named Fallon.'

Standen smiled. 'I know all about her,' he said. His smile became broader. 'I proposed marriage to her three or four days ago. I was refused.'

They all laughed.

'I have an idea,' said Standen. 'It's rather impertinent, but I think we can pull it off. It will take four of us to do it.'

Hiltsch raised his eyebrows. 'Four ...?'

'Yes,' said Standen. 'Four. ... We have another operative here working with us – one of our best men. He has been here for two years as a Swiss waiter. He was the hired waiter who was at the party at Hampstead the night Kane and Guelvada got Helda. Luckily, I have been able to arrange a new situation for him. He is in a position in which he can be

171

of the greatest help to us. At the moment he is the hall porter at the apartment house where Kane's woman friend lives.' He smiled at them. 'Owing to the scarcity of porters, he is also the night porter. He works very hard. He is supposed to be an ex-service man of fifty-seven years of age – Thomas Lang.'

He looked at his watch.

'Now what I have to say will take about five minutes, gentlemen,' he continued, 'and as we shall separate when I have finished, and as we may not have another opportunity to talk at length, you will listen very carefully. ... There must be no mistakes. ...'

v

Hiltsch and Standen stood at the edge of the pavement looking towards the corner building on the other side of the road. It was very dark. The wind whistled through the almost deserted streets. Standen said: 'When one thinks of what London was like before the war ... hey?'

Hiltsch nodded. 'It's not so good,' he said. 'But, by what I can hear, Berlin's worse.'

Standen said: 'Perhaps one of these fine days we might get an opportunity to see ... *one* of these fine days.'

On the other side of the street a blackout curtain that covered the entrance to the apartment block moved very slightly for a second or two. A crack of light showed.

Standen said: 'There you are, my friend. And good luck to you!'

Hiltsch said, a trifle grimly: 'Thanks ... although I've got an idea we're going to pull this off.'

'Of course we shall,' said Standen. 'Well ... so long!' He disappeared in the darkness.

Hiltsch waited a minute. Then he crossed the road. He went into the building by the main door. Just inside, on the right, was the porter's lodge. Hiltsch walked up to it; looked at the man who was sitting inside.

'Hello, Lang,' he said. 'It's cold, isn't it?'

The hall-porter nodded. He looked round; then said with a little smile: 'I've been expecting you.'

'Is she in?' Hiltsch asked.

'Yes,' said the porter. 'She is ... and so's our other friend.'

Hiltsch dropped his voice. 'Is the telephone fixed?' he asked.

The hall-porter nodded.

'I told her it was out of order this afternoon,' he said. 'Nielek is in the apartment next door. He cut the wire and connected it with his line. It's all right. She's not using the telephone. She thinks it isn't put right yet, but any call she makes from now on will go through to Nielek.'

Hiltsch said: 'Is there a house telephone?'

The porter nodded again.

'Ring up on the house telephone and say the telephone's now in order,' said Hiltsch. 'Directly I've gone, get through to her and say it's gone wrong again. Then get Nielek to re-connect it up in the ordinary way as it was before. You understand?'

'Perfectly, said the other. He picked up the house telephone. After a minute he said: 'Is that you, Miss Fallon? This is Lang, the hall-porter. Your telephone will be O.K. in a few minutes if you want to use it.' He hung up the receiver.

Hiltsch said: 'Wait for a minute or two; then ring through to her and tell her I'm here.'

He was wearing a brown raincoat, a bowler hat, brown kid gloves. He looked like a police officer, which was not surprising, because Hiltsch had the ability to look like that when he wanted to. He stood leaning against the porter's box, waiting patiently. After a minute or two he said:

'All right, you can get through now.'

The hall-porter picked up the house telephone again.

He said: 'Miss Fallon, there's someone to see you – a Detective-Inspector Arthurs from Scotland Yard. Shall I ask him to come up ...? Very well, Miss!' He hung up. 'She's waiting for you,' he said. He grinned. 'Good luck.'

'Thanks,' said Hiltsch. He walked towards the lift. He entered it, pressed the button on the indicator for the first floor. During the few seconds that the lift travelled upwards, Hiltsch thought about this new adventure. He wondered what the end of it would be. He shrugged his shoulders. Always at the beginning of a new job he wondered what the end would be. But the end had always been all right – always more or less successful. Why should this be different? Valetta Fallon opened the door of the flat. She looked mildly surprised.

'Are you sure it was me you wanted to see?' she asked.

Hiltsch nodded. 'I'm afraid so, Miss Fallon,' he said. 'I'd be glad if I could talk to you for a few minutes.'

'By all means,' she said. She held the door open for him. Hiltsch went into the flat. He took off his hat, waited for her to lead the way into the sitting-room. It was warm and comfortable, he thought. He sighed inwardly. One of these days, he thought, when this cursed war was over, when he was a Deputy-Gauleiter or something, he'd have warm and comfortable rooms and lots of women – maybe this one. ... Why not? He looked at her quickly. A hell of a woman, thought Hiltsch. Kane certainly knew how to pick them. He sat down on the chair she indicated.

She said: 'I'm feeling a little frightened.' She smiled. 'I'm wondering if I've done anything – anything that would merit the attentions of a detective-inspector.'

Hiltsch smiled reassuringly.

'I don't think *you* need worry, Miss Fallon,' he said, although the business I have come to see you about is rather important. When I tell you what it is I know you'll do your best to help us.'

Valetta said: 'It sounds very dramatic.'

'I don't know about that,' said Hiltsch. 'It may be, although I hope it won't be.'

'Would you like a cigarette?' she asked.

He shook his head.

'No, thank you, Miss Fallon,' he said. 'I'll just get on and tell you all about this business as quickly as I can. The position is this: A couple of days ago we received a telephone message from a gentleman – I think you know him – a Captain Standen. Anyway, he said he was a friend of yours. He wanted to talk to us about another friend of yours – a gentleman by the name of Kane.'

'Oh, yes?' said Valetta. She looked surprised.

'It seems,' Hiltsch went on, 'that this Captain Standen, who, if I may say so, is an officer with a very good record, had, for reasons best known to himself, become a little suspicious about this Mr Kane. Apparently Captain Standen had been trying to find out just who and what this Kane was, and in the process had stumbled on one or two facts which made him think that it was his duty to report the matter to us.'

'I see,' said Valetta. Her voice was very serious. 'Please go on.'

'We did a quick check-up,' said Hiltsch, 'and, candidly, we're not at all satisfied with the position about Mr Kane. That's where we want you to help us.'

Valetta said: 'I don't quite understand what you mean. You seem to suspect Mr Kane of something. Why? What's wrong!'

Hiltsch shrugged his shoulders.

'The information in our hands, Miss Fallon,' he said, 'points fairly conclusively to the fact that Michael Kane is a German agent operating in this country, and that he seems to have been doing it successfully for a considerable time.'

Valetta was very white. She said softly, almost to herself: 'Good God!'

Hiltsch went on: 'I expect it's rather a shock, Miss Fallon, because we understand from Captain Standen that this Kane was rather a friend of yours, which is not to be surprised at, because he seems to be a very plausible and attractive person.'

Valetta said: 'This *is* a terrible shock. You're quite certain, of course? It doesn't seem possible.'

Hiltsch nodded.

'I'm afraid there's no shadow of doubt,' he said.

'What are you going to to do?' asked Valetta. 'Are you going to arrest him?'

'No,' said Hiltsch, 'we don't want to do that. You see, we think the position is something like this: Kane is working over here, coming into this country and getting out periodically. We don't quite know how, but we do know that he has contacts here, and we want to find out who these people are. He seems to be a member of an organisation that's been pretty clever up to date. If we arrest Kane at once we shall have him, but very little else.'

'What do you want me to do?' asked Valetta.

Hiltsch said: 'What I'm going to ask you to do is not very difficult, but it is important. First of all you mustn't let Kane suspect that you're trying to find out anything about him. And even if you think you can find out things, I don't want *you* to try. These people are inclined to be very wary. He'd probably notice the slightest change in your demeanour. But what I do want is for you to let us know when he comes here to see you, so that we can pick him up outside, follow him, see where he goes to, and if possible find out who the other people are. Do you think you could do that?'

Valetta said: 'Yes, I suppose I could. There's no reason why I shouldn't, is there? You mean that if he comes here to see me you want me to telephone you?'

'No, I don't want you to do that,' said Hiltsch. 'We want as few calls from here to Scotland Yard as possible. The hall porter here is a very reliable man. He's an ex-service man by the name of Lang. If, when Kane comes to see you, you could ring down to Lang on the house telephone and give some prearranged signal, such as asking if a parcel had been delivered or something like that, Lang would get in touch with us at once, so that we should be ready for Kane when he left.'

'I see,' said Valetta. 'Very well. ... I'll do that.'

Hiltsch said: 'I'm afraid this has upset you a little bit, Miss Fallon. I'm very sorry. I sympathise with you. It's pretty tough to find out that anybody who is a friend is working for the enemy. But these things happen ... unfortunately.'

Valetta said: 'I suppose they do. It doesn't make it any the less shocking though.'

Hiltsch said: 'There's one other thing I'd like you to do, Miss Fallon. As I just said, we don't want any obvious contact between this place and Scotland Yard.' He got up, took a leather case from his pocket. 'Here's my warrant card,' he said. He handed it to her. 'And I'd be glad if you'd telephone through to Scotland Yard now and just check up on who I am, so that you'll know that it's in order. Would you mind doing that?'

'Very well,' said Valetta. 'The number's Whitehall 1212, isn't it?'

Hiltsch said: 'That's right. How did you know that?'

She smiled. It was a sad smile.

'I've read it in so many detective novels,' she said, 'and I never thought when I saw it in those books that I should be using it for this purpose.' She dialled the number.

In the next apartment, Nielek picked up the telephone. He heard Valetta's voice. He listened; then he said in a brusque voice: 'Thank you very much, Miss Fallon. ... This is the Information Room, Scotland Yard. If you'll hold on for a moment I'll put you through to the Department concerned.' He clicked the receiver handle two or three times; then in a deeper voice said: 'Hello. ... is that Miss Fallon ...? Oh, Miss Fallon, thank you for ringing up. This is to confirm that the officer who is with you – Detective-Inspector Arthurs – is in charge of the business about which he has spoken to you. I do hope you'll be able to give him every assistance. It's rather important.'

'I understand that,' said Valetta. 'Of course I'll do anything I can.' She hung up. The click of the receiver on the handle sounded to her almost like Kane's death warrant. She looked into the fire. She felt terribly miserable.

Hiltsch said: 'Well, I must be going. Cheer up, Miss Fallon, and don't worry. Everything will be all right. Just let the hall porter know when Kane comes here, and if you're feeling unhappy remember you're doing a job for your country – a good job. Don't worry to see me out. ...'

She sat down on the settee. Vaguely she heard the front door close behind Hiltsch. She realised for the first time in her life what unhappiness meant.

Downstairs Hiltsch passed the porter's box. He said to Lang:

'I've seen her, and everything's O.K. She's going to let you know directly our friend comes here.'

Lang said: 'All right. I'm glad things went so well.'

Hiltsch went out into the darkness.

VI

It was a cold day. The bitter east wind made Kane shudder a little in spite of his heavy coat. He wished that he had put up the hood of the touring car. He turned out of Pall Mall into St. James's Street. The speedometer showed that he was doing only eighteen miles an hour. It was not until he turned the corner into Piccadilly and began to drive towards Hyde Park that he realised that he was driving aimlessly about the West End because he was worried, because he was trying to think constructively, and because he knew he had to answer a question. Kane, who had always made it a rule to face facts, was beginning to think that he was trying to avoid facing a fact.

He pulled in to the left, stopped the car just past the main gate into St. James's Park. He lit a cigarette, sat smoking, looking straight through the windshield but not really seeing anything. He was thinking about Valetta.

In an odd way, ever since he had known her, she had become more and more of a habit, and during the last six or seven months a habit that one relied on. Valetta was an anchorage – a haven to which one returned occasionally for just a little while after a dangerous voyage. He realised he had got used to the idea of Valetta being a haven.

And women were dangerous to men in Kane's profession. No matter how delightful, how sincere, how honest, how patriotic a woman might be, she could still be dangerous – even in spite of herself. He remembered the half a dozen occasions since the war had started when women, perfectly innocently, and without knowing anything about what was going on, had been the cause of *something* happening. You could always do things *through* a woman. More importantly, you could always get at a man through a woman one way or another, and if a woman were fond of a man then it was even easier to get at him through her, because women in love sometimes become easily frightened.

Kane was perturbed. He was perturbed about Valetta's attitude. He was perturbed about her sudden curiosity, and he realised that the operative word was 'sudden.' She had been content, because she was fond of him, to go on, to take him and his background for granted, to ask no questions, to want to know nothing. Now suddenly she had become curious. Why? Kane was remembering that at their last meeting, when she had had supper with him, she had as suddenly ceased to be curious. It was as if, having failed to find out what she wanted to know, she had thought that she must not make him suspicious by continuing to be curious. Just as she had suddenly become curious, so she had as suddenly ceased to be curious. Kane did not like that.

He took the cigarette out of his mouth and sat regarding the burning end, looking at the little wisp of smoke that was soon blown away by the wind. He realised that something had to be done about Valetta, and here again he was in a bad spot. The alternatives were to satisfy her curiosity, which was impossible, or to cut her out. At first thought, the second alternative seemed the obvious one, but whilst Kane, who was tough enough to be very tough with himself, would have finished with Valetta if he had thought it the best thing to do, he did not see that the process would serve his purpose. He realised that his sudden removal would intensify her curiosity, and whereas before she had been merely curious, after his disappearance she would be keen to find out *everything* she could.

At the back of his mind all the time a little voice was telling him that it was unlike Valetta to be curious. This thought presupposed the existence of some other personality. Kane remembered that if Valetta knew little about him, he on his part knew little about her. Quite obviously, she had friends. She was a very attractive woman – an alluring woman, thought Kane – and some time some man was going to want to marry her. What would she do then? Surely that would be the time when she would consider and weigh up the possibilities of marriage with Kane. Surely that would be the time when she would would want to know something about Kane.

He threw away the stub of his cigarette, lit a fresh one. He did not like the situation. He had to do something. He switched on the ignition key, let in the clutch. He moved out into the stream of traffic, drove past the Hyde Park traffic lights, turned into Knightsbridge. It was a grey January day. The sort of day that Kane had liked in the years when he had been interested in the appearance of days.

Something had to be done. Kane was irritated. As a person whose habit it was to face facts as and when they presented themselves, he knew that the line of least resistance is inevitably the hardest road in the end. He baulked from creating a situation in which Valetta would appear. Yet, at the same time he knew he must do it. He grinned cynically. He was thinking of the dozens of situations he had created during the past two years – situations which had been ready-eyed for all sorts of conditions of people to walk into. The fact that most of these people had been enemies of his country, enemies of the cause for which Kane fought as hard and as dangerously as any soldier, had made the process simple and easy. But this was nearer home. Kane was realising for the first time just how near it was.

By now he was at the end of the Brompton Road. He drove the car round by South Kensington Station, along the Old Brompton Road. He turned up Drayton Gardens, swung the car right along the Fulham Road. Now he was thinking about himself. The trouble with him, he thought, was that he possessed an over-developed sense of duty, realising at the same moment that an over-developed sense of duty was very necessary to people who did his job – a job permitting no deviation from a strictly mapped-out course. In any event, sense of duty or not, something had to be done.

He began to wish that his temperament was different, that he brought a different outlook to bear on life and things generally, especially women. He continued with this line of thought for some time, pulling himself up with a jerk when he realised that he was crossing Putney Bridge, which was, he thought, not the most attractive place for aimless driving.

He came back to the consideration of himself and women. Perhaps, he thought, there were not enough women in his life – that there was safety in numbers. Lots of people thought there was safety in numbers. Ernie Guelvada, for instance. Right through Guelvada's meteoric career women had sprinkled themselves like stars in a summer sky. Some of them, of course, had been shooting stars – Kane grinned at the triteness of this thought – but, by and large, as Guelvada would be the first to admit, there was safety in numbers. Kane wondered how Ernie, with his peculiar sense of the theatre, his quickness of perception, his intuition, and his extraordinary knowledge of women, would handle the situation which confronted Kane. Now he began to think along those lines – of what Guelvada would do.

The twilight was forming. Kane realised that the darkness came quickly these days. He realised also that he was nearly at the beginning of the Kingston By-Pass. Then something struck him. His driving had not been so aimless after all. It had been attuned to his thoughts, and if he had only consciously thought of Guelvada at the end, well, what did that matter?

Because now Kane realised that all the time he had been thinking, trying to puzzle out this situation, he had been driving towards Tyrrell's Wood.

Guelvada lived at Tyrrell's Wood. So that was it ...! Subconsciously Kane had known all the time that the answer to his problem must come from Ernie – that blithe spirit who had never yet known what it was to be confounded by a woman.

Kane remembered a conversation. A hot afternoon in Spain. ... He remembered stopping to get water for the car, and Guelvada's intimate conversation with the girl at the inn. He remembered when they had resumed their journey, he had said to Ernie: 'One of these fine days you'll get yourself in bad through a woman,' and Guelvada had looked at him sideways, one eyebrow cocked, and said: 'What ... me! Oh no, Michael ... not me. Why should I be afraid of women?' Kane had said: 'Sometimes they get nasty.'

Guelvada had shrugged. 'So what ...?' he had said. 'If a woman gets nasty, well ... you can always duck!'

Darkness came artistically to the Grain Tavern in Tyrrell's Wood. The tavern, as you probably know, stands back off a little side road. Away on the right is the golf course, billowing away into the distance, and on the left, and curving behind the inn, are the woods. Desolate perhaps, but definitely romantic. Many things, historic even if not of great importance, had happened at the Grain Tavern. These things, no doubt, had left their mark, creating the present atmosphere of the place, which atmosphere I have no doubt was responsible for the presence there of Ernie Guelvada.

He was sitting at a table in the corner of the bar parlour. A bright fire burned, and Mrs Soames, the proprietress, for whose trim and well-developed figure Ernie had a supreme admiration, was arranging the black-out. When she had finished, he said:

'I think, Mrs Soames, I will drink a large whisky and soda.'

'Certainly, Mr Guelvada,' she replied, bustling towards the bar. As she poured out the whisky she said: 'You know, we've missed you since you've been away, Mr Guelvada.'

He took his cigarette case from his pocket, selected a cigarette slowly. When he lit it, he looked through the flame of his lighter at Mrs Soames. He said:

'And who is "we," Mrs Soames, please?'

She came towards him with the drink.

'Oh, everybody, I think, Mr Guelvada,' she said. 'It's been sort of general, you know.'

Guelvada said softly: 'Do you mean to tell me that people have come to you and told you that they've missed me?' He smiled at her.

She said: 'Why, I can't say exactly that, but ...'

Guelvada said: 'You mean *you* have missed me. That is as it should be. I like to be missed. Tell me, have you been thinking about me a lot, Mrs Soames?'

She flushed.

'You are a one, aren't you, Mr Guelvada?' she said. 'There's nothing you don't say if you think of it.'

Guelvada said: 'You mean nothing is sacred to me, Mrs Soames?'

'I mean you always say what you think,' she said.

'Isn't that a good thing to do?' asked Guelvada. He smiled at her again. 'I'm sure you approve of that process,' he said.

Mrs Soames nodded. 'I think I do,' she said. 'It's a nice change when people speak their minds. They usually don't.'

Guelvada drew on his cigarette. He said:

'You know, Mrs Soames, one of these fine days – or nights – I'm going to speak my mind to you. I hope you'll find *that* a nice change.'

Mrs Soames did not say anything. She went back to the bar. When she got to the door, she threw Guelvada a quick look over her shoulder. He was still smiling. Behind the bar-counter Mrs Soames put a straying curl back into place. She looked at herself in the glass. She thought she was still a rather attractive woman. She began to think about Guelvada.

Guelvada looked up as Kane came into the bar parlour. He smiled. Although this sudden appearance of Kane, who had never before been to Tyrrell's Wood, meant that something important was afoot, Guelvada evinced no surprise. Surprises were to him the normal attributes of life. He said:

'Have a drink, Michael?'

Kane said: 'Thanks, Ernie. I'll have a whisky and soda – a large one.'

Guelvada walked over to the serving-hatch. He ordered the drink, brought it back with him. He said: 'Do you remember that drink I made in Lisbon – that night when we were looking for Gallat? That *was* a drink. ... You know, Michael, I've come to the conclusion I don't like the winter.'

'What you mean is,' said Kane, 'you like Lisbon.'

Guelvada shrugged his shoulders.

'I wouldn't be *too* certain of that,' he said. 'I used to like it very much, but now ...' He was thinking of Marandal. ... 'I think there'd be too much atmosphere.'

Kane put down his glass. He said:

'There's a job I want you to do, Ernie. It's rather a personal sort of thing. It might be important and it might not.'

Guelvada nodded. He was thinking: 'This is something to do with a woman.' He was thinking that possibly Kane had got mixed up in something and couldn't get out easily. He began to wonder what sort of woman would attract Kane.

Kane said: 'The position is this: Some time ago I met a woman – a rather nice person. Her name's Valetta Fallon. We've been pretty good friends.'

Guelvada nodded. 'I understand, Michael,' he said.

Kane went on: 'We've seen quite a bit of each other ... whenever I've been able to.' He paused to light a cigarette. 'I don't have to tell you, Ernie,' he said, 'that in our business friendship is a rather rare thing – rare because if you get to know people too well they're inclined to want to know something about you. But in this case that angle didn't seem to arise. There were no questions asked. Everything was taken for granted. It was rather a nice situation.'

183

Guelvada nodded again. 'And now ...' he queried, 'someone has asked questions, hey?'

Kane smiled.

'Exactly,' he said. 'Someone has asked questions.'

Guelvada said: 'You know, Michael, it is reasonable enough, isn't it? You can't expect a woman to go on being friendly, to be fond of one ...' he smiled suddenly, 'to love one if you like, without asking questions. Why should she? It isn't right, is it?'

Kane said: 'It was right for this woman, Ernie. You see, she's rather extraordinary. She has that supreme quality which so few women possess of minding her own business.'

Guelvada said wryly: 'I congratulate you, Michael. She must be unique. All my life I have been looking hopefully for a woman who would mind her own business. I don't have to tell you that I have never found one yet.'

Kane said: 'If you go on long enough, Ernie, you might find one.'

Guelvada grinned.

'I shall continue to search,' he said. 'In the meantime, I am intrigued that you have found such a woman.'

Kane said: 'The fact that she is like that made the sudden curiosity on her part more marked. I began to wonder.'

'Precisely,' said Guelvada. 'The same thing's happened over and over again. Life is like that, especially as regards women. One meets a woman. She's delightful. She's pleased with you; she's pleased with herself. Everybody is happy, and then, sooner or later, the serpent enters the Garden of Eden. Usually it's some other man.'

'Quite,' said Kane. 'It's usually another man who starts a woman's curiosity. That is what I was thinking of. ...'

'I see,' said Guelvada. 'So it's like that. You think ...?'

'I'd be a fool if I didn't,' said Kane grimly. 'Just think for a moment how many times have *we* used a woman to get at someone or to find out something that we wanted to know? In nine cases out of ten she's never even been aware of what we were doing. She's been entirely innocent. Yet we've used her successfully, because we had to use her, because that was the only way we could work.'

Guelvada nodded.

'Quite,' he said. 'But, Michael, *we* are unique.'

'Are we?' said Kane. 'I wouldn't be too sure of that. You know I never take chances – not *any* sort of chance – no matter how small or how remote. Too much depends on our not taking chances except when we have to.'

'I follow,' said Guelvada. 'And so you're going to take the point of view that the worst has happened. You're going to believe that –'

'I'm going to believe that somebody is trying to get at me through Miss Fallon,' said Kane. 'I'm going to believe that because it's the safest thing. Perhaps I'm wrong. Perhaps I've been mistaken in my estimate of her character, but I have an idea that someone has been trying to get next to her, possibly trying to make love, possibly proposing marriage. Then, when they've come up against a brick wall – found there's nothing doing – they've discovered about me. After all, it is very easy to start a woman being curious, you know. More especially if the process is merely part of some well-planned scheme.'

Guelvada nodded again.

'What are you going to do, Michael?' he asked.

Kane said: 'I'm going to play this so that if I'm wrong it doesn't matter, but so that if I'm right we're going to get on to something. I shall see Fenton to-night. He'll have to give us a hand over this.'

Guelvada said: 'If you think it's serious, I think you're right. It would be silly to run into something through not taking a little care. And what am I to do, Michael?'

Kane said: 'Supposing somebody was trying to get at me through Miss Fallon. They'd want to use her to find out things about me. But they couldn't do that in any obvious way. They'd have to be very careful – very clever. They couldn't openly ask her to find out things about me. That would make her suspicious. But what they could do would be to use her as a sort of stalking horse, as a means of picking me up, of finding out my movements.'

'Quite,' said Guelvada. 'They'd wait till you went to see her. They'd follow you.'

'That's right,' said Kane. 'And that's how we can find out if I'm right or wrong in my case. When I leave here I'm going to see Fenton. I'll arrange something with him. To-morrow is Sunday. Valetta won't be working at the theatre. I shall ring up in the afternoon and tell her that I'm going to see her at seven o'clock. I shall go there. You'd better be around. You can keep an eye on things and see what happens when I leave the place. See if somebody tries to tail me. In any event, I'll take the usual process to shake them off. But perhaps you can find out where they're going, what they're at, possibly who they are. This may be a wild-goose chase,' said Kane, 'but it's worth while.'

'Of course,' said Guelvada. 'And if you're wrong what does it matter?'

Kane said: 'Miss Fallon lives at the Vallance Apartments in Knightsbridge. I expect you know the place I mean. The entrance is on a corner, but the lay-out is quite good for keeping the place under observation. You had better be around at five to seven to-morrow night, Ernie. See what happens. Telephone me afterwards.'

'Excellent,' said Guelvada. 'It shall be done. It would be amusing,' he said, 'if we stumbled on to something by chance. I find life a little boring down here.'

Kane grinned. 'That means there aren't any attractive women about,' he said.

'On the contrary,' said Guelvada. He sighed. 'I hate to admit it,' he said, 'but I think I'm beginning to find that even attractive women can be boring.'

Kane finished his drink. He said:

'I'll be getting along. I've a lot to do to-night. I'll hear from you to-morrow one way or another, Ernie?'

Guelvada nodded. Kane picked up his hat and went out.

Guelvada felt in his pocket. He produced a miniature pack of patience cards. He set them out on the table. He began to play patience and, when he felt like it, he cheated.

He sat at the table in the corner of the bar-parlour for an hour. Twice during that period, Mrs Soames refilled his glass, commented on his skill with the cards. Guelvada smiled and answered, but his attention was not on Mrs Soames or on the game he was playing. He was thinking about other things.

This business of Kane and the woman was funny, thought

186

Guelvada. Damned funny. He was more than interested. He was intrigued. He began to talk to himself very softly, in French, as was his habit when very interested in some subject. He placed the cards in front of him automatically.

'Consider, my Ernest,' he said to himself, 'this business of Michael. It is most extraordinary and of a pattern which is not acceptable to your intelligence. To use a vulgar expression, it stinks. That being so, why does it stink? It stinks because, though old, it is *not* logical.

'Figure to yourself,' he continued, 'that suddenly the woman friend of Michael develops a curiosity. Quite suddenly she develops this curiosity. The presumption being that someone, someone interested in Michael, desires through her to obtain information. It is, of course, understood that the person desiring information about Michael is working for the Boches. ...

'Very well. ... That being so, the matter becomes even more illogical. More illogical because the individual desiring information about Michael, and those for whom he operates, is, presumably, intelligent. Being intelligent, this individual will surely expect that Michael will be intrigued at the sudden curiosity on the part of the lady. The lady who has not been curious on previous occasions, or, at least, not to any extent that matters. Being intelligent, the individual who desires the information must surely guess that Michael is a person of extremely acute perceptions, of most refined instinct, of an intuition of the utmost celerity and sureness. If the individual desiring information knows anything at all of Michael, or the work he has done, of the superb *coups* he has achieved, then he must guess these things. Is it not so, my Ernest?'

He placed another card.

'It is so,' he continued, 'and being so, it is entirely obvious that the individual desiring information was certain that Michael *would* be interested and intrigued at this sudden curiosity, and therefore he quite obviously has some *arrière pensée*. He does not expect the lady to obtain any information from Michael, but he does expect that, as a result of her curiosity, something may happen, or that he may be able to achieve something.'

He yawned. 'In any event,' he continued, 'what does it matter? Whatever is fated will most assuredly happen, and will be, in the long run, quite logical. Of that you may be certain.'

He gathered up the cards, shuffled them, began to lay them out again. He was thinking about women – women who, for one reason or another, had projected themselves into the 'business' activities of Kane and himself; who had been used for the furtherance of such schemes as were necessary or desirable at the moment.

There was the woman at Soissons – the blonde woman, the woman who walked so alluringly, who was so lovely that it was almost impossible for any man – any normal man – not to be infatuated with her. Her name was Yvonne, and she came to Soissons after the German occupation. She lived in a small house in the Rue Lafarges and, apparently, kept very much to herself. She was said to be a good Frenchwoman and loathed the Germans with the most complete hatred.

But it was Fenton who smelt her out. It was one of Fenton's bright spirits who had discovered that the attractive and demure Yvonne was one of S.S. Reichsführer Himmler's 'specials' – one of the charming and delightful ladies that were 'put in' to keep an eye on the comings and goings, the sayings and doings, of highly-placed German officers in occupied territory.

And then Kane and Guelvada had descended upon Soissons. Descended was the right word, for they had been dropped just before dawn from a British plane and had melted into the atmosphere to reappear some three hours later as inhabitants of Soissons with identity papers and backgrounds arranged promptly through the organisation of Fenton. Guelvada wondered if Yvonne's ears had burned that morning.

Four days' quiet work had enabled Kane to discover that the Town Commandant was one Captain von Fiersch, a Prussian of middle age, a roving eye and a wife who, luckily, had permission to spend three weeks with him. It was lucky, or natural, thought Guelvada, that Frau von Fiersch should be jealous of her husband and his roving eye.

They had worked quickly, expertly and ruthlessly. Guelvada remembered the afternoon of Kane's secret interview with Frau von Fiersch when, almost with tears in his eyes, Kane, posing as a member of the City Surveyor's office, had entreated the good Frau to do something about her husband, who was casting ardent glances at Mademoiselle Yvonne, to whom he was engaged, and more than that, writing her letters which were more forthright than tactful.

Guelvada smiled pleasantly to himself. From there the situation had progressed wonderfully. From Frau von Fiersch's first suspicions to jealousy, to the watch that she and Kane had kept upon the *appartement* of Mademoiselle Yvonne; thence to the making of the keys to the apartment; then the rifling of Mademoiselle's private papers by Kane whilst the Frau kept guard on the street door; then – without the knowledge of the good Frau – the planting of some of the less important papers in the Captain's room. All that had been very nice. A week later Kane and Guelvada were back in London with a haul of secret instructions from Himmler to the local agents of the Gestapo through Mademoiselle Yvonne.

And a week after that a little bird had told Fenton that the anonymous letter that had been dispatched to Yvonne had borne fruit, that Captain von Fiersch's apartment had been searched, the incriminating documents found, and the Captain shot as promptly as such things were done under the taut organisation of the S.S. Reichsführer Himmler.

Guelvada sighed. Never, he thought, would the good Frau von Fiersch realise the part she had played in that small comedy, never would she know that she had assisted so expertly in the liquidation of her husband and the theft of the complete Himmler organisation scheme that operated throughout France, occupied or unoccupied.

Guelvada took out his cigarette case, lit a cigarette. He drew the smoke down into his lungs with satisfaction, held it there for a few seconds and then expelled it slowly. He watched the cloud of tobacco smoke as it disappeared in the warm atmosphere of the bar parlour. In it he thought he could discern faintly the outline of the charming face of the

Fraulein Marta Szelginger – the delightful Marta – unconscious heroine of the affair of the Bürgerbräu Keller, where Hitler had missed death by twelve minutes.

If Marta had not been born half a Jewess. If for that reason she had not been treated so cavalierly by an S.A. Group Leader who had thrown her over when the 'stain' of her birth had become publicly known, she would never have found herself in the state of mind in which she could listen to the ardent pleading of Sigrid Wirt – that blonde and handsome Norwegian who, working with Kane – who was actually in the Beer Hall when the explosion occurred – had suborned the cleaner, drilled out the bricks in the main platform pillar and cleared the way for the insertion of the time bomb by Kane. Guelvada grinned. It seemed that the Führer had as much to fear from the jealousy of women as from the bullets of the enemy.

It was a great shame, thought Guelvada, about women; and the crosses they had to bear by reason of their sex, their beauty, their allure, were more than heavy. Most of their lives, he thought, they were being used, consciously or unconsciously, by someone.

A woman was like a harp. You could play tunes upon her if you knew how to do it. Because most women never ceased to think in terms of love; they laid themselves open to the operations and schemes of all sorts and conditions of men. For a woman – especially when she loves deeply – is unable to think logically – whatever feminists may say. Guelvada, for his part, thought this a good thing. He began to consider some aspects of this thought. For instance how annoying it would be if a woman deeply in love *were* able to think logically. What bad times many men would have.

Beauty, he considered, exacted a harsh tax. The more beautiful a woman was, the more she attracted men. To be admired, loved, desired, by many men, was not good for any woman's logic. It was obvious that after a few months of such process she would cease to think at all mathematically. She would think only in terms of love, of admiration, of marriage, and of her own desires.

And that was the time to strike. Because when a woman was subject to the admiration of men, her mentality ceased to help her. Guelvada could remember a dozen women (women who had been through the mill, who had served under the Himmler system, the Italian system, or even that outmoded and amusing service that the Vichy Government liked to describe as 'Secret' – the operations of which were all so obvious that they were invariably laughable) who had all of them come up against the problem of falling in love with the right man at the wrong moment.

Guelvada sat back in his chair and lit a cigarette. His eyes were on the cards, but his mind was elsewhere. He was thinking of the little brunette, Gala Ziek, who had ruined a period of six years' service in one of Karl Hildebrand's Special Sections by falling in love with a railway traffic manager, and as a result, endeavouring to stop him travelling by a train which was to be derailed. Hildebrand had been very tough with Gala about that. They said she had gone mad eventually. And Guelvada, knowing something of Hildebrand, could believe this.

And there was Zoe Garin and Stehren Muller and Sabine Hertzmin and Helda Marques ... yes, there had certainly been Helda Marques. ... Helda who had decided that it would be safe just for one little night to amuse herself with the oddly attractive Pierre Hellard, and who had thrown her astuteness, her intuition, her logic, and her life on the unstable altar of desire.

Love, thought Guelvada, was an odd thing. Love, assisted by Messieurs Kane and Guelvada, was sometimes a dangerous thing. Dangerous, at least, for those ladies whose paths strayed from the prosaic sphere of everyday life into the labyrinth wherein the Fentons of this world dwell.

Curiosity it was that killed the cat. And curiosity it was that had killed more women or, at least, wrecked their *amours*, than women knew or even dreamt of. Guelvada began to think about Valetta Fallon, who had decided – for some reason which would at some time be plain – to be suddenly curious.

She did not realise, he thought, what a stone she had thrown into the pond when she had been curious. She did not realise what circles in the water, what whirlpools, were even now stirring as a result of that stone. Perhaps she would be trapped in the whirlpool of her own making; perhaps she would escape.

If Kane were *very* interested in her she would be beautiful. And she would be beautiful in her mind. Guelvada – who was no fool about women – knew that women who appealed to Kane were of the first order. They had to be. Kane was a *connoisseur*. And why not? When each woman one met was just as likely as not to be one's last experience one might as well be a *connoisseur*. ...

Guelvada sighed. He got up from the table and collected his cards. He put them away. Then he went over to the service hatch and peeped through at Mrs Soames, who was busy on the other side. She looked over her shoulder and saw him. He smiled at her. A bland, childlike smile.

'And what can I do for you, Mr Guelvada?' she asked.

He said: 'First of all I think you should call me Ernest, which is my name, and which I like to be used by women as completely delightful as you are. And secondly, if I were to tell you what you can do for me you would probably have me thrown out. ...'

She laughed. 'You *are* funny, Mr Guelvada,' she said. 'I meant what would you like?'

Guelvada sighed. 'You must ask me that question in private,' he said. 'Then I should be able to answer it adequately. In the meantime, a whisky and soda from your hands – a nightcap – would satisfy me for the moment.'

She gave him the drink. Guelvada looked at it and sipped it; then, carrying the glass in his hand, he went out of the bar-parlour and up the stairs to bed.

VII

Guelvada braked the taxi-cab to a standstill just round the corner, off the main road. He got out of the driving seat, stamped his feet on the snow-covered pavement after the manner of taxi-drivers, and began to bang his woollen gloved hands again t his sides. The flag on the taximeter was down, and to all appearances he was waiting for his fare to come out of one of the entrances of the Vallance Apartments.

He was wearing two overcoats, a woollen scarf pulled well

up round his chin, and an old felt hat. His licence-plate with its number hung from the conventional top buttonhole of his uppermost coat. He had omitted to shave, and his face looked red and rough. He looked at his watch. It was twelve minutes past seven. Then he clambered back into the driver's seat and sat, hunched-up over the wheel, after the approved fashion of taxi-drivers on a cold day, and waited.

From where he sat he could just discern, in the blackout, the main entrance of the Vallance Apartments. Guelvada yawned and watched his breath turn to steam on the cold air; then he fumbled in one of his coats, produced an old tin box, took a cigarette from it, lit it, smoked silently.

Two minutes passed. Then the blackout on the door of the Vallance Apartments shifted for a moment and a man came out. He turned towards Guelvada's cab, passed it, went down the street. It was Nielek. Guelvada switched off his engine quickly. He listened intently. After a moment the footsteps of the individual who had come out of the apartments stopped suddenly. A minute after that Guelvada heard a motor started.

Guelvada listened. The purr of the car down the street went on. Someone had started the engine and was waiting.

The blackout on the entrance door moved again. Someone came out and stood outside the doors. It was the hall-porter. He stood looking up and down the main street.

Guelvada let in his clutch and drove the cab slowly round the corner. As he appeared, the hall-porter shouted, 'Taxi!' Guelvada pulled into the kerb by the entrance.

Kane came out. He said to Guelvada: 'Drive to Philmore Street. It's near Notting Hill Gate Station.' He got into the cab.

Guelvada drove off. Just down the street he slid back the glass panel behind him and turned his head. He said:

'Michael, just before you came out, a man came out of the apartments. He passed me and started up a car just down the street behind me. He may have been waiting to tail you when you came out. Is there anything behind?'

Kane said: 'Yes... there's a car trailing us now. He's having to keep pretty close up because of the blackout. Keep on driving and I'll see if he keeps after us.'

He sat back in the corner of the cab and lit a cigarette. Guelvada accelerated. They were moving now at a good thirty – a fast rate having regard to the snow and the frozen roads.

When they were in Church Street, Kane said: 'He's still after us. It's a tail all right.'

Guelvada said: 'Shall I shake him off? It would be very easy.'

'No,' Kane replied. 'Just carry on. By the way, d'you think he got your number when he passed you while you were waiting? D'you think he was at all interested in you?'

'No,' said Guelvada. 'He walked straight past. It was too dark for him to see the number unless he stopped and looked. He didn't stop.'

'All right,' said Kane. 'At the top of this street, on the right, there's a one-way street. It's "one-way" into this street. Chance it and drive round the corner; stop, and I'll get out. Then run through into the main road, turn left, and with luck you'll catch him as he runs into Notting Hill Gate. He'll think he's lost us. Drive after him for a bit to see what he does and then get back to the Vallance Apartments as quickly as you can. Park the car somewhere and keep an eye on the place. If he drives back there, and parks the car, see if he uses the Vallance Garage. If he does, it's a certainty that he's living in the Vallance Apartments. That'll give us plenty to work on. Telephone me afterwards and tell me what happens.'

'All right," said Guelvada. He pushed the accelerator down and drove quickly. When he came to the one-way street he was momentarily out of sight of the car behind. He swung the taxi quickly round the corner on the wrong side of the road and slowed down. Kane jumped out while the taxi was still moving and ducked into a doorway. Guelvada accelerated, shot round the curve and disappeared. A few seconds afterwards, from his doorway, Kane saw the tailing car appear and drive straight up the main road.

Guelvada pulled round into Notting Hill Gate with a sigh of relief. He drove slowly along for a few minutes but could see no sign of a car that was moving slowly, or stopped. He drew into the kerb, lit another cigarette, refused a fare on the grounds that he had not any petrol, turned the cab and drove quickly back to the Vallance Apartments by way of Park Lane.

He stopped in the street behind, parked the taxi in a cul-de-sac with the flag down, walked quickly round the block and stood a few yards from the entrance-doors. He stubbed out his cigarette and leaned against the wall, invisible in the darkness.

He waited ten minutes; then a car appeared. It passed the entrance-doors, turned the corner, drove slowly down the side street. Guelvada walked quickly after it, stepping softly. The car stopped fifty yards down the street and, as Guelvada came up, he saw it turning down the ramp that led to the Vallance Garage.

Guelvada smiled. He lit a cigarette and walked slowly back to where he had left his cab. He started it up, backed it out of the cul-de-sac and drove slowly back to the garage near Jermyn Street. People were very silly, he thought. That very old idea of planting someone in a place in order to be on the spot to tail someone else was too old-fashioned. Yet what could *they* have done? It was quite obvious that *they* would not be able to have much notice of when Kane appeared. *They* would have to keep an eye open to see when he left and it was necessary that they should be able to follow immediately.

This explained the car planted down the street, the car that was started up just before Kane came down to the entrance-floor, and this presupposed that whoever it was had tailed them had known before Kane got down to the entrance-floor that he was leaving the apartments.

Very amateurish, thought Guelvada. But what else could *they* do? It was tough working under such conditions. But then the Boches were not very good at last-minute organisation.

That was their trouble. In the last war they were at the gates of Paris, and then, at the last moment, had lost their heads, had decided to retreat. In this war they were unable to follow up their initial success against the French quickly enough. The British had got away at Dunkirk, and then the Boches had wasted fifty-five days before turning their attention to England. Whereas if they had struck at once ...

Guelvada took his hands from the wheel for a moment and banged them together. That was the trouble with the Boches. They had to have a cut-and-dried organisation. Even in their secret service and undercover work they relied on a set plan. While the plan worked everything was all right, but if the slightest thing went wrong, they went to pieces.

In this case they thought they were safe. Either they believed that Valetta Fallon would not, by her sudden change of attitude, arouse Kane's suspicions, or they had thought that even if he did suspect something he would not regard the matter seriously. He would dismiss it as a temperamental outburst of a woman who was in love. Even if he did suspect that something was afoot, they would think that he would do nothing at once; that he would probably wait to see what further evidence of curiosity Valetta showed; that he would try and discover through any further questions on her part exactly what she was trying to find out. If further questions were not forthcoming then, they surmised, his suspicions would be lulled.

Such people, thought Guelvada, were not worthy antagonists to people like Kane. They were not worthy of his steel. There was something childlike in their make-up and their planning. And they were not last-minute experts.

That was the difference between the opposing forces. The British undercover services worked by themselves with little official backing and on schemes adapted to circumstances, often at the very last moment. Operatives were trained from the start to work by themselves, to rely on themselves. Astuteness and impertinence were the main weapons of the British agents, and against these weapons the consistent planning, the thoroughness, the ruthlessness, and the admitted bravery of the German services were not effective.

Guelvada swung the car round into the mews and sounded his horn. In the dim light of his headlights he saw the garage doors open. He drove the taxi in.

Searle limped out of the office in the corner. The limp was a memento of six months in the Haltz Concentration Camp and then, after having him for six months, the damned fools had let him go – without even discovering who and what he was!

He said: 'Hello, Ernie. Everything all right?'

Guelvada said yes. He went into the office and took off his overcoat, his wrap, and his battered hat. He put on his own things. 'Start up my car for me, Searle,' he said. 'She will be cold and the exercise is good for you!'

Searle grinned and went out. Guelvada picked up the telephone and dialled Kane's number in Queen Anne Street. When Kane came on the line, Guelvada said:

'Listen, Michael, I came back to the Vallance, and ten minutes afterwards a car returned and went into the garage. I *think* it was the same car. It sounded the same.'

Kane said: 'All right. ... In any event we'll take it that it was the same. That means that they've got somebody planted in the Vallance Apartments and that somebody must have been waiting for me to leave so that they could get down first and get the car going. That means that they're in an apartment close enough to Miss Fallon's for them to have seen me leave her apartment, slipped down the back stairs and beat me to the front door.'

'That's what I thought,' said Guelvada. 'It looked like that to me.'

Kane said: 'Tell Searle to get on to the right person and have a check-up on the Vallance Apartments. We want to know who the inmates are. We want to know of any new arrivals. We want to know all about the staff, who they are and where they come from. Tell Searle to get all that stuff from the Special Branch officer and have it all telephoned through to me here before ten o'clock to-night.'

Guelvada said: 'Understood.'

'You go back to Tyrrell's Wood,' said Kane, 'and play some more patience. I'll let you know when I want you.'

Guelvada said: 'All right. By the way, I've been thinking about this business. I wonder if it would be Hildebrand?'

'It's Hildebrand all right,' said Kane. 'It smells of him. Besides, I think he's the only one who could get 'em over here. This bunch came from Eire. I'll bet anything on that. If that's so, then it's Hildebrand. I've just learned that he pulled in there about three weeks ago.'

Guelvada said: 'Sometimes Hildebrand is clever. But not often. You remember that business at Heyst?'

Kane laughed. 'I remember,' he said. 'Maybe we'll settle the account this time. So long, Ernie.'

Guelvada hung up. He went out into the garage, talked to Searle. He got into his car, said good-night to Searle and backed out of the garage.

He drove slowly in the black-out towards Putney Bridge. He was thinking about Hildebrand.

VIII

Carson, a young detective-sergeant borrowed from the Special Branch, yawned, shifted his cigarette from one end of his mouth to the other and traced his initials on the window-pane with a stubby forefinger.

He was planted on the first floor opposite the Vallance Apartments, from which position of vantage he could watch both the front and the side entrances of the apartment block.

Carson, who was still young enough to be romantic, wondered what the devil it was all about, wished that when you were given a job to do you knew a little more about what was behind it. He shifted his cigarette back to its original position; then took notice as Valetta came out of the main entrance opposite.

That's her ... thought Carson. He put out his hand and grabbed the telephone. He called a priority number, his eyes still on Valetta.

A hell of a woman, thought Carson. What a piece! He wondered if, one of these fine days, he would be able to get himself a woman like that. Carson had a nice eye for the finer attributes of femininity, and he liked the way she moved. A graceful one, that one, he thought. A sight for tired eyes.

Valetta stood on the snowy pavement just outside the entrance. She wore a double-breasted Persian lamb coat cut on military lines, with a smart toque of the same fur. One white kid-gloved hand was ensconced in a muff, and there was a small bunch of violets pinned in the high collar of her coat. Russian boots set off the neatness of her feet. A brusque voice at the other end of the line said curtly: 'So what?'

'She's just come out of the main entrance,' said Carson. 'She's standing on the corner. Looks undecided. Looks as if she doesn't know whether she's going to wait for a cab or walk. ... Wait a minute ... she's decided to walk. She's moved off ... towards the Park. She's going to take the left-hand side ...'

'What's she wearing?' asked the voice.

'A black Persian lamb coat and a hat to match,' said Carson. 'She's got a bunch of violets pinned in her collar. She's wearing high Russian boots and she's got a small-sized muff – Persian lamb – on one hand and a white kid glove on the other. She's carrying a fair-sized black handbag under one arm, and if it means anything to you she looks like a million dollars to me. ...'

'It doesn't mean anything to me,' said the voice. 'You're sure you've got the right woman?'

'Unless she's got a double she's the spit of the photograph I was shown,' said Carson. 'And, anyway, there couldn't be two women as good-looking as that one.'

'All right,' said the voice. 'You can lay off, Carson.'

'Thank you for nothing,' said Carson. He hung up.

A car was standing fifty yards down the street from the Vallance Apartments. It was a Morris twelve saloon. Inside two plain-clothes men sat and smoked. They listened attentively as their instructions came through on the radio:

'A woman has just left Vallance Apartments in Knightsbridge,' said the radio. 'She is a brunette, five feet eight inches in height, good figure, good carriage. She is wearing a black Persian lamb coat with a bunch of violets pinned in the collar, a Persian lamb hat and Russian boots. She is carrying a Persian lamb muff and a black handbag. She is walking towards Hyde Park on the left-hand side of the road. Go after her at once and keep her in sight. If she takes a cab follow it. Be careful. Other persons may be trying to keep her under observation. Tail her until she goes into a shop or a side street; then pick her up, identify her yourself and bring her in. Use great care not to be observed by other parties. That is all.'

The driver let in the clutch. The car began to move slowly towards the Park.

Valetta was not quite certain where she was going or what she was going to do when she arrived there. At the back of her mind was a vague idea that she was going to do some shopping. The idea persisted because like most women she thought that the process of choosing and buying something might, possibly, take her mind off a subject from which she was trying, rather vainly, to escape. The subject of Kane.

The small and not unpleasant world – she realised now that it had not been at all unpleasant – in which she had been living for the past months had tumbled about her ears, and the process had done something to her that was as definite as it was horrible.

Michael was a spy. Michael was an enemy of her country. He was a person who must be trapped and disposed of. A person whose associates must be discovered and eradicated. And she had loved this man.

She had been trying to persuade herself that it was unnecessary and impracticable to make a mountain out of a molehill, that such things had happened before and would happen again; that all she had to do was to remove the picture of Kane from her mind, to help the authorities as much as possible and, her duty done, to forget a man who had the ability to hide appalling treachery under the appearance of a normal, smiling, sometimes amusing man.

Why should this thing happen to her? The question persisted in spite of the fact that there was no answer. Such things did happen, and the reason for their being was of no importance. The reason for their being meant little compared with the pictures that came unbidden to her mind.

They would trap Michael. They would trap him, and they would try him. The trial would be secret; the evidence would be produced and they would sentence him to death. He would be shot. That would be the end of Michael. And he deserved to be shot. He was a traitor. And she had been in love with – and loved – a traitor. A man who worked for the enemy. A man who plotted and planned so that his own fellow-countrymen might be snared and die, so that British ships might be torpedoed and British soldiers taken unawares. This was the man she had loved. Valetta thought that it seemed a little ridiculous that such things could really happen. That they could be true. Especially that they could happen to her. They were the sort of things that one saw on the cinema and didn't believe. But it *was* true. It had happened – and to her.

She walked down Piccadilly. The pavements were covered with snow. Across the road St James' Park looked like an old-fashioned Christmas card. Normally its expanse of smooth, white snow, with one or two children throwing snowballs at each other, would have been attractive and amusing. ...

And she had seen Michael last night. He had telephoned and had come to her. He had brought a box of chocolates, pointing out that in these days they were more precious than diamonds, and he had talked for a little while and been amusing, and then said, quite suddenly, that he had something to do – that he must go.

Valetta felt quite numb. Not only her body but also her mind. This, too, was quite ridiculous. This must stop. After all a logical person (she remembered Kane and his amusing and cynical wisecracks about 'logical' people) should not find it difficult to reorientate her mind and adapt herself to a fact. Facts were things that must be faced. The line of least resistance was always the most difficult line in the long run.

She smiled bitterly. Even the things she thought were the things that *he* had said. Not only had this traitor possessed her body but even now a part of her mind belonged to him.

There was a crowd of people at the bus stop opposite the Ritz Hotel. Most of them looked cheerful. Valetta thought how willingly she would change places with any of them – even the poorest. At least they were normal and happy. Their discontent – if it existed at all – was concerned with little things. None of these women could even guess the misery that possessed her.

She turned into Bond Street. She walked a little way and then stopped. She stood looking vaguely into the window of a shop that sold men's shirts and ties. After a minute she went inside and asked to see some handkerchiefs. She did this, not because she wanted handkerchiefs, but because her mind sought action – no matter how trivial – so that it might escape from the miserable routine of her thoughts.

When she came out of the shop a man was standing by the entrance. He was a short, plump fellow, in a grey overcoat and bowler hat. He said to her quietly:

'Excuse me, Miss Fallon. I'm a police officer. I wonder if you could spare a few minutes to come to Scotland Yard. It's rather urgent. I've a car here.'

Unobtrusively he showed her his warrant card.

Valetta said: 'Yes ... if it's necessary.' She thought, 'Here is some more questioning, more talk about Michael and his treachery ...! Probably the detective-inspector who had come to see her – Arthurs – wanted to talk to her. Probably they had found out more about Michael. ...'

She got into the car. It turned, drove quickly over the Piccadilly intersection, down St James's Street. Valetta sat in the back seat, her hands in her muff. She wondered what was going to happen now. What new mischief was afoot.

Fenton was sitting at a desk in the corner of the room. He looked up when Valetta was shown in.

His face wore its habitual frown, but when he looked at Valetta the frown disappeared, giving place to a small cold smile. Fenton was thinking that women were a damned nuisance. He was thinking that Valetta was beautiful, but that she looked intelligent. He was wondering whether she was going to be sensible.

For a moment Fenton thought about his own wife. It had taken him ten years to get *her* into the frame of mind that he described to himself as 'sensible,' the word meaning to him a process of mind under which a woman was prepared to accept everything that happened, no matter how dramatic or cruel, as normal – a process of mind under which *nothing* could surprise her.

If one had argued with Fenton that such an attitude was unreasonable, he would probably have agreed. He would have countered with the fact that the work that he and Kane and the rest of them did was also unreasonable, but that the temperaments of women, unless suitably controlled, superimposed on such work, could make life even more unreasonable – if not impossible.

He got up from his chair. He came round the desk. The detective-constable who had shown Valetta into the room departed, closing the door quietly behind him. Fenton moved an armchair nearer to the fire. He said: 'Sit down, Miss Fallon, and smoke a cigarette.' He produced a cigarette-case. 'There are both Turkish and Virginia here,' he said.

She chose a cigarette. He lit it for her. Then he went back to his chair behind the desk. He said:

'I expect you're curious about a lot of things, Miss Fallon. Perhaps I'm sorry that I've got to satisfy your curiosity to a certain extent. I'm doing that because I've *got* to do it. I'll make myself as clear as circumstances permit.

'First of all you are wondering why I had you brought *here*, and why I adopted the peculiar method of having you picked up by a squad car in such an odd fashion, instead of telephoning you. Well ... I had to bring you here, to Scotland Yard, so that you might see me surrounded by the panoply of the law' – Fenton smiled his cold smile – 'so that you might know just who your friends are and who are *your* and our enemies. I had to use the odd method of bringing you here because I think it more than possible that the telephone line at your flat is tapped. I had to allow you to know that when I say 'we,' meaning myself, the organisation for which I work, an organisation that is important to the successful carrying on of the war against the enemy, I include our mutual friend Michael Kane, who is, I would like you to know, one of the most courageous, astute, and unselfish operatives working – usually at the risk of his life – against the enemy. ...'

Valetta said in a strangled voice: 'But ...'

Fenton went on talking. His quiet, monotonous voice seemed to her to be coming from a distance. She felt suddenly faint.

'Miss Fallon,' he said, 'I've a definite idea that somebody has been trying to get at you ... that's the usual expression. Last evening Kane came to see you. When he left the Vallance Apartments, an attempt was made to follow him. He came there for the purpose of discovering whether such an attempt would be made. We believe that there is some con-

203

nection between that attempt and yourself. I wonder can *you* help us?'

Valetta smiled. A warm surge of happiness permeated her body. She felt almost hysterical with joy. Her eyes filled with tears of which she was utterly unashamed. She said, almost to herself: 'So that's why he would never say what he did. That's why I never knew what he did, where he went, when he was coming back.'

'Precisely,' said Fenton. 'Now will you tell me anything that has happened to you, Miss Fallon, during the last few days; anything that you might consider to be odd or strange.'

'A great deal has happened,' said Valetta. 'I'll tell you from the start. ...'

She told him. She told him of the visit of 'Detective-Inspector Arthurs' – of the arrangement with Lang, the hall-porter. Fenton listened. When she had finished he said:

'It seems to me, Miss Fallon, that you are in a rather unfortunate position. You know a little but not much. You will know from what you have told me, and from what I have told you, that some attempt is afoot, probably an attempt on the life of Kane, and some of the people who are associated with him and his work.' He smiled wryly. 'You must realise, Miss Fallon,' he said, 'that there are many people in the pay of the enemy who would give a great deal if Michael Kane were dead.'

Valetta said: 'So he's as important as all that?' She was smiling. Fenton noted the smile. It pleased him. Here, he thought, is a 'reasonable' woman.

'Yes,' he said. 'Kane is important.' He got up. He walked over to the window, stood for a moment looking out. 'I should think Kane and one or two other people have been a thorn in the side of the Germans for the last two years,' he said. 'There are not many men with the ruthlessness, courage, and ability that Kane possesses. That is why he is valuable. That is why I shouldn't like anything to happen to him.'

'And you think something will happen?' asked Valetta.

Fenton smiled. 'Quite obviously, someone in the person of Detective-Inspector Arthurs is trying to make something happen,' he said. 'And you will also realise, Miss Fallon, that this man and the people working with him are not fools.

The system they have used with you, whilst not being original, was the best one they could use in the present circumstances, placed as they are.

'A certain amount of information about the people residing in and employed at the Vallance Apartments has come into my possession this morning. There is no doubt that there are at least two people working for our friend the pseudo detective-inspector, inside the Vallance Apartments. It is obvious that someone whose flat is either above or below, or on one side or other of your own flat, ran a connecting line through from your telephone to enable you to believe that you were speaking to Scotland Yard, confirming the authority and business of our friend the "Detective-Inspector." There are probably some others working outside. The point is are you prepared to help?'

Valetta said: 'I'll do anything I can. I don't care how dangerous it is. I would like it to be dangerous. I want to make amends to myself for having even thought that Michael could be a traitor.'

Fenton said: 'I'm glad you think like that. But I shall have to ask you to do a great deal. You see, now that we know roughly what the position is, we can take steps to meet it. Now that Kane knows what he's up against, I think he will manage to find a solution himself.' He smiled. 'I hope he will. Therefore I would like you to do what he, or any agent of his, may ask you to do.'

He took a pocket-book from his pocket, opened it, took out a photograph. He brought it round to her. She took it and looked at it.

'That,' he said, 'is a gentleman you will meet. His name is Ernest Guelvada. He works in close association with Mr Kane. I think it probable that he will be seeing you shortly. If there is anything that you *can* do to help he will tell you. In the meantime, carry on quite normally. Do the things that you would do in the ordinary course of events, but don't use your telephone. And thank you for being so helpful.'

Valetta got up. She said: 'Thank *you*. I was so very miserable. Now I'm so happy that nothing matters.'

Fenton said: 'I'm glad you're happy. There isn't too much of that commodity about these days.' He held out his hand.

'Good-bye, Miss Fallon,' he said, 'and thank you for what you've done.'

'The detective-constable will show you out by the Embankment entrance,' Fenton went on. 'There'll be a cab waiting for you. I don't suppose any one noticed you come here, but it's best to go out by a different way. Good-bye, and good luck.'

When she had gone, Fenton went back to the desk. He took a pipe and a dilapidated tobacco pouch from his pocket. He began to fill the pipe.

Women, he thought, were a damned nuisance.

IX

Valetta sat on the silk-cushioned stool, her hands folded in her lap, and looked at herself in the reflecting mirrors of her dressing-table. She was not displeased with the picture. She qualified the compliment to herself with the thought that it was not for herself that she was glad that she was not plain, or ill-figured or ungraceful.

She wondered if Kane would come. If he would make an attempt to get into touch with her. Possibly, she thought, the tired-looking Mr Fenton would have seen him, told him about her interview of the morning. She wanted to see Kane, to ask his forgiveness for her doubts – even if they had been the result of the carefully-planned scheme in which she had been merely a pawn, with Kane as the eventual prey.

She remembered what Fenton had said. There were many people in the pay of the enemy who would give much to liquidate Michael Kane. He was a thorn in their flesh. There was a price on his head. This quiet, often whimsical, man who had such joy in her company; this odd, tough person who found happiness with her and a means of escape.

And there must be much that he desired to escape from. Most of the time, thought Valetta, his nerves must be strung up, attuned to situations, schemes in which life – his own, his associates' – were at stake. When he had told her that she was important to him he had meant just that. She *was* important to him. She was a solitary link with peace and contentment.

The ivory clock on the mantelpiece struck nine. She smiled to herself when she remembered that this was the first night that she had ever been 'off.' But the theatre had no appeal to her to-night. She had wanted to keep away from it, to think, to try and think out some pattern for her life. A new pattern, and one which, for better or for worse, would please Kane.

She had sent a note to the theatre in good time, remembering Fenton's instructions not to use the telephone, and now, at this moment, her understudy, pleased for the chance, would be playing her part. She had thought that to-night Kane might want to talk to her. In any event the excuse was good enough for her to take the opportunity to think and to plan. Even if there was little to think about, and planning impossible.

There was a sudden click. She spun round on the stool. Behind her the French window opening out on to the balcony opened slightly. A hand appeared. The window continued to open. Valetta leaned back against the dressing-table. Her heart was pounding. Then she began to smile.

The cheerful countenance of Guelvada appeared round the edge of the window, followed by the rest of him. He slipped into the room, closed the window quickly behind him, rearranging the velvet blackout curtains.

He said: 'Miss Fallon, I am desolated at being forced to make use of such an undignified entrance. Please don't be frightened. The name is Guelvada.'

She got up. 'I'm not frightened, Mr Guelvada,' she said. 'And I'm very glad to meet you. If you will come into my sitting-room, I'll give you a drink. And you can leave your raincoat in the hall.'

She led the way into the sitting-room. After a moment Guelvada appeared. He had shed his dilapidated raincoat and hat. The suit beneath was elegant, as always, and his air of smiling amiability was that of an old friend.

'Consider my difficulty, Miss Fallon,' he said. 'I must speak to you and I must do so without telephoning you, and without passing through the hallway downstairs in case my friend the night-porter – who is *not* really a friend – should recognise me. So there was nothing for it. I came by way of the roof next door and the balcony. And here I am – entirely and absolutely at your service.'

Valetta smiled at him. There was something very pleasing about Mr Guelvada, she thought, something very happy and infectious. And he was someone near to Michael and, therefore, must be a friend of hers.

She said: 'Can I give you a cocktail or a whisky and soda? Which will you have? And please sit down by the fire.'

Guelvada said: 'I will drink the whisky and soda, if you please.' He sighed. 'What a lucky man I am,' he said.

Valetta laughed.

'Why?' she asked. 'I think you're rather delightful, Mr Guelvada. You enter my flat through the bedroom window, after climbing over all the roofs in the neighbourhood as if it were the most ordinary thing in the world, and as if you did it merely for the purpose of telling me that you are a lucky man. Or was there something else?'

'Oh yes,' said Guelvada. 'There was something else, but that will keep.'

Valetta put the whisky and soda on the small table at his elbow, and a box of cigarettes. She took one herself. Guelvada lit it and his own. He looked at her quickly, smilingly, as she sat in the chair opposite.

'First of all I would like to tell you why I think I am lucky,' he said. 'You must realise that all my life I have been a worshipper of feminine beauty. From the earliest times I have been enchanted by the sight of beautiful women. Well ... facts must be faced, and when I learned from Michael that you were a friend of his – an important friend – then I was greatly concerned. You will want to know why I was concerned, so I will satisfy your curiosity immediately.'

Guelvada drank a little whisky and soda. He replaced the glass on the little table. But all the while he was looking at Valetta with the same delightful smile.

'You will realise,' he went on, 'that Michael is a close friend of mine. He and I have been in all sorts of things together. We understand each other very well. Imagine therefore how curious I was about this mysterious woman who was important to him, and who was so busy creating situations that were urgent and must be dealt with. I wondered what she would be like. I *hoped* she would be beautiful. And now I see her and discover that she is utterly enchanting.'

Valetta said: 'Mr Guelvada, you are an experienced flatterer. You make it sound almost like the truth.'

'It *is* the truth,' retorted Guelvada. 'You know, all one's life there is an idea in one's head. An idea of the perfect woman. To me there has often come such an idea. I have visualised such a one. A woman of delightful figure, dressed as you are dressed, wearing a black velvet house-coat, with a delightful frill at the throat and wrists, with little georgette shoes with diamond buckles, with the delightful low, soft voice – "like a husky flute" – that one reads about in books but never meets. And behold ... I see this picture. I see it in the flesh. I am carried away with joy. I, Guelvada, am happy!'

He finished his drink with satisfaction.

Valetta laughed. 'I see that you are a very clever person, Mr Guelvada,' she said. 'Why are you tempting me into such an agreeable frame of mind? Is that part of some deep scheme? Or is it to prepare me for something serious?'

Guelvada shrugged. 'Do not believe,' he said, 'that life is ever really *serious*. Sometimes it is a little dramatic. Sometimes merely boring. But seldom serious.'

She said: 'It's been serious for me during the last few days ... dramatic and serious and horrible. ...' She shivered at the thought.

Guelvada shrugged and smiled.

'That was merely one act of the comedy,' he said. 'Now we may progress to the second and the third acts.' He leaned forward in his chair. 'You have a part – a most important part – to play in the second act. Important because, if you play it well, then I have no doubt that Michael will be able to finish off the third – and possibly last – act successfully and quickly.'

Valetta said: 'I will play any part to the best of my ability, Mr Guelvada.'

He nodded.

'Excellent,' he said. 'I assure you that Michael is a very good stage-manager. You could not have a better one.'

He stubbed out his cigarette, lit a fresh one.

'Now,' he said, 'it will be good for you to know what we think has happened, what we intend *shall* happen. Because what I shall tell you is important, you will please listen very carefully, because it is necessary that there should be no mistakes.'

Valetta nodded her head. 'I am listening,' she said.

Guelvada drew on his cigarette.

'I have talked with Michael,' he said, 'and Mr Fenton, who saw you this morning, has also talked with him, and so it seems that this is the position. ... The Boches have been clever for them – as clever as they could be – but that is not clever enough. This is the way they wanted to play their scheme:

'Consider the situation: Standen arrived. He gets to know you. He gets to know you because he has been advised that you are a close friend of Michael's. He sets out to be attractive, and I have no doubt he *was* attractive. I imagine him to be a delightful and charming person. He would have been picked for those qualities. Very well ... having secured your interest, he proposes marriage.' Guelvada laughed. 'He knows perfectly well that you will refuse, but the fact that he has done so gives him the right to ask why. He hopes you will say something about Michael. Very naturally you do. You also tell him that you know nothing about Michael, which is what he wants you to say. But before he leaves you he suggests that it might be to your advantage if he found out something about the mysterious Mr Kane.

'So the ground is prepared – well prepared. And you are not surprised when the second actor appears on the scene – the pseudo Detective-Inspector Arthurs. He informs you that Michael is a spy. You are ready to believe this because he is able to tell you that they were put on Michael's track by Standen; because he produces evidence of who he is, and because he has arranged for you to telephone through to Scotland Yard in order that that evidence may be confirmed.'

Guelvada drew on his cigarette again.

'All this was very good whilst we did not suspect,' he said, 'but when we did suspect, it was not good. It was not good for them because it showed us there was someone else in this building – someone who had been able to disconnect your telephone wire; someone who had pretended to be the official at Scotland Yard.

'Last night,' Guelvada went on, 'an attempt was made to follow Michael. He came here to see you in order to give them an opportunity. The attempt was unsuccessful. Therefore they will try it again. But next time we must arrange that the attempt is made in such a way that it reacts to our advantage.'

Valetta nodded.

'How will you be able to do that?' she asked.

'This is what we shall do,' said Guelvada. 'First of all the hall-porter, Lang, is a German. He is working with someone else who is living in this block – a man named Thomson in No. 17 to the left of this flat. It is certain that your telephone line is tapped, so that the only use we can make of your telephone is to plant ideas into their heads. Now these two people inside this place must have help from outside. That help will probably consist of the pseudo Detective-Inspector Arthurs and Standen, but it is reasonable to suppose that Arthurs, having once appeared as a police-officer, will not appear again until the end of this little comedy is in sight. So,' continued Guelvada with an amiable smile, 'we propose to bring it to an end quickly – to ring down the curtain in the hope that, when it falls, these gentlemen may make their last bows.'

He stubbed out his cigarette carefully.

'Now, Miss Fallon,' he said, 'listen carefully. ... To-morrow you must not go to the theatre. You must be indisposed. Early in the evening Michael will telephone through here. He will suggest that he comes to see you. You will agree.

'Then he will say that he has an important appointment to keep later in the evening with his employer. He will ask your permission to leave a case containing some important documents in your care whilst he is away. You will agree to this. He will impress on you the importance of these documents, and you, in your turn, will impress on him the fact that they will be quite safe in your keeping.

'Immediately he has rung off, you will ring downstairs to Lang, and, as you arranged with our friend "Detective-Inspector Arthurs," inform him that Kane is coming at seven-thirty. You will inform him that Kane has said that he will be leaving important documents in your care.' Guelvada grinned. 'This, I think, will delight our friend Lang, downstairs,' he said.

'Very well then, Michael will arrive carrying a locked document-case. He will stay with you for a little while and leave just before eight. Our friend who followed him last time, will follow him again. But this time he will be successful. Michael will take good care that he is properly followed, and that his destination is noted.' Guelvada grinned cynically. 'Now,' he said, 'this is where you make your entrance. ...

'Let us consider the position. Michael has gone. He has been followed by Thomson, and you are left alone in your flat, with the case containing documents which they will think are important. What is the obvious thing for them to do? Surely Lang, the hall-porter, will get into touch with our friend "Detective-Inspector Arthurs." He will come round to the flat for the purpose of collecting those documents from you. It is also fairly obvious that before he does so, he will communicate with the fourth member of the party – Standen – and tell him what he proposes to do. If they consider the documents to be sufficiently important they will make their getaway there and then. At least they would hope to make their getaway. ...'

'I understand,' she said. 'It seems that my part is not a very difficult one.'

'Nevertheless,' said Guelvada with a smile, 'being an actress, you will know that small parts are often quite important. So, with your permission, we will hold a rehearsal. First of all, we must rehearse your telephone conversation with Michael, and then we must rehearse the scene when, as we hope, our friend "Detective-Inspector Arthurs" pays you a sudden visit to retrieve the documents. Shall we do that?'

'Please,' said Valetta. 'I should like to be word perfect.'

The rehearsal began.

x

Lang, the hall-porter, sat in his glass-fronted office, on the right of the main-entrance doors. He was reading the *Evening News*. He was interested in the situation in Libya.

Lang, whose name was Adolf Hierchel – he was a Bavar-

212

ian – had been in England continuously for eight years. He was a specialist in accents, and could speak English with a Scots, Irish, Welsh, or provincial inflection as he desired. He had been sent over originally by Herr Doktor Goebbels, who – even at that time – realised the importance of propaganda for the coming Nazi struggle in Germany, and had later been transferred to one of the Special Sections of the Intelligence Department. He had worked all over the country and in Ireland and Scotland. He was a first-class agent, calm, deliberate and intelligent, and had been working under Hildebrand for the last two years.

The telephone rang. Lang picked up the receiver, answered. It was Kane speaking:

'Hello,' said Kane. 'Is that the Vallance Apartments? Put me through to Miss Fallon, please. I've been ringing on her own line but can't get through.'

'Hold on, sir, and I'll put you through on this line,' said Lang. 'Miss Fallon's own line has been a bit troublesome for the last day or two. ...' He put the call through, keeping his own line connected. He listened carefully.

When Valetta answered, Kane said: 'Hello, Valetta. This is the first chance I've had of speaking to you. I've been busy. How are you?'

'Very well,' said Valetta. She had her 'part' word perfect. Her voice, after a dozen 'rehearsals' with Ernie Guelvada, was easy and confident. 'When am I going to see you again, Michael?'

'Do you *want* to see me?' asked Kane.

'Of course,' she answered. 'You know I do. Can you manage it?'

'Well ... yes ...' said Kane hesitantly. He paused for a moment. 'The fact is,' he went on, 'I've got a document-case full of most important papers which I want to park somewhere. The papers are so important that I don't like carrying the case around in this blackout. You see, I've an urgent engagement which will take me about an hour. I'd like to come straight to you now and leave the document-case with you – I know it'll be all right in your flat – and then go on and keep the appointment. Afterwards I could come back to you. How would that suit?'

Valetta said: 'That's all right. But what a shame you've got that appointment. It's such a beastly night – so cold and snowy. Couldn't you possibly get out of it?'

'No,' said Kane, 'I couldn't. You see, the appointment is with my boss. And he's tough. I must keep it. But I shouldn't be with him for more than an hour and I'd come straight back.'

'Very well,' said Valetta brightly. 'You come along here now and leave your papers or whatever it is with me, and then get your business done and come back afterwards. That'll be nice.'

'Right, I'll be with you in ten minutes,' said Kane.

Lang waited until they had both hung up. Then he plugged his line in to Nielek's apartment. Nielek answered the telephone quickly.

Lang said: 'He's coming here in about ten minutes. He's going to leave some papers with her and then going to see someone he calls his "boss." You'd better go after him. I'll look after everything else.'

'Right,' said Nielek. 'I'll get the car out and park on the other side of the road. I don't want to lose him this time.'

'All right,' said Lang. 'But keep close to this place. It's dark outside and he won't see your car. If he does it's quite normal for people to park round here.'

Nielek hung up. So did Lang. A minute afterwards his 'house' buzzer sounded. He picked up the house telephone. It was Valetta.

'Is that Lang, the hall-porter? It is. Oh, Lang, Mr Kane has just telephoned me. He's coming here in ten minutes' time. He's going to leave some papers here and go off and keep an appointment. That will take about an hour. Then he's returning here. I expect Inspector Arthurs would like to know that.'

'Thank you, Miss,' said Lang. 'I'll telephone through and tell Mr Arthurs.' He hung up. He smiled a little. Hiltsch had played his part beautifully, thought Lang. She'd fallen for the story – hook, line, and sinker –was doing her best to help.

He rang a Primrose number. Hiltsch answered. Lang said quickly: 'Listen .. this is Lang. Kane is coming here in a few minutes. He's going to leave some papers with the woman.

214

They're important. Then he's going off, and will return after about an hour.'

Hiltsch asked: 'Is this absolutely right?'

'Yes,' answered Lang. 'I listened in to the conversation between Kane and the woman. Afterwards she called through and told me. She thought "Mr Arthurs" might like to know.'

'All right,' said Hiltsch. 'I'll come along. I'll give Kane twenty minutes to arrive and leave. I'll see her and get those papers. Standen will be standing by near the Apartments. We've got to finish this business and get away. Everything's hanging about much too long.'

'All right,' said Lang. 'I'll talk to you when you come.'

He hung up. He left the little office, walked down the corridor, stood in the shadow. A few minutes afterwards Kane arrived. He was carrying a big document-case. He walked straight into the lift and ascended. Two minutes afterwards Nielek came down by the back stairs. He passed Lang, who said:

'Hiltsch is coming for the papers. Standen will be here. We're going to clean up and finish to-night.'

'That suits me very well,' said Nielek. Lang thought his face was rather white and drawn. He grinned cynically. Perhaps the strain was beginning to tell, he thought. These super-trained young Nazis were all damned well operating in Germany, but when it came to jobs like this they cracked too easily. Why didn't they use more old-timers with seasoned nerves like himself ...?

He went along to the second entrance-door. A car was parked outside. That would be Kane's car, he thought. On the other side of the road, in the darkness, he could just discern a rear light. That would be Nielek.

Lang went back to his place along the corridor. A good thing to finish it off. He was tired of it anyway. Eight years was a long time to be away from the Fatherland.

He heard the lift descend. Kane passed by the end of the corridor and went out of the main door. Lang went back to his hall-porter's office. He pulled the blackout curtain half an inch to one side and peered out. He saw Kane's rear light turn the corner and Nielek's car go after it. Nice work, thought Lang. Nice organisation. By and large, the British were bloody fools. They had become soft and easy and casual. You could get away with anything in their accursed country.

He replaced the blackout curtain, sat down, lit a cigarette. As night-porter he was allowed to smoke – a war-time privilege. He was only half-way through the cigarette when Hiltsch came in. He came straight to the office. He spoke quickly.

'Call through to her and tell her Detective-Inspector Arthurs is here,' he said. 'I'm going up to look at those papers. If they're important we're going to get out to-night. Standen is in the car in the side-turning on the other side of the road. When I go upstairs I'll take a quick look at the papers. If they're what we want I'll wait for Kane to come back. I'm going to give it to him when he comes back. Directly I've gone upstairs, go downstairs and put on your overcoat and hat. Take anything you want and go over and join Standen. Tell him everything's all right. He'll want to post a note maybe. Then wait for Nielek to return. When Kane comes back I'll be waiting for him. Stop Nielek from coming up and take him over to the car. Then you all wait for me.'

Lang said: 'What about the woman?'

'I'm going to finish both of them,' said Hiltsch. 'She'd only make a damned noise. You understand what you have to do?'

'Perfectly,' said Lang. He picked up the house-telephone. After a minute he said: 'Miss Fallon, Detective-Inspector Arthurs is here. Shall I send him up? Very good, Miss. ...'

He hung up. He looked at Hiltsch.

'You're to go up,' he said.

Hiltsch went towards the lift.

Lang locked the hall-porter's office. He turned down the right-hand corridor and walked to the end. He began to walk down the stairs towards his room in the basement. He was thinking that he would be glad to finish off with this hall-porter job. It was boring, and the hours were long. He had had a much more amusing time as Veteria, the free-lance waiter.

He walked along the basement corridor, unlocked the door of his bedroom, went in, switched on the light.

216

Ernie Guelvada was sitting in the corner of the room, smoking a cigarette. His right hand was in his pocket. He said curtly in German. 'Put your hands on your head and don't move. You get a week or two longer that way.'

Lang thought quickly: 'Curse it ... so they weren't such damned fools. ...' He began to raise his hands. Somehow, he thought, he must try and warn the others. Well ... he must get this goddamned fellow to shoot. There was just a chance – a remote chance – that Hiltsch *might* hear the shot. The building was very quiet. There was just a chance he *might* hear.

He dropped his hands quickly. Guelvada fired through his pocket. There was no noise. The bullet hit Lang just above the waistline. He fell over against the wall. Guelvada got up and came over to him. He stood looking down. He was smiling amiably.

'I suppose you thought I'd make a noise and let your friends hear. What stupid fellows you are,' said Guelvada. He brought his hand out of his pocket. Lang saw the silencer on the barrel.

He struggled to get up. He tried to speak. He said:

'Heil ... Heil. ...'

'Exactly,' said Guelvada. '*Heil Hitler!* Let *me* say it for you.' He put two more bullets into Lang, looked at him for a moment, switched off the light, closed and locked the door and went upstairs. He was humming softly to himself.

Hiltsch sat at the small table in Valetta's sitting-room. He had opened the lock on the document-case with a spider key from his key ring. He was looking through the papers inside. His expression was almost uninterested, but his heart was thumping. He admitted it to himself. His, Hiltsch's, heart – that heart attuned to boredom by a thousand excitements and tight corners – was thumping. God ...! What a haul ...! he thought. There was practically everything in those papers that Hildebrand wanted. Practically everything. ... He replaced the documents in the case, snapped the lock.

Valetta said: 'Is it as you thought, Mr Arthurs ...? Those documents ...?'

'They are absolute proof of Kane's treason, Miss Fallon,' said Hiltsch. 'I shall wait and arrest him when he returns here.'

He got up from the table. He stood in the centre of the room looking at her. A damned pretty woman, thought Hiltsch. Rather a pity to let her have it too ... but duty was duty. He'd finish her off quickly anyway.

Valetta said: 'My God ... how terrible. ...' Her face was ashen. Her hands were locked in anguish. Valetta, 'produced' by Ernie Guelvada, was giving an excellent performance.

Hiltsch sat down so that he was facing the door.

He said: 'I'm very sorry you were fond of Kane, Miss Fallon. It's a terrible thing to happen to a woman. I can't think of anything worse. You'll just have to forget him. He's a bad one. Black through and through. A man who'd sell his own country. ...'

He slipped his right hand unobtrusively into his overcoat pocket. His fingers closed round the butt of the automatic. By now, he thought, Lang would be away. He would be with Standen, who was sitting in the car with the engine running. When Kane returned he would come straight up. Nielek would join the other two. Then Kane would knock at the apartment door. Valetta would open it for him, and they would come into the room together.

The rest would take about ten seconds. No one would hear. A minute afterwards he, Hiltsch, would be away. And to-morrow, according to Standen's perfectly organised time-table, they would be in Occupied France. ...

Hiltsch said: 'You know, Miss Fallon. ...'

He stopped suddenly. The door had opened. Kane was in the room. The automatic in his hand spurted with a noise like a champagne cork being pulled.

Hiltsch looked down at his right arm. The bone was smashed. He could feel the blood running into his pocket.

Kane said easily: 'Go into the bedroom, Valetta. ...'

She said: 'Yes, Michael ...' She went away quickly.

Kane said in German: 'Well ... now or later?'

Hiltsch began to curse thickly. In spite of the pain, he struggled to get his left hand round into his right-hand pocket. Kane watched him. 'Don't be a fool,' he said quietly. 'You can't make it. You'd better take it easy.'

Hiltsch was still cursing. Damn it, he thought, I can do

this. I am Hiltsch ... one time commander of the Twenty-fourth *Standarte* of the Bremen S.A. I *can* do it. ... There is still a chance ...

With a superhuman effort he pushed his left hand into the pocket. His fingers pushed past his shapeless right forearm and hand ... but he dragged out the pistol. ... *Sieg Heil*. ...

Kane shrugged his shoulders. He fired again.

Hiltsch pitched down on the carpet. His body twitched. He lay still.

The door opened behind Kane. Guelvada came in. He looked at Hiltsch. Kane said: 'The others?'

Guelvada said: 'There were two. The one who came after you and another. They had a car waiting on the other side of the street. I think one of them is the Commando Captain.' He smiled a little. 'The other one – one of those young and very ruthless Nazis – is crying about something. I think Searle must have told him that we're still old-fashioned enough to shoot spies in England. Perhaps he didn't realise that.' He sighed. 'Someone should have told him,' he concluded.

'What about Lang?' Kane asked.

Guelvada shrugged. 'He tried to be funny,' he said. 'He's downstairs in his bedroom.'

Kane said: 'Get the outside doors locked. Get through to Fenton on the porter's telephone. Ask him to get a mortuary waggon round here and get this mess cleared up quickly without any of the residents here getting wise to it. Tell Searle and Minneys to take the other two down to Cannon Row. Ask Fenton, when you speak to him, to lay a formal charge.'

'Very good,' said Guelvada. 'Oh, by the way, Michael, our Commando friend had a letter in his pocket. Written in English – apparently quite harmless – to a gentleman in Eire. I've got it for you. I wonder. ...'

Kane said: 'Hildebrand ...!'

'That's what I thought,' said Guelvada. 'They thought they were going to pull this job off. They'd probably planned to get out off the coast and get themselves picked up. It's nice and foggy for that. Probably they were for France. If so, they'd advise Hildebrand. They'd write an ordinary letter containing a twist that would tell him, a letter that would get past the English censor because it would apparently be quite harmless. One never knows. ...'

He held out the envelope. Kane·took it, put it in his pocket.

'Get a ripple on, Ernie,' he said.

Guelvada went away.

Kane stepped over Hiltsch and went towards the bedroom. He opened the door. Valetta was sitting on the bed.

She said in a funny voice: 'Oh, Michael ... oh, Michael.'

Kane smiled at her. He said: 'Don't worry ... it's all right. ... Take it easy ... pal.'

He caught her as she fell.

CHAPTER IV

SOUVENIR

THE HOUSE was lonely. It stood in the bend of a little river. A path from the dirt road led through the snow-covered orchard and lawn to the front door. A wisp of smoke came from the red chimney. The countryside round about was peaceful. The snow lay like a thick, white-velvet carpet. The moon was full.

Guelvada, standing in the shadow of a tree, just off the dirt road, smoked a cigarette, thought that it was nearly as light as in the daytime. He looked at his watch. It was nine o'clock.

He shrugged his shoulders. Perhaps it was too much to expect. It would be too lucky if it came off. But you had to try things. Whatever happened, you had to try things – no matter how remote the chances seemed.

Twenty minutes passed. Guelvada heard the car as it came round the corner. It was a small car. It was moving slowly. Perhaps, thought Guelvada, the driver was trying to find the house.

The car stopped. The occupant opened the off-side door and looked out. Then he closed the door, drove the car off the road on to the snow-covered verge in the shadow of some bushes. He got out, put a rug over the bonnet. He crossed the road, opened the gate, began to walk through the orchard towards the house. Guelvada smiled. He lifted his upper lip off his teeth like a wolf. He threw his cigarette into the snow. He waited for a few minutes; then slowly he began to walk towards the house.

Hildebrand walked across the flat expanse of snow that covered the lawn towards the house. His gloved hands swung easily by his sides. He walked with a supple movement. When he came to the little porch that guarded the door, he knocked his shoes against the iron mud-scraper, watched the powdered snow fall off them. He put his hand on the door, pushed it open. He went in.

He was standing in a large hallway. A little light came from a lamp suspended from the ceiling. On the other side of the hallway was an open door. Hildebrand walked across the thick carpet. He looked into the room, went in.

A fire was burning in the grate. Kane was standing in front of it, his hands behind his back. He smiled.

He said: 'Hello, Hildebrand. Sorry I'm not Hiltsch. So it came off. ...'

For a moment Hildebrand's body relaxed. Then he smiled. His smile was not unattractive. He shrugged his shoulders.

'It happens like that sometimes,' he said. 'My congratulations ... Mr Kane ...?'

'Correct,' said Kane. 'I am Kane. I had the advantage inasmuch as I had seen a photograph of you.' His smile broadened. 'Once seen, never forgotten,' he said, 'in spite of the fact that in the picture you were in S.S. uniform. No one could fail to recognise you.'

Hildebrand said amiably: 'I think you've done very well. When I read the letter I would have sworn that it came from Hiltsch – that he had written it. Also this was a house he had used before. That substantiated the letter.'

Kane nodded.

'Exactly,' he said. 'We were lucky to know about this house. When we got Hiltsch and the other three, the one called Standen had a note in his pocket addressed to a gentleman in Ireland. It seemed, although the note was apparently innocent, that it was a tip-off that the job had been done here, that they were getting out – an unfortunate anticipation. I spent a lot of time on that note,' said Kane, 'and eventually I got the idea. I had another one written. The man who wrote it was once an expert forger. He made a good job of Hiltsch's handwriting. Anyhow, it achieved its purpose.'

Hildebrand said: 'So it seems.'

Kane said: 'You had better sit down. I imagine you're unarmed.' He grinned. 'Otherwise you'd have tried something by now.'

Hildebrand nodded.

'Your surmise is correct,' he said. 'I came over on a stolen passport, but I had the sense to realise that if the Customs people found a weapon they might be suspicious. Unfortunately,' he smiled a little wryly, 'I haven't been able to get one.'

He sat down on a high-backed wooden chair by the side of the table.

Kane said: 'Hiltsch and Lang, the hall-porter, who was once Veteria, the waiter, are dead. Standen and Nielek were sentenced yesterday. They will be shot in a few days' time. Kane took out his cigarette-case, lit a cigarette. 'Nielek went very soft,' he said casually. 'He talked considerably. He thought it might save his skin.'

Hildebrand nodded.

'That's a chance one always takes with these young men,' he said. 'Although, you know, he was well trained. ... I'm surprised at Nielek.' By the sound of his voice one might have gathered that he was talking about an erring schoolboy.

Kane said: 'Guelvada has seen you arrive. He'll be telephoning. We'll take you back to London very shortly.'

Hildebrand said: 'The formalities are really rather ridiculous, aren't they?'

'In a way ... yes. ... Kane answered. 'Except that here we like to do things in an orderly way when we can. We're still rather old-fashioned, you know. And, according to our lights, you're entitled to a fair trial. Anyway, it'll give you another chance to study our English methods.'

A voice from the doorway, a staccato voice, said: 'No!'

Hildebrand looked round. Ernie Guelvada was standing in the doorway. His hands were in his overcoat pockets. His shoulders were slumped forward. His face was drawn. Kane thought he had never seen Ernie look like that before.

Guelvada spoke. He spoke in a peculiar monotone. He said:

'Michael, he is not to be tried. It is unnecessary. I am going to have this one. ... You understand ...?'

Kane said easily: 'I'm afraid I don't, Ernie. What's the matter?'

Hildebrand said: 'This is most interesting. I take it that this is the notorious Mr Guelvada?' He smiled pleasantly. 'I am wondering why he seems dissatisfied with the carrying out of your normal arrangements in cases such as this.'

Guelvada said: 'Listen, Hildebrand ... perhaps you remember when the first S.S. Panzer Squadron arrived at Nicolas, in Belgium, you were in charge. You were very pleased with yourself, weren't you, Hildebrand? Everything was going well for you and for Germany.

'You were keen and enthusiastic, Hildebrand. Nothing stopped you doing your work – nothing. ... Not even that one unfortunate woman who stood up to you. I expect you don't remember her. I expect there have been so many, that the name of Mariette Defors means nothing to you. ...'

Hildebrand smiled. He said:

'On the contrary, I remember her very well.' He continued to smile.

Guelvada said: 'That is good. ... You were very unkind to Mariette, Hildebrand, weren't you? You were angry because she wouldn't talk. You thought she knew a lot. Perhaps she did. Particularly you wanted to find out where some of her countrymen were and she wouldn't tell you. You did all sorts of things to her, didn't you, Hildebrand ... but she wouldn't talk. So you killed her, *after* you had cut her breasts off. ...' Guelvada sighed. 'It was unfortunate for Mariette,' he said, 'that she had not the pistol – the little automatic that I gave to her as a present. She might have been able to use it on herself to save herself much suffering, much indignity.'

Guelvada put his hand in his overcoat pocket. When he

brought it out there lay in the palm a small ivory-handled automatic pistol.

'There were three shells in it when I found it,' he said. 'It was in the place where she kept it hidden. I have saved them for you, Hildebrand. Each month, each week, each day, I have told myself that one day I shall use those bullets on you. I have promised myself that treat. The time has come ...'

Hildebrand shrugged his shoulders. He said:

'Very interesting ... but if you will excuse me, it bores me. Except that I find a certain satisfaction in having been able to annoy you.'

Guelvada looked at Kane. He said:

'Well ... Michael?'

Kane shrugged his shoulders. He picked up his hat from the mantelpiece. He put it on. He began to walk towards the door. He said:

'You didn't telephone for the car, Ernie ... ?'

Guelvada said: 'No!'

Kane said: 'You had better use Hildebrand's. Your instructions are to take him back to London, to hand him over to the proper authority. In the event of his resisting or endeavouring to escape you will take the usual steps. ...'

Kane took the short cut across the orchard. He removed the rugs from his car bonnet. An east wind was blowing. He turned up his coat collar. He got into the car, started up the engine. He drove slowly towards the dirt road. The sound of three shots came from the direction of the house.

Kane smiled. He drove towards London.

THE END